"The elements of a classic horror tale, harking back to dracula."

Associated Press

IT awakened. IT was blinking in the darkness. Then it brushed against the narrow confines of the culvert, smelled the damp, chill must inside there, felt the cobwebs. It was instantly on guard. It hissed toward one end, then the other, staring at the blackness out there. It saw the moon now, and it stiffened, hissing; felt the pain and terror swelling up, and it was howling. Food. It needed food. It hadn't eaten since . . . and it was studying the rangeland. Then it turned and saw the town across the road there. With its urge too great to be controlled by caution, it was shuffling through the ditch. The town was calling. . . .

THE TOTEM

David Morrell

FAWCETT CREST • NEW YORK

for Herb Katz

PART
ONE

Slaughter stepped inside the bar and tried to keep from looking nervous. It was Thursday, ten o'clock at night. The place was half full, people sitting at the tables or the bar, but though the jukebox played a mournful country-western tune, the customers themselves were silent, glancing furtively at Slaughter before turning toward the far right corner once again. A man sat by himself there, whiskey bottle in his hand, his cowboy hat shoved back upon his head.

But what the people mostly stared at was the handgun there before him on the table.

Slaughter took a breath and walked across to lean against the counter. He was trying to appear relaxed and wishing he could have a beer, but knew that he could never justify it later. Not because he would be drinking while on duty, but because the beer would really be to calm him, and he couldn't tolerate that weakness. People might suspect, and so he simply told the barman, "Coke."

The word, despite the jukebox, came out loud, and people—those who weren't already looking at him—turned to him expectantly. He glanced away as if he hadn't noticed. Then he sipped his Coke: the barman had been so distracted that he hadn't thought to put in ice, but that was all right. Ice would only rattle. Slaughter peered around the room, and then, as if he hadn't seen him until now, he nodded, smiling, toward the man alone there in the corner.

"Hi there, Willie."

"Hi ya, Chief."

"You mind if I sit down with you?"

"No, I don't mind. As long as you don't block my angle on the doorway."

"Well, if *that's* your only problem."

Slaughter walked across and sat near Willie's right arm where, if necessary, he could grab it, but the man already shifted toward the other corner of the table, making sure the gun went with him.

Slaughter sipped his Coke and, though his hands were almost shaking, kept them spread out on the table.

"All alone here, are you, Willie?"

"Yeah, that's right. *I'm all alone.* Just where the hell are you two going?"

Slaughter managed not to flinch as Willie grabbed the gun and aimed it at the two young cowboys walking toward the doorway.

They both stopped and looked across the room uncertainly.

"We have to go to work tomorrow morning."

"No, you stay. You have another drink. I'll even pay."

"But we don't—"

"—listen too good."

Willie cocked the gun, and they both looked at one another. Then they walked back toward the counter.

"There, that's right. You have another drink."

And Willie slowly set the gun down.

Slaughter watched him. Slaughter, by most standards, was a big man. Willie was much bigger, and his eyes were mean-drunk. Slaughter didn't want to fight him, but he knew that Willie wouldn't give the gun up, and if Slaughter drew his own gun, there'd be shooting.

Slaughter pointed toward the two young cowboys. "What's the matter, Willie? They just want to get some sleep."

"There's lots of time for sleep. They're young yet. They don't need it."

"From the looks of things, you maybe need some sleep yourself."

And Willie turned to him. "You want to sit there?"

"I'm just making conversation."

"Well, I didn't say I wanted conversation."

Slaughter shrugged and sipped his Coke then. "Fair enough." And Slaughter waited. "Any reason for the handgun, Willie?"

"Yeah, I've got a reason. I'm just waiting."

"Anybody I might know?"

But Willie didn't answer."

"Anybody—?"

"Yeah, you know him, all right. Yeah, I'm waiting for my brother."

Willie's eyes were narrow as he drank now from the whiskey bottle. Slaughter almost moved to grab the gun, but when he saw the way that Willie looked at him as, bottle raised, he drank, Slaughter simply kept his hands spread on the table.

"That was smart, Chief."

"Yeah, I thought so."

"I don't want to shoot you."

"Well, I'm comforted. You know, these people here—"

"They're staying."

"If your brother comes in—"

"Oh, he'll come. He always comes. He's late already."

"But these people . . . if there's trouble . . . you don't want to see them hurt."

"And I don't *want* them going out to warn him, either."

"Yeah, I understand that, I suppose. He must have—"

"I don't want to talk about it. Play that song. You let it stop."

And Willie turned now toward a man beside the jukebox.

"Dammit, play the song."

The man put in a quarter, quickly pressed a button. He was awkward, upper torso stretched off in a different angle than the lower.

Now the same sad tune scratched from the jukebox.
"There, that's better."
Willie smiled and sipped his whiskey.

I can't help it if—

"You caught him with your wife?"
"I heard about it."
"Heard is hardly fact."
"I heard it from the desk clerk at the Highway Motel."
"Well, that's different."
"You're damn right it is."
And Slaughter concentrated on the handgun before glancing at the doorway. "Willie, you don't want to do this."
Willie snickered.
"I mean, let's say that you kill him."
"Yeah, I'm with you so far."
"Then you'll only have to deal with me and lots of others."
"I don't care about that. Once I kill him, nothing matters."
"Think about it. If you'd meant to kill him, you'd have waited in the bushes. No, you came in here to prove that you meant business, but you hoped that someone like myself would change your mind."
"You know, I ought to kill her too, but she was never strong. She always liked him."
"People won't think less of you if—"
"Slaughter, why not shut your mouth?"
And Slaughter felt his stomach burning.
Willie pushed back from the table.
Slaughter flinched, and then he saw that Willie's brother, Orval, was now standing in the doorway.
"Stay right where you are, you bastard."
Orval, worse than that, came farther in, and people scattered.
"Willie!" Slaughter shouted.

Orval raised his hands, and Willie aimed as Slaughter surged up from his chair to grab the handgun. It was pointed toward the ceiling. Slaughter fought to keep the gun from going off.

"Hey, that's all right, Chief. Let him shoot me," Orval told them.

And the two men froze then, staring at him.

"What?"

"You heard me, Willie. I deserve it."

"You're damn right you do."

"I screwed her. Hell, I won't deny it, though if truth be told it's her who did the screwing. Damn near raped me, if you want to put a name to it."

Now Slaughter's grip was stronger.

"She's my wife!"

"That's something else I want to talk to you about. She's on the bus right now. If I were you, I'd smile with thanks at your good fortune."

Slaughter had the gun. He stepped back, hoping no one noticed that his hands were shaking.

Willie started toward the door.

"Hey, let her go, for Christ sake. Where you been, kid? I looked everywhere to find you."

Willie stopped and stared at him. "I waited here for you."

"I should have figured, since you're always in here after ten yourself."

And Willie kept on staring. Then he suddenly was grinning. "You dumb bastard."

"Hey, don't call me that. I'll go home, get my gun. No, never mind. I'll just use yours. Hey, Chief, let's have that gun a minute."

"It won't do you any good. It isn't loaded," Willie said.

"It isn't what?"

And they were laughing.

Slaughter glanced down at the handgun. When he pushed the cylinder, he saw it wasn't loaded.

They kept laughing.

"Yeah, I figured that you'd pee your pants."

And Slaughter was too sick for anger. He just stared down at the gun and then, his hands yet shaking, slipped it underneath his gun belt. He could drive with Willie to the station, charge him with disturbance, but he didn't see much point in that. The gun was empty. No one had been hurt. The people in here were beginning to appreciate the situation. They'd be making jokes about it for at least a couple of months. He let it go and started walking toward the brothers.

"Willie, I should—"

"Hey, Chief, no hard feelings."

"Maybe next time."

And he tried to look like he was laughing with them.

Both were walking toward the bar. "I'll buy a chaser for you," Orval said.

And Slaughter started toward the door.

"Hey, what about my gun?"

"I think you lost it, Willie."

"Let him have it," Orval said. "A joke like that, you ought to lose it."

Slaughter kept on walking. At the door he saw the owner.

"Well, I'm glad you came," the owner said. "It could have turned out different."

"Yeah, we're lucky," Slaughter said and nodded. He was going through the doorway.

As he did, he heard the brothers talking: "Really she was awful. How'd you stand her all these years?"

And Slaughter closed the door, and he was in the moonlight. Those two brothers. He'd had trouble with them several times before. The way they drank, the jokes they liked to play. He should have understood that nothing much would happen. Now they'd drink till closing, find a whorehouse. Really that was all they cared about. The wife was just distraction, though for all that Slaughter knew she'd set the brothers off against each other so that she would have a chance to leave. He couldn't tell. He'd never thought that she

13

was smart enough to try a ploy like that. For sure, though, Willie never would have let her go if she'd been screwing someone other than his brother.

Slaughter looked down at his trembling hands and shook his head. And two young punks like that had spooked him. It was something to be shamed by. He was walking toward the cruiser, got in, staring at the moon that shimmered through his windshield.

Yeah, this town was full of lots of people like those brothers. You and they deserve each other, he was thinking. Hell, it wasn't even loaded. He kept shaking, couldn't stop himself. There was a time when you would never have been caught like that, he told himself and fumbled with his keys to start the cruiser. *Yeah, but that was in another city.*

And at last he had the key inside the slot, and with his knees yet weak, he started driving slowly toward the outskirts.

He had come here from Detroit five years ago. He'd never said what happened there to make him leave. He only let on that he'd tired of living in that city, tired of being a policeman where he saw too much brutality. In need of something better, much more peaceful, he had come here to Wyoming, and with money he had saved, he first had tried his hand at raising horses. But he couldn't make a go of it, and when the old chief died, he'd given in and asked the council for the job. After all, police work was the job that he was trained for, and a small town such as this, he didn't think that there'd be trouble that he couldn't handle. So he told himself, at least. But every time he stopped a fight or came upon a twisted car wreck, even walked inside a store at midnight when its back door was unlocked, he felt that subtle tensing in his stomach, sometimes not so subtle, felt his hands begin to sweat, and often he suspected that he'd gone back to police work to face up to what had happened.

No one knew, and no one noticed. At the start, a few had feared, thinking of his name, that he would be too

14

tough for them, that coming from the East he would treat them as if he were in the city, breaking heads as if this were Detroit. But members of the council had been quick to phone Detroit, and word about him there was even better than he claimed. He had never had a charge against him. He was never one to push. So they had tried him on condition, and they'd liked him ever since. At least in terms of lack of crime, the town had never had things better. What was more, he saved the town some money, and that cinched it.

And in truth he liked the town as well. Oh, he might sometimes tell himself that he had fallen awfully low to have to ride herd on two people like those brothers, but in fact he even liked the brothers. Although stupid, even careless, they weren't mean, at least. The mass of people here were blessed with plain good nature. Any problems that he found here were his own, he'd brought them with him, and he had his ranch, though "ranch" was only what he liked to call it, just five acres and two horses. But the house was very nice. He had his friends: the people whom he worked with. He'd been married once. His wife, though, had divorced him, which was common with policemen who were married to their work. She had kept the children, one boy and a girl, and now he hardly ever heard from them except when he insisted that they come out for a visit. That had been a month ago, and since then he'd been lonely. But aside from that, this place was awfully good for him. Though he might be afraid of dying, he was certain that he'd never end up bleeding out his life in some black gutter.

He was glancing at the mountains all around the valley: snow-capped jagged peaks, the moonlight glinting off them. Then he concentrated on the road where he was driving past the outskirts toward the highway, checking for some speeders coming into town, and there he saw the object slumped along the shoulder. First he thought it was a bulky burlap sack which had been dropped along the road. But then he moved a little

15

closer, headlights glaring, and he saw the backpack and the body sprawled beneath it.

He was stopping, tires crunching on the gravel at the side. He kept the motor running, headlights glaring, even switched the searchlight on to get a better view of this. He glanced away a moment, and that trouble in the bar had been cathartic. Nervous once tonight, he was now calmer, empty, as he stepped out from the cruiser, flashlight ready, and he heard the crickets in the long grass by the gravel. With the moon now stark upon him, he just rubbed his mouth and glanced away another moment before starting toward the body.

It was male. He saw the face where it was sideways on the gravel. Twenty-five or even thirty. Hiking clothes. A pair of woodsman's boots.

When Slaughter stooped, he saw the eyes were closed. He felt one wrist but found no pulse and noted that the wrist moved freely. This had happened recently. No sign of rigor. *What* had happened recently? He saw the dried blood on the arm, the hip, and guessed that this was hit and run. But if this happened recently, there wouldn't have been time for blood to dry. He didn't understand it.

Slaughter searched among the objects in the backpack, found the nylon tent but not much food. He shook the canteen. Not much water. Sure, this hiker had been camping in the mountains. Several days at least, considering the stubble on his face. In need of food, he'd started walking into town but didn't reach this road till it was dark, and someone hit him. Maybe he'd been thumbing for a ride and, with the backpack, couldn't scramble from the car or truck in time. Poor bastard. With his face in death so peaceful. Slaughter drew a breath and straightened, glanced once at the long grass, then the moon. He'd check the wallet for I.D. For now, though, he was walking toward the cruiser.

He was going to need some people from his office and the morgue out here.

2

The blind man sensed the danger, even as the dog did.

"What's the matter?"

She was tense beside him, edging closer.

"Someone there?"

But no one answered. They were on a side street, half a block from home. This section of the town was old, as he was, and he knew from talking to the owners that the houses all were well kept, high and wide, with trees and bushes.

Now the dog was growling. He had gone out with the dog to try to get more tired. Sure, his Braille watch told him it was nearly midnight, but this time was always good for him, few sounds or people, just a pleasant stillness, and he'd gone out like this many times before but never felt endangered. Now he heard the rustling in some bushes and a car that went past at the corner.

"Someone there?" he said again.

He felt the guide dog tug to lead him back toward home. She kept on growling, and he couldn't figure what was out there. After all, his dog was big, a German shepherd. Surely no one would be dumb enough to come at him. He'd put his old clothes on. He didn't look like he had money.

Could this be an animal she saw? But what kind here in town would bother her so much? She was conditioned to ignore some tempting small game or a stray cat or a passing dog, and even so, she wasn't pulling forward; she was tugging backward.

After ten years, he had never heard her growl like this. The bushes yet were rustling. Her insistence was determined.

He gave in and let her take him, footsteps scraping on the sidewalk. Now she moved much faster, and he had to work to stay with her. He tried to keep from being frightened, but he couldn't help it, for the rustling had increased back there.

He stumbled on the sidewalk, felt the dog veer over toward the house now, touched his cane against the steps, and he was going up them. He was rushing, knew the quality of how she had been trained. She wasn't being cowardly. Her whole life's purpose was his safety.

He came to the door and fumbled with his key.

Then he was in there.

3

Slaughter stood behind the ambulance and watched the two attendants lift the body from the back and flip the wheels down on the stretcher cart. They rolled it toward the rear doors of the hospital. When they had earlier been at the scene, they'd hurried to inject the body's heart with stimulants, to put a mask for oxygen upon the face, but there was no response, and after they had satisfied themselves that death was really present, they had been in much less hurry.

Now they almost seemed to shuffle as they went in through the swinging doors. Their lassitude was not indifference, Slaughter knew from seeing this behavior many times, both here and in Detroit. They'd hoped they could revive this man, and now their energies were slowed by disappointment.

Inside, there were nurses waiting, staring at the

sheet upon the body; and in the back of them, the old man, Markle, frowned and looked at Slaughter.

"Bad night, Nathan?" Markle said.

"Not really. Until this."

"The dispatch called it hit and run."

"That's what it seems like. I've got Polaroids in case you need them."

Slaughter handed him the envelope.

"My men are out there now. They'll check for skid marks, anything that might have fallen in the long grass by the road. Until we know for certain, that's my best guess. Hit and run."

"You've got an I.D.?"

"In his wallet. I don't know him. Joseph Litton. Twenty-eight. From Omaha, Nebraska. From the looks of things, he was a camper. No sign he was married, and no mention of a next of kin."

"Well, that could make things easier—no rush to get in touch with someone."

"But I'd like your information by the morning. If this *does* come out as hit and run, I want my men to check the body shops as soon as we can manage."

"That's no problem. I'll be finished. Hell, it's only Thursday. What's the weekend going to be if trouble starts this early?"

They both stared down at the sheet across the object on the stretcher cart. The two attendants now were wheeling it along the corridor, and Slaughter shook his head as he went with the old man toward the elevator.

Slaughter glanced across to study him. The man was haggard, moving slowly, small thin body almost stooped, his white hair dull and lifeless. Folds of skin hung here and there along his cheeks and neck. The last two months since Markle's wife had died had really aged him. Slaughter didn't like his strident breathing, didn't like the ashen color of his face and hands.

"I thought you planned to take things easy, didn't want the night shift."

"Well, it's hard to break a habit."

"But the night shift—"

"It's a way of keeping occupied. There's nothing home to do that. I just sleep all day and work all night. Like when I was an intern. I'm all right. Believe me."

Slaughter didn't. But he knew this old man, knew that he was tough and stubborn; and he knew as well that nothing he himself could say would change the old man's patterns.

So he stopped before the elevator, pressed the button.

"What I said about the morning. There's no rush on this. You've got all night."

"It shouldn't be too difficult. I tell you what. You still go home at two o'clock?"

And Slaughter nodded.

"Stop by on your way. I'll maybe have some news by then."

"I wish I had your energy."

"You do. You just don't know it. Look, don't worry. Accum's back from that convention in Seattle. He'll be working double-shift this weekend. I'll have lots of time to rest."

"I hope so."

Now the elevator doors slid open. Slaughter watched as Markle went in with the two attendants and the body. Markle turned to press the inside button; winked at Slaughter. Then the elevator doors went shut, and they were starting toward the morgue down in the basement.

Slaughter lingered. That old man. That wink. And Slaughter smiled. He went out past the nurses toward the cruiser. He had first met Markle in his early days as Chief here. There had been a gunshot killing which the old man proved was suicide, and Slaughter had been reassured to know that, while this town was simpler than Detroit, at least he had the kind of expert help that he was used to. Two of them, for Accum was the main pathologist, and he was even better than the old man. But the old man was more friendly, helpful not just in his job but socially as well. He guided

Slaughter through the web of local politics. He showed him who was who and helped him ease in to his job, so that in time they got to be good friends. They visited on weekends, went out for some chili after work, or simply phoned if they got lonely. Slaughter liked him, mourned his wife, whom he had liked as well, and wished that he could soothe him in his grieving. Well, he'd see him yet again tonight, and maybe on the weekend they could spend some time together as they used to.

Slaughter drove out from the parking lot. The radio beneath his dash began to crackle.

"Yeah, it's Slaughter here."

"We've got a prowler out where you are."

"Let me take it. What's the number?"

Slaughter listened, hung the microphone back on the dash. He almost flicked his siren but thought better. Yeah, the old man had been right. What kind of weekend was it going to be if trouble was already starting on Thursday?

4

Markle watched the two attendants wheel the body into the morgue. The place was three rooms in one basement corner of the building. First, a kind of antechamber, sinks for scrubbing down, a cabinet for lab coats, things like that. The second room contained three tables, gutters in them and a drain for blood, a microphone above them. There were cabinets for instruments, a counter, green tiles on the walls, fluorescent lights across the ceiling. Everything was strong with disinfectant. Far in back, the third room was the cooler where, if necessary, bodies could be stored with minimal decomposition.

Now, his nostrils flaring from the smell of disinfectant, Markle watched them set the body, sheet across it, on the middle table.

"Do you need some help?" the one man said.

"No, all I needed was for you to get his clothes off. I can manage it from here. But leave the cart out in the anteroom. We'll want that when I'm finished."

They were nodding.

"Funny night out there."

"Oh? How is that?"

"The moon. It's like we didn't need the headlights on the ambulance."

"The season's changing, summer's coming. After all the storms we've had, you don't remember what a clear night looks like."

"Yeah, I guess it's something like that. Well, we'd best get back on duty. I don't think we'll have another call tonight, but we should be upstairs. Just in case."

"I'll see you later."

"Yeah, come up and have some coffee."

"In a while."

Markle concentrated on the sheet across the body. Then he heard the door close as they went out through the anteroom. He heard the hall door close as well, and he was all alone here.

He was wincing from the pain, the effort not to show it as they talked with him. He had to lean against the nearest table, gasping, fumbling in his pocket while the pain shot through his chest. At last he found a tablet, shoved it in his mouth, his tongue too dry to swallow. He was listing toward the counter, pouring water in an empty beaker, drinking. Water rolled across his chin. He gripped the counter, waiting as the seconds passed, became a minute. Gradually his chest relaxed, and he was breathing much more freely.

Not completely free from pain. Sufficient, though, for him to straighten. He was taking out his handkerchief, wiping at his chin, his forehead.

This was crazy. He should go home, but he knew

that Slaughter needed that report, and Accum wouldn't be on duty till tomorrow. Never mind the damn report. You know that, if they find out you've got pain, they'll never let you work here. *Then* what would you do? Stay home until you died in bed one morning? No, the pain is just angina. You can beat it. You don't have to let them know about it.

He was standing straighter, much less shaky. In another minute, he felt strong enough to try to reach the anteroom. He did that with no problem, sat and told himself that, with his medication working, he was fine now. Even so, he had some further trouble breathing as he washed and put his gown on, then his face mask and his bonnet. There was little need for them, especially the face mask, which made breathing even harder—clammy and constrictive—but his years of habit once again controlled him, and he powdered, put his rubber gloves on, went in toward the tables.

Where the middle room was empty.

Markle glanced around. He felt his chest begin to tighten.

On the floor, he saw the sheet where it lay crumpled. "What the—?"

He'd been certain that the man was dead. He'd heard the ambulance attendants. He had tested for some life signs on his own. But there was nothing.

"What the hell—?"

His eyes now focused on the far door that led to the cooler. It was almost shut, but not quite. If the man had somehow been alive, reviving he would have been puzzled, frightened. He'd have tried to find some people, and with two doors to select from, he had picked the wrong one, gone in to the cooler. There was nothing in there, but he surely must have guessed by now that he was in the morgue. He would be terrified. The door swung slowly open, and the naked body snarled at him.

"My God, no."

Markle stumbled back. He saw the gashes on the

arm, the hip, the gashes which, when he had watched the ambulance attendants take the body's clothes off, had seemed strange to him. Not what a car would do to someone, but he'd held off judgment till he'd have the chance to take a closer look. But watching now the body shambling toward him, staring at those eyes—those eyes which couldn't bear the lights, which needed one arm raised to shield them—he was certain that no car had injured this man. Markle lurched back farther, struck the wall. The pain surged up his arm, and he was praying.

"Oh, dear God, no."

In a crazy lengthened second, he could almost see his wife. He thought of Slaughter, wished that he had said good-bye. He thought about so many things. The body loomed before him, arms out. Markle gasped and started slipping down the wall. He felt a rupture in his chest. A portion of his mind flew out to watch him, and then, for both watched and watcher, there was nothing.

5

Slaughter searched among the bushes, one hand near his gun loose in its holster. He was five blocks from the hospital. The houses here were run-down, huge trees in the back, no fences, lots of bushes, dense and tangled, as if he were in a forest. He was probing with his flashlight, but the moon was high enough to shine down through the trees, and there were spaces where he didn't need the flashlight. Even so, he often stumbled: on a pile of rocks, a crumbled sandbox, once a rusted birdbath which had toppled. There were far too many hiding places. Someone could be waiting out here, and these bushes were so thick that Slaughter easily might pass him. He was glancing at the moon, then all around him. He suspected that these yards were overgrown like this, both up and down this section. He could search all night, keep going farther, right, then left, and still not find a prowler. Hell, the guy would just keep shifting back and forth to places Slaughter had abandoned. This was getting nowhere.

Just make sure you understand your motives, Slaughter told himself. You want to stop. That's fine. The guy, if he was here at all, is likely home and sipping beer by now. But maybe he's nearby you, waiting for a chance to jump you. Could be that you're quitting 'cause you're nervous.

No. I've stayed here half an hour. There isn't any point in this.

You're sure now?

Yes.

Okay then.

But if he was hesitant, the roses that he brushed against and scratched him made him resolute. He turned and faced the back porch of the house that he had left. The lights were on inside, the porch light on as well, and he could see the lady staring through the screen door at the darkness of the yard back here.

He brushed ahead through bushes toward the lawn, which wasn't mowed. He didn't like his back exposed and almost turned to face the darkness once more, but he knew that he was being paranoid, so he kept walking, reached the porch, went up its creaky steps, and looked in through the screen door.

"I found nothing, ma'am. I'm sorry."

She was maybe sixty, hair dyed red, lipstick thick, her bathrobe clutched around her.

"Well, I know I saw him, Mr. Slaughter. Someone crouched low in those bushes. He was crawling."

"I don't mean to say you're wrong, ma'am. But it's dark. That could have been a dog you saw."

She only shook her head. "I saw him."

"Well, I doubt he'll be back. Just keep your doors locked and this porch light on. If you get frightened, call the station. I'll leave word that you should have priority."

"That's *all?* You mean that's *it?*"

"We don't know who he is. He didn't bother you. He maybe was a drunk just crawling home. I'll have a car sweep through here several times tonight."

She just kept staring at him.

"All these houses. There's no reason he should bother this one. Get some sleep. This happens sometimes."

"Not to me."

"I understand that. Really it's not fair."

And Slaughter said a few more words to reassure her, stayed until she'd locked the door, and he was leaving. As he stepped down from the porch, he faced the darkness once more. Then he walked along the side, and she was in there, turning every light on. Well, that wouldn't hurt, he guessed, and if she got some sleep . . . He reached his cruiser, driving down the street, and glancing toward the backyards.

In Detroit, this kind of night was normal, even quiet, but out here it was uncommon. Oh, a prowler by itself was nothing, if there was even a prowler. He was used to calls like that from time to time. But after Willie and the body, things were forming in a cluster, and he didn't like his apprehension.

He was four blocks over, in the newer section of the town, neat homes down both sides, their lights off. But the tenth house on the right was lit up, in stark contrast with the darkness, and that wasn't what he had expected. Thinking of the prowler, of the woman he had just left who was turning on her lights, he drove down that way, pulling up and stopping. When he got out, he was frowning, checking both sides of the house before he climbed the stairs and rang the doorbell.

He could hear the bell in there. He waited. No one came. He rang the bell again. He almost tried the door but saw her coming.

"Officer?"

"There's been a prowler. When I saw the lights—"

"I'm all right. Thanks for warning me . . . I'm making bread. You want some?"

"I'm on duty."

"You can take it with you."

Slaughter nodded, smiling, stepped inside and kissed her.

She was tall, though not so tall as he was, body pressed against him, breasts insisting.

Then she leaned back, and she smiled at him.

"Now that's the way to greet a girl."

"It's just my standard service."

"Don't talk dirty, Nathan."

She was pressed against him once more. This time when they kissed, her tongue was probing.

"Hey, I said I was on duty."

"Not ten minutes?"

"There's a way to make it last that long?"

He grinned, and she was laughing.

"Better eat your bread before your conscience is offended."

Reaching for his hand, she walked him down the hallway toward the kitchen. Slaughter liked the new white walls she'd painted and the clean smell that was always in here.

When he saw the kitchen, though, he started laughing once again.

"Who wrecked this place?"

"I don't make bread too often."

"God, I hope not. You'll be all night cleaning up."

"Unless you come back later to assist me."

"There's a mess up in the bedroom too?"

He breathed the yeast smell, looking at the floured hand print on her jeans. He watched the way her arm moved as she cut the bread, then watched her bring it over to him.

"You're some lady."

There were specks of flour in her long dark hair. He reached to brush them off.

"I cook too. And I sew—"

"And this damn stuff is good. I take it back. The mess is fine."

He chewed the bread. The sweet yeast taste was wonderful. His mouth was full. He swallowed.

"Want some coffee?"

"I can use it, Marge."

She turned to him. "Some trouble?"

"Well, this prowler—"

"That was true?"

He bit another piece of bread. "If what the woman says is accurate." He chewed.

"I thought that you were kidding."

"There was trouble in a bar tonight. I found a body near the highway. Hit and run. I hate to think what else will happen. In Detroit when things got started, sometimes they kept going."

"It's the moon."

And he was frowning.

"It affects them. Full moon rising."

"I'm not sure, Marge."

When she poured the coffee, added cream and sugar, he went over.

"I don't have much time to drink this. Old Doc Markle's waiting for me."

"Well, then, skip the coffee."

Marge leaned close to him again, her thin tanned face against his, as he felt his body start to sink.

He loved the bread smell on her.

6

It was lurching up the stairs. The light was blinding. One hand raised to shield its eyes, it clutched the other to the railing, groping higher. Even with the lab coat on, its body shivered, and it needed to get out of here.

It reached the door and waited, listened. There was nothing on the other side, and it was fumbling with the doorknob. White hall out there, brighter lights, and it was groaning.

Voices, and it stiffened. Down there at the far end of the hallway. It was squinting through the crack the door made.

But those voices. Women's voices. So low, thin, it couldn't hear what they were saying. It was angry. But it had to get away from here. It saw the door across the hall, the red sign and the window, and the blessed night beyond that. It was almost in a rage now. Then it heard the footsteps, speaking, going fainter.

No more voices.

It was peering out the doorway, saw a woman in a white dress and a pointed cap. Her back was turned as she was writing on some papers at a counter. She was small down there. It stepped out, bare feet cold upon the smooth tile of the hallway.

If she turned, it judged how fast it had to be to reach her before she could start her screaming.

7

When she heard the noise, she turned, but there was no one.

What's the matter? That was just the other door down there, some intern likely going out to have a smoke. She'd like to join him.

Yeah, she knew the one she'd like to join.

And she was smiling.

Then she heard another noise, this time from the

swinging doors beside her. When she looked she saw Slaughter come in, nodding to her.

"Dr. Markle isn't finished yet," she told him.

"Well, he might have gone up to his office without telling you. I'll check in case he's waiting."

Slaughter passed her, and she watched him. He was tall the way she liked a man, square-faced, solid, in his forties, and her luck was always good with men that age. But there was little money in his job, and she was not about to ruin all her chances with that intern just because she screwed a cop for one night.

All the same, she watched him as he pushed the button on the elevator; liked his short-cropped sandy hair, his lively eyes. She scanned his light brown uniform, his low-brimmed cowman's hat, his boots, the badge upon his shirt. She narrowed on the gun belt snug around his waist, and when he turned, she smiled at him. He nodded. Then the elevator doors came open, and he stepped inside.

She thought a moment. Then she went back to the chart she was preparing.

8

Slaughter walked along the upstairs hallway. This part of the hospital was offices, and when he saw the old man's light on, he went in, but Markle wasn't waiting for him. Markle sometimes did that—left his light on, even when he didn't plan to come back for some time. On the other hand, the old man might have stepped out briefly to the men's room.

Slaughter shrugged and poured himself a cup of coffee from the warmer on one table, sat and flipped through the journals of the Medical Association. When he reached the bottom of the pile and yet had not found anything he understood, he saw that he had drunk the cup of coffee. Almost two o'clock. He could have stayed at Marge's longer, but he planned to go back later, and he knew this was his place here.

Anyway, the old man wasn't in the men's room this long, that was sure—unless the old man's health was even worse than Slaughter guessed. Then, thinking of that possibility, Slaughter went out, glancing in the men's room, but the stalls were empty, and he told himself that he was being foolish. Markle was still working on that body in the morgue. Two o'clock had not been time enough; and bored from waiting, Slaughter started down the hallway.

Bodies didn't frighten him. It was the unpredictable that frightened, and although he didn't find the mess of autopsies attractive, he did not avoid them either. If the old man had an early judgment by now, Slaughter'd like to know it, tell the station, get tomorrow's duty sheet prepared. Then, with his job completed for the night, he could go back to Marge's.

On an impulse, now impatient with the slowness of the elevator, he decided on the stairway, pushed through to the damp chill concrete steps and went down to the first floor, then the basement. When he came out in the hallway, he turned toward the door which wasn't marked and paused now in the anteroom. He heard no noises in the middle room. A man in calm dissection wouldn't make much noise, regardless. Slaughter pushed through to the middle room and saw the crumpled sheet, the empty tables.

Markle must have finished. Where the hell then had he gone? He knew that Slaughter would be waiting. Rudeness wasn't normal with the old man. Slaughter tried to keep from being angry, almost stormed out to confront him, and he never knew why, as a last thought, he stepped farther in and let the door swing shut.

He sensed the object to his right and turned toward where the door had earlier restricted vision. Slaughter

31

couldn't move a moment. Something cold knifed through him. Then he hurriedly was crouching, recognizing clothes but hoping that the face mask would reveal another person.

But it didn't. Markle's face was twisted in its final grotesque effort. Eyes stared upward, bulging. Slaughter felt a wrist. He listened for a heartbeat. Gasping "Jesus," he was running.

9

They were staring at the old man's body on the table in Emergency. The tubes hung from his neck, his arm, electroshock pads near him on the counter, but the EKG was neutral, one straight steady line, its buzzer sounding. Slaughter turned toward Accum, and his voice was broken. "Nothing else?"

"The interns did the best they could. It's what I would have done if I had been here. He was dead before you found him."

Slaughter glanced back now at Markle, and the body's stillness was so final, so impossible. That pained and twisted face. "We ought to close his eyes, at least."

"They should have done that when they started working on him."

Accum leaned across to switch the buzzer off. He closed the eyes, and Slaughter felt that chilling knife again. He loved this old man. He was going to miss him.

"In a way, I feel responsible."

"I don't see why."

"I had a job for him tonight."

"That didn't make a difference. It was clear that he was dying. Simply putting dishes on a table could have killed him."

32

"Well, I knew that he was tired, and his wife's death—"

"No, the signs were unmistakable. I knew from merely looking at him."

"But you let him go on working?"

"What would be the point of stopping him? A man like that, you take away his work, he only dies much sooner."

Slaughter turned and studied Accum. Tall like Slaughter. Thin, though. Always in a dark suit which contrasted with his skin, the shade of talcum. Dark eyes, almost black. Long dark hair combed straight across. As coroner, he must have understood that he looked almost dead himself or like an undertaker. Accum didn't care much for appearance, though. He mainly did his job well, almost too well. It was really all he did. He seldom went out, seldom saw another person outside work. He had no family. That kind of single-mindedness could not be healthy, Slaughter thought, but then the two of them were in the same position, not to mention that they both came from the East, where they had been through crises. Slaughter never let him know about his own, though. But he felt a sympathy with this man: more than that, an understanding based on their devotion to their business. All the same, this man had calmly watched as Markle showed more symptoms of his heart disease, and Accum maybe had been kind to let the old man keep on working. On the other hand, he maybe had been clinically detached, from working too much with the dead, a fatalist.

Slaughter didn't know. He didn't want to jeopardize their strange relationship by judging him.

Now Accum frowned as Slaughter kept on staring. "It's a heart attack, but if you want to know in detail, I can tell you in a couple of hours."

"No, there's lots of time for that. I hate to think of him cut open. You can do it in the morning."

"What about the job you gave him?"

"I don't know. He had his mask and cap on, but no gown. He likely never started."

"It's important?"

"Hit and run, we think. I need to know for certain."

"I'll get on it."

Slaughter understood that anyhow: the need for occupation, to keep busy.

"Yeah, I guess the world can't stop because a friend dies. Not in our jobs anyhow."

"I'd only lie awake and think about him."

"Thanks for coming."

"Hey, he was my friend. I know that you and he were close, but I was friends with him as well. I rushed here hoping there was something . . ."

But there wasn't, and they both stared down at Markle once again.

"The poor old guy. His face."

"It sometimes twists like that. I wouldn't worry that he suffered. From the signs, his death was quick."

"I hope. For his sake."

Slaughter reached to touch the old man's hand. The skin, already cold, was soft and unresponsive, but he squeezed the hand regardless, wished him luck on his long voyage, and slowly turned to face the doorway.

"Well, I think I'd like to drive a little."

"We're as close to him as anyone. I guess it's up to us to make arrangements."

"In the morning."

Slaughter started toward the doorway, paused once, looking back at Markle. "Hey, I'll see you." But he didn't know if he meant Accum or the old man, and he tried to shut his mind off as he passed the nurses, walking toward the swinging doors, the night outside, the cruiser.

10

Accum watched him disappear, then turned to Markle, gave instructions to the interns, but he lingered. He had grown so used to watching Markle's steady sickness that he understood now he had almost thought of Markle as already dead. He wasn't sure if he felt grief or only a facsimile, and that to him was bothersome. He'd spent his adult years so close to death that living seemed ephemeral, too temporary to put faith in. All the same, he lingered. Then he left the room and took the elevator to the basement. He was feeling grief, all right. Indeed, despite his efforts, he was almost crying. That was why he had few friends, why he had never married—to avoid this kind of feeling. If he wasn't close to people, then in dying they would never hurt him. He had learned that long ago the hard way.

Now he needed to keep busy, went inside the anteroom and almost put a gown on, but he thought he'd better check inside to guarantee that everything was ready. So he went inside the middle room. He saw the crumpled sheet, the open cooler door. The body must be in there, and the old man was too weak to close the door. The old man. Accum tried to push his feelings down. He checked inside the cooler. It was empty. He was puzzled, grief now muted as he wondered where the old man would have put it. In Receiving while the old man made his preparations? That was hardly standard practice, but the old man could have been confused by then.

He crossed the room to reach the telephone. The nurse up on the first floor answered.

"Dr. Accum here. Chief Slaughter brought a corpse in earlier."

"That's right."

"It isn't down here. Check Receiving for me, will you?"

"But I saw them take it down there."

"You're quite certain?"

"Dr. Markle went down with it."

"Just a second."

Accum went out in the hallway, crossed, and glanced inside another room. He saw a pile of clothes upon a table, folded neatly, dried blood on them. He checked several other rooms. He came back in to reach the telephone.

"It's Dr. Accum once again. You'd better ask around because we've either got a corpse in with a patient or else someone's playing games here."

11

Clifford stumbled up the street to take the shortcut, though he almost went the other way to see a friend, but that guy had left town he now remembered. Funny he'd forgotten that. But Clifford's wife was always claiming that, when he got drunk, he never came home, so he'd go home now and shock her.

He was lurching toward the stock pens, toward the field before them where he'd cut across, when he was almost blinded by the moon. It loomed out from a cloud, and with its nearly perfect circle, it was radiant. He stopped and squinted up there, closed one eye, then opened it, and closed the other. No, he knew it was the whiskey. He had never seen the moon so large before, and he was certain that the drink was magnifying it. He started singing:

By the light . . .

And he was walking.

Of the sil-
very moon.

And then he stumbled in the field, and he was falling. He lay gently in the weeds and bushes, rolling on his back and staring at the moon again. It swelled above him, seemed to swirl and grow to join him as he shook his head and fumbled to his hands and knees and then his feet. He listed, arms out for his balance, kept on shuffling through the field, his arms yet out—he walked a tightrope he imagined. But the wind, though calm, insisted, and he heard its whisper in the bushes, felt the magnetism of the moon. He missed his step. He fell and kept on falling. When he landed, he was stunned and couldn't raise himself. A hollow. He had fallen twice the distance he expected, lying down here, staring past the rim toward where the moon kept watch upon him. Clifford blinked in whiskey-filtered pain as, hand upstretched to touch the moon, he wearied of his effort and was sleeping.

When he woke, the moon was even brighter, though it had descended slightly. And the wind had ceased, although he heard its whisper in the bushes yet, and then he saw the dog emerge from moonlight and the bushes.

It was there upon the rim, the moon behind it, obscured by the radiance, a halo all around it, pitch black in the middle. It was staring at him, and he felt its strength, its hugeness, more than that, its presence.

"What?"

He didn't know what he was seeing. Yet drunk, stupefied by sleep, he saw it double, saw it shimmer and expand, and then it left the ground as, screaming to avert it, he felt all its weight upon him. He was sightless.

"Not my face!"

But it was shredding, tearing. One cheek wasn't there now.

"Not my face! Oh, Jesus, not my face!"

12

He woke up screaming.

"Nathan, what's the matter?" Marge said.

Slaughter turned and looked at where her hand was on his shoulder. He was sweating, upright, and he took a moment to remember where he was.

He shook his head. "It's nothing." He was rubbing at his face. "I had a nightmare."

Then he glanced around the room and tried to calm himself.

"You're sure that you're okay?"

Slaughter shrugged and drew a breath.

"You haven't had one in a while."

"It likes to sneak up when I'm off my guard."

He crawled from underneath the covers. He was naked, putting on his underwear, his trousers.

"It's the same one?"

And he nodded.

"From Detroit?"

"That's right."

He didn't like to talk about it. He was walking toward the light switch, almost flicked it. But the moon was on an angle, shining through the window, and instead he walked across to stare at it.

"I've never seen the moon so bright before."

He turned to her.

"You've got a cigarette?" he asked her.

She was sitting up in bed, her naked breasts above the sheet around her waist.

The moon was full upon her.

"It's that bad?"

They hardly ever smoked but kept a pack nearby in case of some remembrance of the old days. Slaughter, thinking of the old man, thought as well of that first case that he and Markle worked on: gunshot death that turned out suicide. The suicide was Marge's husband. That was how they first had met, and in the years that followed, they had gradually sought comfort in each other. Lately he had seen a lot of her, his children having come and gone, the loneliness grown full in him, but though she understood, she had no accusations. He had been with her when she required help, and she was pleased to give it. After all, they both had nightmares.

Marge, instead of waiting for an answer, fumbled in the nightstand. "Just a couple left."

"A year old, they'll be choice."

She tossed the almost empty pack to him.

He thanked her, lighting one and staring out the window toward the moon again.

"You ought to get some help."

"It's just the old man. Going in that morgue to find him."

"Like the two kids in the grocery store?"

She knew that much. He'd never told her more than that. "A little. . . . Mostly it's just death."

Now he was drawing on the cigarette. The smoke was stale, as if from crumbled leaves. His head felt light and swollen.

"Well, there's nothing I can do about it."

"What? Your dream? The old man's death?"

"The both of them."

He turned to her. "You ever get the feeling something's going to happen?"

She was staring at him. "When my husband died . . . before, I mean . . ."

"That's right."

And he was turning toward the window once again,

the backyard. He saw something crawling through the bushes.

13

It was freezing. Everywhere it turned, the lights were bright, the moon oppressive. Hand upraised, it lurched across the street. it jerked its head and moaned, and everywhere before it there was concrete, white lines in neat patterns, high lamps, and a row of buildings. It was stumbling toward them, lab coat flapping as it passed a sign, the large block letters WESTSIDE MALL, and then it reached the windows. Dishes, lamps, and sofas, tables. It was snarling, stumbling farther. Books and records. Aspirin bottles. Radaranges. All these it remembered, but its bare feet cold upon the concrete, it was trembling, jerking in the damp night air. A mist was forming, and it wanted only to rush toward the comfort of the dark night forest, but it shivered as it found what it was looking for. Another window, coats and shirts and pants. It didn't bother to protect itself. One elbow raised, it cracked against the pane. The glass was breaking. Now a bell was clanging, and it raised its fist and smashed more glass. It snarled and stepped inside there. Warmth. A coat. The forest. When its feet began to bleed, it only snarled down at the glass and gripped a coat rack.

Three drunk driving, two assaults.

A break-in at a clothing store.

A missing person.

And the other items. Slaughter scanned the night sheet. In his five years as the chief here, he had never seen a night sheet like it. Prowlers, barking dogs, and stolen cars and fights and family quarrels. There had been a holdup at the Piggly Wiggly, not to mention Willie and the hit and run, the prowler he himself had seen from Marge's window.

And the old man. Don't forget your friend died. No, there wasn't any way he could forget that.

Keep your mind on what you're doing.

He was standing, moving from his glassed-in section of the office.

"Marge, you've seen this?"

She was turning from her desk beside the doorway. She had been here part-time with the old chief. When her husband died, she'd needed work, and Slaughter kept her on full-time now. He was well aware that, in a small town, gossip traveled fast, that people guessed they slept together, but he'd made a special effort, as had she, to separate their work and leisure, and the only comments he'd received were that they handled things with dignity. The point was, her employment wasn't based on nepotism. She just did her job damn well, and in the context of the office, that was all that mattered.

She was nodding, dress on now in place of faded blue jeans.

"Christ, I haven't seen a night sheet like this since I left Detroit. What's going on here?"

"I don't know. But other calls are coming in."

"If this keeps up, we'll have to run a double shift today."

"I phoned the men off duty. They're back working."

That was what he meant. She did her job well.

"And the coroner's been calling."

"I'll get back to him."

He knew what Accum wanted. There would be some news about the old man, what the autopsy revealed, but Slaughter didn't want to hear it. He had gone out last night searching for the prowler he had seen at Marge's. He had not slept well before that. He had not slept any afterward. He didn't want to think about arrangements with the undertaker. That next step was far too final, too much to adjust to.

"Better hear this."

Marge was pointing toward the two-way radio upon the desk beside hers. There was something in the way she looked at him. He frowned and listened.

There were two policemen in the room with them, typing up reports, and they were glancing toward the radio as well.

He surely hadn't heard right.

He was leaning toward the upright microphone, the morning sunlight glinting through the eastern windows.

"Accum, this is Slaughter."

"It's that hit and run you brought in last night."

"What about him?"

"I've looked everywhere. As near as I can tell, somebody stole it."

She was Phoebe, this week anyhow, and she was huddled in one train compartment corner, staring at this tortured man who still was sleeping in the pull-down bed. He'd said his name was Dunlap—Gordon Dunlap—but since she herself changed names as often as her moods, she had no reason to believe him. What she did know was that he was haunted, and though she was frightened, she felt nonetheless compelled to stay with him, not out of charity, but as a rabbit, spell-bound, views the snake about to strike, chill fascination. If she grabbed her things and left now, there was no way to get off the moving train. He might wake up and miss her, go through, searching. . . . No, she'd better not provoke him.

Stay cool, she was thinking. Play this through. The train will have to stop soon.

She had met him as the train pulled from Chicago. With the cocktail lounge now open, she had left her seat to go there, and she'd seen him all alone against the window. He was smoking, staring at his glass—of what? It looked like scotch or rye or bourbon. Though the outskirts had turned into farmland, he had not glanced out, and she had watched him for ten minutes before picking up her wine and going over.

"Mind if I sit down with you?"

At first, she thought he hadn't heard, but then a moment passed, and he was slowly peering up to stare at her.

He kept on staring, but she didn't mind. Indeed she was accustomed to that, even craved it, liked the way a man's eyes took her in, moved up and down, and welcomed her.

But this man only focused on her eyes, went past them, through her.

He was nodding toward the empty seat.

She frowned but didn't show it, sitting. Didn't know why she had even walked across. Partly she was lonely, partly bored. But mostly, she suspected, she was curious. She'd long ago stopped choosing men because their looks appealed to her, though this man was attractive in a stark way—gray hair (but he didn't look past forty), steel eyes, brooding cheeks and forehead. He had on a business suit, a club tie, white shirt, well-buffed shoes, but while he should have looked successful, while the suit was pressed, the shirt unwrinkled, while his cheeks were shaved, his hair trimmed neatly, there was something wrong, as if the suit were six years old, the only one he owned, as if he kept himself together with some effort.

Gordon Dunlap. Going to Seattle. And he didn't volunteer that, only answered when she asked him. She was puzzled, used to eager statements, hooks to keep her once she'd made the starting effort. And that must have been why she remained—because this man was something different, in a sense a test for her. She felt that, if she didn't speak, this man would be content to keep on staring at his glass and take her presence next to him for granted.

Why not fly? Because he wasn't in a hurry. What was waiting for him would remain there.

What was that? He didn't answer.

She was going to Sun Valley.

And he nodded.

She had friends there.

And he nodded.

Hated flying. Actually it terrified her.

He just shrugged and asked the waiter for another drink, a second glass of wine for her.

"If you'd prefer I didn't sit here."

"No, it's fine. I like the company."

"You hardly show it."

44

"I don't show much anytime."

And parry, feint. She should have seen her chance and left then, but the lounge was almost empty. Dunlap was the only solitary male. She had no choice.

They went to his compartment three drinks later. In the end she had to ask him, and that made her more determined. And he had a bottle. Bourbon, she had earlier discovered. Shifting from the wine to liquor, she helped finish half the bottle. And they screwed and screwed. She had expected sex without involvement, simply cynical mechanics, but instead he lunged at her with frenzy, desperation, as if he were concentrating to be nowhere else but here. He wailed in climax, almost pained. He took no satisfaction, sought her out again and then again. They drank the bottle's second half. He fumbled in his suitcase, showed another bottle. And they drank. The train moved into South Dakota. Dark now.

And it started. His capacity for bourbon now achieved, he talked—not all at once. His words were fueled. The more he drank, the more the words came out until, a steady stream together, one out, one in, he expatiated, he expounded. He became the opposite of what he had been, and he told her he was going to Seattle, to a clinic, to dry out. That he had recently been through a breakdown, that his marriage too was breaking down (she'd looked but seen no wedding ring), that he was broke in other ways, a has-been, once a famous photojournalist (and now she understood the tape recorder and the camera), a *Life* reporter, *Look*, the *Post*. But they were gone now.

"No, I see them on the stands," she told him. "*Life* is back."

"It's once a month. No, *Life* is gone now."

And he laughed hysterically, and that was when she really started getting frightened.

"Hell, I write for *Rolling Stone* now."

Which at last was something that she knew. "I haven't seen your name."

"You wouldn't. After everything.... I use a pseudonym. I'm Geoffrey Clinker."

"Oh." And he might just as well have said that he was crazy. She moved inward, on her guard. She knew his essays: twisted and frenetic, forays to the borderline of madness. She was powerless. His eyes were like two hands which held her rigidly. She thought, you're twenty-three, a drifter, useless. All you like to do is pick up men, and one night you stare face to face with one wrong choice who's going to kill you.

But he didn't. Frenzied babbling became isolated outbursts. In the measured clatter of the rails, his eyes sank now. They shut, and Dunlap drifted.

But she didn't move, afraid that, if she did, she'd wake him.

And an hour later he was screaming, lurching out of bed to crouch, defending.

He was staring at her. "Did you see it?"

"What?"

"The antlers."

She just shook her head.

"And something..."

"Something what?"

He wouldn't tell her, couldn't. He was sweating, sinking toward the bed.

"The antlers," he was saying, only this time he was in dismay. He frowned and moved his head from side to side. "The antlers. They...My Jesus. God, I'm sorry."

And the different meanings in that were too much for her to sort.

But he was turning to her. "Really. Look, I'm sorry."

"What? You mean you're saying that to me?"

"I have this dream. It... Never mind. I'm sorry. Did I scare you?"

"Yes."

"I scare myself. That's why I'm going to Seattle."

He was staring at her. Without thinking, she reached out and held his hand. She never understood

46

her gesture, but it calmed him. It was what she should have done. She held him, and in time he went to sleep. She watched his knees, at first drawn up, move down, and gradually she crawled from bed and huddled in this corner, watched the sun come up and saw the mountains.

They were looming. Then the train ascended, reached the tree line, straightened, and the snow-capped jagged peaks were so close that she felt the need to walk among them. When she glanced toward him again, she saw that he was blinking at her.

"Did I dream?"

"You don't remember?"

"No."

"You had a nightmare."

And he seemed to make a choice. "Where are we?"

"In the mountains."

"I can see that. Where? What state?"

"Wyoming."

He kept looking at her.

Now the train was in descent. She glanced out, saw the valley, mountains all around it, saw the town there in the middle.

She was hoping. If the train stopped, she was going to leave.

He crawled from bed. He washed and shaved. He dressed, and as she watched, she understood how right she'd been. The effort.

And the train passed through the rangeland now. It slowed, the town before it, passed the sign that told her POTTER'S FIELD. It slowed some more.

She reached to lift her suitcase as he told her, "I'll be getting off here."

"But Seattle?"

"No. There's something . . . I'll be getting off here."

And she watched him close his suitcase, grip his tape recorder and his camera. "Here's my ticket. You can keep the sleeper."

He was going out the door. She followed, went along

47

the corridor, the windows on this side which showed the old-time depot. Through another door, and they were on an exit platform.

Train stopped, he was turning to her. "Hey, I... Friend, I'll see you."

He leaned close. Her cheek. He kissed her.

Then they smiled at one another, and he pushed the exit door. His suitcase, tape recorder, and camera held against him, he was stepping toward the gravel, stepping on the depot's platform, and she watched him disappear around one crowded corner. She had smiled, but really she'd been frowning. Now she showed it, kept on staring at that corner, thinking of the way he'd moved with purpose, as if he were not a stranger here.

16

The town was much the same. Of course, it had been winter then, the streets obscured by snow, the wind chill almost sixty below zero. But his eye for detail was still good, and he remembered how he'd stepped down from the train back then and gone around that corner. One block over, and he saw the long main street as he'd expected, neat two-story buildings down both sides, all painted white and glaring in the sun. The street was wide, as he remembered it—a vestige from the cattle drives back in the old days. And he saw the signs for rodeos, for cattle shows and specials on alfalfa, stores with fancy cowboy clothes, bars with names like Trail's End and The Hitching Post. Yes, he remembered Potter's Field, all right. It was the last place he'd been healthy.

Potter's Field. He thought about that winter and the photo essays he'd prepared, the last ones before he had been informed that *Life* was finished. They had been among the best work he had ever done, for sure the best that *any* writer here had done, and there had been a lot of other writers. But he didn't understand what he was doing here. He'd meant to reach Seattle. Truly. He had made that promise to himself. Of course, he'd broken many promises, but this time he had been determined. He had gone to Jackie, told her what he planned to do, and she had told him he was crazy which, considering what he had done now, maybe was the truth. He'd even managed to convince her that, if he dried out, she'd try to make a life with him again.

So why the hell then had he left the train to stop here? That made no sense whatsoever.

He was walking down the main street toward the courthouse, burdened by his suitcase and his other things, his body awkward from the bourbon. Though the summer wasn't here yet, he was pressed down by the heat. His eyes hurt. In the sun, he squinted toward the mountains, sweating, and the more he walked, the more his shirt clung sticky to him. Then his suit began to lose its shape, and he knew, as he passed his image in a window, that he looked the way he felt. Indeed he felt as if he might be sick. He thought that, if he stepped in now to have one drink, he'd find the strength to put his act together, but he hadn't come here just to have a drink—he could have drunk some more back on the train. No, it was something else, and he was puzzled. Then he glanced across the street and, through the midday traffic, saw the building, saw its large block letters POTTER'S FIELD GAZETTE, and he knew where he planned to go now.

He was moving through the pickup trucks and rusty Fords to reach its shiny all-glass front, its glinting imitation marble steps. And he was thinking of the man whom he would see there, if the man were still around—the man whose weight seemed like blubber till you saw him walk and realized that he was like a heavyweight or some gigantic dancer, who, near fifty, was in charge here, who had been in charge for many

49

years and used his power with a skill that many senators and congressmen would envy, who could be a threat, a danger—if the man were still around.

His name was Parsons.

17

"We met in December. Nineteen seventy-one."

"Yes, I recall what happened then. I don't remember you."

"I was a newsman on that story."

"Yes? I still don't understand."

"I'm here to do a follow-up."

And Dunlap wondered if that really was his motive.

"But the story has no interest now."

"The bodies, the disaster. But what happened to the others?"

Parsons leaned back in his chair and squinted past the flesh high on his cheeks. "I understand now. Do you mind if I'm direct?"

"It's what I hoped for."

Hoped for what?

"You plan to start that trouble once more."

"Trouble?"

"It's no secret. People on the outside blamed us. Hell, it's not our fault if lunatics think they can beat the mountains. If they'd backed off, kept away, we would have welcomed them. But all those others in the town? The rejects? If they hadn't settled here in town and made that trouble."

"But that isn't what I came for."

"Well, what is it then?"

And Dunlap wished he *did* know why he'd come here.

"So it happened. Who can say where fault should go?

You're right. Despite what happened here in town, they should have known they couldn't beat the mountains."

All those frozen bodies, spread out through the snow-bound woods as they had tried to go for help, arms and legs gnawed off by wolves and coyotes—and the compound, like the horrors of a concentration camp, the children wailing, starving, adults with their ears and noses, fingertips and feet turned black and rotting from the frostbite. Dunlap shivered.

"What's the point then?"

"That's the point. We've got a Brook Farm in our century, okay? We've got a man like Quiller, rich. He's got ideals. He thinks he's, I don't know, some kind of Trancendentalist. He turns his back on worldly goods. He leads his caravan out here, sets up his compound, and he says he's going to live with nature."

"Goddamn college kids."

"Not all of them."

"It doesn't matter. Hell, they thought they were so goddamned smart. They didn't know what every six-year-old around here knows instinctively. You try to take on nature. It'll kill you."

"That's my story then." But Dunlap wondered. "Sure, there never was a follow-up. They learned a lesson. So what happened to them?"

"No one's there now."

"What?"

"They made it through the spring. One rancher's kid went up to join them. When the father found out, he raced up to get him, turned a little crazy, pulled a gun, and shot a guy. No, everybody's gone now."

Dunlap stared at him.

18

The two boys ran across the vacant lot. They'd sweltered in the school all day and knew that this was Friday, that tomorrow was cartoons and two weeks later was the start of summer recess. They were laughing, eager to get home and have cake, then play some baseball. They had brought a ball and gloves with them to school, and now one ran ahead, the other threw the ball, the first boy caught it.

He was grinning as he threw the ball back, braced to turn and run a few more feet before he'd stop and catch the ball again.

"A high one this time," he was shouting as he turned, and he was startled.

He blinked dumbly at the body in the hollow.

At the blood, the face. Then he was screaming.

19

It was sleeping.

It had stumbled this far to the edge of town by sunrise, but then, blinded by the growing brilliance, agonized, it scurried to find shelter, some protection. It was by the road, a truck came roaring closer, and its hands up to its eyes, it tumbled in the long grass, crawled along the ditch. It saw the tunnel that went underneath the road. It scrambled toward the entrance, crawled in, panting, whining.

52

But the sun had gone.

Except for dim light at the far ends, it was safe here, and it huddled on its side, the culvert narrow, wet, and musty, laced with webs. Its pain diminished. In a moment, it was sleeping, and it dreamed of being in the mountains, in its other recent life when it was camping.

When it had needed food and set out hiking toward the town here.

Just two days ago.

So brief a time. . . . When everything was different.

20

Slaughter flicked the siren and the flasher. He was squealing from the parking lot behind the station, racing toward the main street and the intersection that would lead him to the vacant lot beside the stock pens. He was trying to control himself. He felt his stomach burn, his heartbeat quicken. Accum hadn't found the body yet. The undertaker had been at the station about Markle. Other calls had come in—vandals last night, broken windows, and a deer had somehow wandered into town where, in a panic, it had rampaged. Slaughter hadn't known which problem he should handle first, but then this other call had come in, and he knew for sure, and he was skidding around the corner.

21

Dunlap watched the cruiser, flasher wailing, skid around the corner, rushing through the center of the town. He turned to focus on the big man driving, frowned, and almost thought he knew him, but that surely wasn't possible. The cruiser door was marked POLICE CHIEF, but he'd met the chief when he was here before, and this big man was someone else. All the same, that driver. Dunlap couldn't shake the feeling that he'd seen him other places.

He was heading up the sidewalk toward the station's entrance.

This was crazy, he was thinking. He had just come from the paper's morgue. . . .

Why? What was he doing here?

He'd sampled whiskey from the bottle in his suitcase while he'd smoked and read the microfilm, the local pieces about Quiller and the compound. In the darkened room down in the basement, just the dim haze from the microfilm machine, he had been frightened, sensed the image of his nightmare, seen those antlers and that other thing. He'd never seen it in the daytime, while awake. He'd sensed it hunching over him, and to preoccupy himself, he'd kept on drinking, reading. Hell, it's what you've got instead of insects or pink elephants. You've got the D.T.s, friend. You should have kept on going to Seattle.

But he didn't understand his strange compulsion. Was it just that he was at the top when he was here and ever since he had been sinking to the bottom? Was he trying for some crazy comeback, picking up his skills where he had left them? He had done his last best work here, but he'd never seen it printed. *Life,* to save its money toward the end, had published only what was in its backlog, and that market for him gone, he'd scrounged and hustled, but the other markets gone as well, he'd started his decline. A man like him whose work was all that mattered, he had drunk to ease frustration, and he'd ended finding solace.

But no more. He knew he never would have reached Seattle. As his nightmare took possession of him, he'd have killed himself and maybe that girl, Phoebe. There had been no choice. He'd had to leave, to stop here. *Life* is back, and maybe you can pick up where you ended. Though he didn't need to be reminded, he had read the microfilm, regardless. Something. There was something that was nagging at him. He recalled the caravan, the ragged string of pickup trucks and vans and buses, Quiller's red Corvette before them, as they set out from the City Hall in San Francisco. July Fourth. Independence Day. The Exodus. He'd read about the thousand people Quiller had evicted from the compound, read about the trouble in the town, the battle in the park, the state police, the buses that came in to take the vagrants out. He once more learned how people in the town were so resentful that they wouldn't deal with Quiller's people which, as food and clothing ran low, led to all those frozen bodies in the mountains. Then the stories from the compound stopped altogether. Well, not altogether, for in June, about the same time as right now, there was the murder.

And one other thing, an early thing that Dunlap hadn't known about or else did not remember. After Quiller's people first came here and settled in the mountains, Quiller had them bring down all their trucks and vans to sell, which Dunlap thought was logical—a nature group, they had no need for vehicles—but in the record of the bargains that the local people had acquired, there had been no mention of the red Corvette that Quiller drove as vanguard. Dunlap scanned the reels of microfilm. A red Corvette, a classic 1959, its sale would have some interest, but there wasn't any mention. What was going on here?

He was walking up the sidewalk toward the station. To the left, he saw the big, stone, pillared courthouse. Straight ahead, though, was the brick, two-story headquarters that he had known so well when he had last been here. He viewed the rich, well-tended lawn on each side of the walkway. From the shadow of the trees, he guessed. The sun could not get in and scorch it. He was thinking of the brown grass on the rangeland,

55

thinking of the cruiser, what in this small town would merit such commotion. Probably an accident, he thought. A bad one, rush hour and all that. He reached the stairs that led up to the entrance, brick just like the portico and walls, old and dark and weathered. He went in, and there were stairs that led down to the basement, stairs that led up to a kind of center hall, wide and tall and spacious, treelike plants in pots along the walls and in the middle, doors that led off on each side. The wood was old and dark and solid, and the place gave off the not unpleasant must that comes with many years. He saw a door wide open to his right. He saw the sign on top, POLICE CHIEF, NATHAN SLAUGH-TER, and he knew for certain that he'd met that big man who was driving. What the hell was *Slaughter* doing here?

He started moving faster, going in the room. He saw the bright walls, windows, lights on all across the ceiling. To the right, he saw the tall, slim, dark-haired woman at a desk beside a bulky two-way radio. She was attractive, and at first she didn't notice him. She only sat. He moved, and then she turned to him.

"Yes, may I help you?"

He was glancing at the empty room. "I'm looking for the chief."

"I'm sorry. He's not in right now." She once more stared down at the speaker, and he couldn't tell if she were simply rude or just distracted.

"My name's Gordon Dunlap."

"You're the writer from New York?"

"That's right." But Dunlap frowned at her. Despite their conversation, Parsons had been leery of him, phoning people to make sure that they were ready for him, that he didn't cause some trouble. But *what* trouble? Dunlap didn't understand this. "Do you know when he'll be back?"

"It's after five. He might come in this evening. At the latest, in the morning."

"Well, I knew him in Detroit."

56

And Dunlap didn't know why that should matter to her. She was staring at him quickly, frowning, as the radio began to crackle. They were turning to it.

22

"Christ, he's dead, all right!" the voice was saying, garbled by the static. "Lord, he hasn't got a—"

23

Slaughter skidded to a stop behind the other cruisers. He was getting out and putting on his hat even as he reached to switch the motor off. His siren faded. Over to his right, he saw them standing in a circle in the middle of the field, staring down toward what appeared to be a hollow—several members of his force, a few civilians, Accum. They were glancing at him as he came around the cruiser. Then they turned back toward the hollow, went on staring.

He was stepping up the curb, rushing through the stiff brown grass. You'd better get control, he told himself. Again, it wasn't bodies that disturbed him, though he didn't like to look at them, but there was something more, and he was concentrating on the stock pens over to his left, smelling cattle droppings, mounds and mounds of them, the one thing out here that he still was not quite used to, cattle milling in the pens, brought in to be force-fed and then shipped. He was walking fast as he came up to them and looked down in the hollow. No one spoke.

"Good God," he said and turned away and then looked back again. "You're sure that this is him?"

And someone nodded to his right. He looked and saw the husky blond policeman who was Rettig.

"Here's his wallet."

Slaughter opened it and read the driver's license. *Clifford, Robert B.* Sure, this was him all right, unless somebody pulled a switch.

Clifford had been on the night sheet Slaughter read this morning. All those times his wife had called and said that he was missing, fearful something happened to him, when in fact he'd just gone out to have some drinks and get away from her.

And this time, dammit, anyhow, her fear was justified.

What made him think about a switch, what made him read the license, was the body splayed out stiffly in the hollow. Eyes and lips and nose and cheeks and chin and forehead, everything was ripped and mangled. There were bits of chin- and cheekbone showing through, sockets where the eyes had been, but mostly what was shocking were the teeth, bared there with no flesh around them, white against the dark and dirty, crusted, bloody mess.

Almost sick, he had to turn away again. "All right then, what's the story?"

Rettig stepped a little closer. "He was drinking last night at that bar down on the corner."

Slaughter looked. The Railhead. Where the stockyard workers went for lunch and after five. He nodded.

"He was drinking quite a bit. He stayed till closing, bitched awhile because they wouldn't serve him. Then he left."

"Was he alone?"

And Rettig nodded.

"No one saw him after that?"

"Nobody I can find."

And Slaughter tried to look as if he had control. He glanced down at the wallet, searching through it. "Two

58

fives and a one. We know he wasn't robbed, at least." He thought and turned to Accum. "Tell me what your guess is."

"I won't know until I get him on the table."

"Hell, it's obvious," a man nearby them said.

And Slaughter turned. He saw a young policeman. Redhaired, bothered by what he was staring at. His name was Hammel. Slaughter'd interviewed him several months before, and now he guessed he'd have to start to teach him. "No, it isn't. There's just three ways this could happen. One: he was already dead when something came and ripped at him. Two: he fell unconscious, and it happened. Three: he got attacked while he was walking. Now if he'd been dead already, then we have to know what killed him. Someone might have slit his throat, and then an animal came by and smelled the blood." He kept on staring at the young policeman, who was red-faced, blinking, looking one way, then the other. Slaughter knew that he had shamed him, that he shouldn't press it anymore, but he was powerless to stop himself. "In case you haven't noticed, there's a difference between dog attack and homicide. If that's what kind of animal to blame."

He turned again toward Accum. "That's what you think did this?"

"I don't know. I'll have to measure all those lacerations. You can see there are no claw marks on the body. That rules out a cat or something like that."

"Cat? You mean a cougar?"

"That's right. Sometimes things come down here to the stock pens where the cattle are. But not too often. Not in twenty years. There aren't too many cats around here anymore."

"You think it was a dog then?"

"That's my guess. I'll have to check to see, though, as I said. One thing I want to look at are those pant cuffs. You can tell where they've been torn. It could be something nipped at him and brought him down."

"It could be. On the other hand, they could be old

pants that he didn't bother changing when he left the house. I'll send them to the lab and in the meantime go around and ask his wife about them." He was thinking that he'd have to go and see her anyhow, and then he didn't feel like talking anymore. He turned. He saw the young policeman who yet stood there, red-faced, blinking.

"—never saw a thing to beat it."

"I did," Slaughter told him. "Back in Detroit, working homicide. Bodies one and two days old, bite marks all across their arms and legs, their faces and their necks. Rats in tenements. We got so we expected them. If we weren't out there fast enough, we sometimes didn't find too much."

He frowned and looked at Rettig. "Go down to those houses on the corner. See what people know. Screams. A dog that's loose. Anything they might have noticed."

"Right."

And Rettig started walking off.

Slaughter glanced toward Accum once again. "I'll call and have the ambulance brought out." He paused and watched as Rettig crossed the barren field. "You know what I've been thinking?"

"I'm not sure."

"I'm thinking of that hit and run we haven't found."

"There's some connection?"

"I don't know. But old Doc Markle and now this."

"Look, Markle had a heart attack."

"I understand that. But there's too much going on here. I can't shake the feeling something's wrong."

And Accum stared at him. He glanced down at the body in the hollow. Then he peered at where the sun was slowly dipping toward the mountains.

24

It awakened. It was blinking in the darkness. Then it brushed against the narrow confines of the culvert, smelled the damp chill must inside here, felt the cobwebs. It was instantly on guard. It hissed toward one end, then the other, staring at the blackness out there. Night again, and it was crawling, unconcerned about the puddles and the spiders. It went tumbling toward the ditch. It rose up swirling to defend itself, but there was nothing. Once a car roared past, its headlights glaring, but the long grass was a shelter, and it straightened once again. It saw the moon now, and it stiffened, hissing; felt the pain and terror swelling up, and it was howling. With its right hand raised to shield itself, it had to turn away. It saw the rangeland, stark with moonlight, saw the mountains, saw its home. It had to get there, shambled up the ditch, and stopped then. It was trembling, shaking. Food. It needed food. It hadn't eaten since . . . And it was studying the rangeland. Then it turned and saw the town across the road there. With its urge too great to be controlled by caution, it was shuffling through the ditch. The town was calling.

25

Warren scrambled down the bank. The slope was steeper than it looked. He ended with one sneaker in the stream. The moon was stark upon him as he lurched back on the shore. He had no socks on, and the water sloshed within his sneaker, cold and slippery, draining out. He shook his foot to drain some more, but then his skin adjusted, and he eased the foot down on the shore. It sank in mud as had the other. He revolted, and the sneakers made a sucking sound as he stepped onto firmer ground. Now he'd really fixed things. He had mud upon his sneakers, and his mother couldn't help but know that he had snuck out from the house. He almost panicked. Then he thought of water, he could wash them, and his worry was relieved.

He stepped a little closer to the reeds, but they were thick and dark, and even with the moonlight, he would never see the hole. He crouched a good deal closer, pulled some crackers from his sack, and threw them. They were rattling in the reeds. He tossed a few more and then listened, but there wasn't any movement.

What to do?

He peered as close as he could manage, thought that he would reach in with these crackers. As his hand went in the reeds, he heard the hissing over to his right and saw it coming down the bank. It seemed to be off balance. "Here's some crackers," he was saying, but it didn't stop. It just kept coming, and he'd never heard a sound quite like it, something like a cat but not exactly. It kept coming, hissing. Warren had his hand out with the crackers, thinking it was going to eat, already knowing how he'd reach to grab it hard behind the ears, but it was past the crackers, teeth sunk in his hand.

"Aaiieee!"

He jumped up, stumbling in the stream. He felt the raccoon's sharp teeth biting, tearing, scraping on a bone, his flesh now ripping from the weight of what was hanging from him. He was splashing, jerking with his arm, and then he swept around and flailed, and he was free of all that weight. It toppled through the air and thudded on the other bank. The force of flinging it away had dropped him, and he scrambled to his feet now as it came for him again. It must have hurt itself when it had landed. It was limping, listing to one side as it came surging through the stream to reach him. It was hissing, and he struggled with his back against the slope, staring down and kicking at it with both shoes. It snapped and bit and got one shoe and wrenched its head from side to side. He felt its teeth go in, and he was kicking with his other shoe, ramming down against its nose, and then his shoe was free, and he was clawing farther up the bank.

That pointed nose, those bandit eyes. He'd thought that they were cute, and now he couldn't stop from screaming at the terror of them.

26

Dunlap took the first punch in the face, the second in the rib cage. He was sliding down the brick wall of the alley. There were three men. Two had used their turn now. He was waiting for the third as he kept sliding, coughing. He was drunk. He had been since he'd found the first bar after leaving Slaughter's office, and the odd part was how painless this all was, but more amazing was the uselessness. He actually had picked this fight. He'd drunk and stared around the room at cowboys, TV tennis, pool games. He had listened to the tinny music, squinted through the cigarette smoke. Soon he'd started making bad remarks. At first he had been low-voiced. But he'd gradually been louder, and the men around him had gone silent. Yet they hadn't moved until he'd asked the barmaid that rude question, so obscene that even now he couldn't quite believe that he had said it, and the men had gathered near him. One more statement, and they had him in the alley. He was sinking lower, waiting, and the boot that struck his stomach forced his wind out. He was gasping. "That's enough," the one man said, though Dunlap couldn't tell whom he was talking to. It might mean different things, but then the one man added, "He's just some damn drunk," and they were walking down the alley. He lay gasping, but he hadn't managed what he wanted. Drink would not sedate him. Beating wouldn't render him unconscious. Even now awake, he still retained the image of his nightmare.

27

After crawling from the culvert, it had stumbled into town. It was now peering through this window as the woman took her clothes off. Though the lights were out, the moon was slanted toward the window, and it saw the outline of her nipples clearly. It was moaning, watching as she took her pants off, raising up its fist to smash the window. Then it heard the bushes close behind it, and it turned, enraged. It saw the dog emerge from darkness. They were leaping, fighting in the bushes, snarling.

28

"No, it was a dog, all right. There isn't any question."

"That's what ripped his face, or that's what killed him?"

"Both. The cause of death was loss of blood from massive wounds around the face and neck."

And Slaughter put his beer can down and looked at him. "You mean there really is a chance his throat was slit?"

But Accum only shook his head. "No, I remembered what you said back in the field. I checked the throat especially. The jugular was ripped, not cut. Oh sure, some nut might still have gone at Clifford with a hand rake, something like that which would tear, but *that* would leave a different set of marks than all those bites you saw on him."

And Accum looked down at his beer can. Slaughter shrugged.

"Okay then," Slaughter told him. "Let's try this. The nut rips Clifford's throat and runs away. A dog finds Clifford and starts chewing. That way all the first marks are obliterated."

Accum only shook his head again.

"Well, why not?"

"All the wounds showed evidence of bleeding."

"Oh." And Slaughter leaned back in the chair and rubbed his forehead. That was final. Only living bodies bleed, so Clifford must have been alive when he was mangled. If some nut had ripped his throat, Clifford would have lived for just a couple minutes more, but hardly long enough to bleed from what a dog might later do.

He sipped his beer and shifted in his chair to face the darkened window as a dog out there began to bark. A howl came shortly after, then some sounds which he could not identify. He listened for a short while, fascinated, at the same time deeply troubled once again.

"You know," he said and turned and paused because he saw that Accum too was looking toward the window, concentrating on the sounds out there.

"You know," he said again. "Since we saw Clifford in that field, I kept remembering the night sheet that I read this morning. Something bothered me about it. I went back and read it through again. A couple lines above where Clifford's missing, there's a note about a dog that kept on howling."

"So?"

"The dog complaint was from that neighborhood."

65

And Accum turned now from the window, glancing at him.

"Not quite near the field, but close enough." And Slaughter looked down at his beer can. "How drunk was he anyhow?"

And Accum shrugged, not even checking through the paper there before him. "Point-two-eight percent, and he'd been drinking like that several years. His liver looked like suet."

"Could he walk, though?"

"I see what you mean. Did someone drag him to that field, or did he walk? I found no evidence of struggle. Could be you'll find something different in the field. I found some bruises on his right forearm that are compatible with his position in the hollow. Also bruises on his shoulder."

"And?"

"Well, think about it. All those bruises were quite fresh, so fresh in fact that he incurred them just before he died."

"Not after? Someone kicking at him once he'd died?"

"No, bruises are just localized internal bleeding. If you strike a corpse, you'll cause some damage, but not bruises in the sense we mean them. Only living bodies bleed, hence only living bodies can develop bruises. Now a bruise will take a little time before it starts to color. Half an hour as an average. . . ."

Slaughter sipped his beer and stared at him. "You mean he landed in the hollow at least half an hour before he was attacked?"

"That's right. But bear in mind the words I used. I said the bruises were compatible with his position in that hollow. Could be he received them earlier some other place. But it's my educated guess that they're from where he fell down in that hollow. Now it's possible that someone pushed him. If so, I don't know what point there would have been, because the cause of death was dog bites at least half an hour later."

"What time?"

66

"Three o'clock. Three-thirty at the latest."

"Yeah, the people at the bar said Clifford left a little after two when they had closed. Fifteen minutes' walk up to that field. Half an hour or so beyond that. Yeah, it brings him pretty close to three o'clock."

"You're understanding then?"

"I'm getting it. There wasn't any other person, as the untouched wallet more or less suggested. He came lurching from that bar and stumbled up the street. He had to piss, he tried a shortcut, maybe he was just confused. We'll never know exactly why he tried that field. But halfway through, he passed out from the booze. That's how he got the bruises. Then he slept a little, and at last the dog came on him."

"That's the way I reconstruct it."

"But how many?"

"What?"

"How many dogs? One? Or several?"

"Oh. Just one."

"You're sure about that?"

"You know how the language goes. My educated guess."

"Sure, but on what basis?"

"Well, the teeth marks were all uniform. But let's assume for argument that we've got two dogs with the same sized teeth. Their enzymes would be different, though."

"Their what?"

"Their enzymes. Their saliva. Hell, the crud inside their mouths. A dog can't plant its teeth in something and not leave saliva. All the enzymes in those wounds were uniform. They came from just one dog."

And Slaughter looked at him and slowly reached to grab the pop tab on another can of beer. The snap seemed louder than was usual. He sipped the foam that swelled up from the can. "And not a coyote or a wolf?" he said and looked now toward the dark and open window.

"No, the teeth were too big for a coyote's. Yes, all
67

right, a wolf, I'll give you that. A wolf would be a possibility. No more than that, however. No one's seen a wolf down here in twenty years. It's hardly worth considering."

"All right, a dog then," Slaughter said, and he was suddenly exhausted. "Tell me why."

"You've lived here, what, five years now?"

"Just about." And Slaughter turned to him.

"Well, I was born and raised here. Dogs are something to be frightened of. People take them in the mountains, camping—lose them or abandon them. The weak and spoiled ones die. The others turn more wild than many animals who live up there. You see a dog up in those mountains—get away from it. You might as well have stumbled on a she-bear with a cub. I've heard about some vicious maulings. Hell, I've seen some victims with an arm or leg chewed off."

"But this is in the town."

"No difference. Sure, they live up in the mountains, but they come down here for food. The winter was a bad one, don't forget. You know yourself, the stock pens put on guards at night to make sure that the steers are safe from predators. The field is near the stock pens. Some dog from the mountains came down near the stock pens and found Clifford."

"Nothing tried to eat him. He was just attacked."

"Without a reason. That's the point. We're dealing here with totally perverted animal behavior. They just like to kill. They'll sometimes come down here and chase a steer for several miles just to get some exercise. They'll bring the steer down, kill it, and then leave it. In a human, we would call that kind of killing 'pathologic.'"

Slaughter put the beer can, vaguely cold yet, up against his forehead. He was thinking now of old Doc Markle.

"You don't look too good."

"I need a few hours' sleep is all." He stood and headed toward the door.

68

"Hey, what about the beer? There's still a six-pack left."

"You keep it. Hell, you've earned it."

"Something's going on, you said?"

"That's right, and what, I wish the hell I knew." He turned the doorknob, stepping in the hallway.

29

"Yeah, okay, I'm looking."

Now the man stepped out the back door with his flashlight. He had been asleep before the television when his wife had wakened him. "There's someone at the bedroom window," she had said. "A dog out there."

He'd blinked as slowly understanding came to him. "Which is it? Someone or a dog?"

"It's both, I think."

He'd mumbled as he struggled from the sofa. She had lately been imagining that she was being watched, or else she'd been forgetting things or waking up at early hours. She was grating on his nerves, and he was tempted just to tell her so, but then they'd start to fight, and it was better if he went ahead and calmed her. He was stepping out the back door, scanning with his flashlight.

"Nothing's out here."

"Check the yard next door. I can't sleep if I think that someone's out there."

"You won't sleep no matter what I do."

He started toward the bushes.

But he didn't need the flashlight. With the moon so full above him, he could see as if the night were day.

The dog was spread out wide before him. It had been a Doberman, though he was really guessing. It was mangled, one leg here, the other over there, its midriff gaping, guts in far-flung clusters. As he stared down at the twisted neck, he had to turn away, and he was choking.

30

"Something's with the cattle."

Now they turned toward Peter squinting in the doorway. He was eighteen, tall and heavy, though when wakened he still seemed the small boy they remembered.

"Did we wake you?"

"No, the cattle did. You're going out there?"

Bodine nodded.

"Yeah, I figured," Peter told him. "Count me in."

And Peter was as strong as Abby. Bodine couldn't argue with him. What was more, the boy was even better with a rifle than his mother.

They were going out the back door, and the night was cold. The lights from town were glowing in the distance. With the moon, they saw the Appaloosa nervous in the horse pen.

"Sure, she senses something all right."

Bodine climbed up in the truck while Abby got up in the other side and Peter brought his rifle. Bodine flicked the lights, and they were heading west beside the barn. The rangeland stretched beneath them.

When he saw the rabbit stunned before the headlights, Bodine swung to miss it and then gathered speed. The noises from the cattle had been coming from where he had found the bones and guts this morning. He was guessing that he'd catch whatever did that near the same place in the foothills, something that lived in the mountains was coming down for easy kills. But

70

not tonight, he told himself. Tonight would not be easy for it.

Now he heard the cattle quite distinctly. They were terrified. He saw them galloping to get beyond him; saw the shadowed outline of the foothills, snow-capped peaks above them, glinting in the moonlight.

And the bushes moving in the forest.

"There. You see them?"

"But what are they?"

He was almost stopping, jumping out to shoot in toward the bushes, but his father had been angry when he once, at twelve, had shot through the bushes. "Wait until you've got a target." And remembering, Bodine continued driving, angling toward the bushes where he planned to push up through and use the headlights.

He was crashing through the bushes now. He winced to feel the jolt, but he was caught up in the action, and he meant to see this done tonight. The bushes closed around him as, above the motor's roaring, he heard clicking in the forest. He saw antlers in the trees, and Lord, he'd only found some deer, and they must be as panicked as his cattle. Then he saw what seemed to be a bobcat, and he slammed his brakes on, jumping out to aim at it. The deer were coming at him, though, their antlers closing, driven by the bobcat. He was in their stampede, lurching toward the truck, and then he heard the howling as, too late, he felt the antlers pierce his stomach. He was coughing, and while Abby screamed, he started falling. He was thinking that he could have saved the deer if they had let him, and then understanding how inconsequent that thought was as he died, he heard the howling once again. A wolf or coyote with a bobcat? That made no sense whatsoever. Then he saw the evil staring through the antlers at him.

Abby kept on screaming.

Slaughter didn't know what he was doing here. He told himself that he should go home, check his horses, told himself that he had put in too much time today already, even told himself that someone else could do this. But he knew the answer to his question. He was frightened, and he had two choices—he could run, or stay to face this. Something's going on, he kept repeating, and he knew that, if he didn't stop it now, he'd never have control again. Those two kids in the grocery store. And he was stepping from the cruiser.

He was walking toward the Railhead bar, and to put off what he intended, flashlight in his hand, he checked the doors, but they were locked as he'd expected. To be certain, he checked all the windows too and then the back. He even checked the garbage bin to see that all the bottles had been broken. Now you're really wasting time, he told himself, and switching off his light, he walked back to the cruiser.

It was three o'clock now, just about when Clifford had been killed. Of course, the man had gone up in that field at least a half hour earlier, and maybe, if he'd fallen, sleeping, closer to an hour. Now, though, was when he had been attacked, and Slaughter stood there by the cruiser, staring up the street and toward the field. There were houses all along the far side of the street, run-down mostly since this section was the closest that the town had to a slum: listing porches, dirt instead of grass, cardboard here and there in place of windows. But the people, although poor, were peaceful, and he'd never had much trouble from them—from the bar, of course, but that was mostly workers from the stock pens. Slaughter looked up past the bar and field on this side toward where he could dimly make out silhouettes of buildings at the stock pens. Three of

72

them: the cattle stayed outside except for special auctions, and there wasn't any need for more than just an office and two showrooms. In the stillness, he could hear the low of cattle coming faintly from the far side of the field, and he was waiting, thinking. Then he started walking up the sidewalk toward them.

In the open like this, he had no use for his flashlight. There were stars, a swollen moon. They gave the night a silver glow which made it almost magical. So Clifford would have thought, he guessed. He himself was trying hard to think like Clifford. Last night had been bright like this, and Clifford had come from the bar and walked this way toward the field. Clifford had been drunk, of course. With that much alcohol inside him— point-eight-three percent—the glow would have been just about the only thing he noticed. And he wouldn't have been walking. He'd have *staggered*, lurching slowly up the street, and maybe that was why he'd tried the awkward shortcut through the field instead of going twice the distance down around the block. Because he knew that he would never otherwise have managed to get home. He had stumbled slowly toward the field, and anything that might have crouched low in the weeds here would have seen he was an easy target. No, the timing was all wrong. Those thirty minutes between when he fell and when he was attacked. Anything that saw him come and knew he was an easy target would have tried him right away. There wasn't any reason for the thing to put off lunging. Could be that it had no interest, that it tried the cattle next and didn't like the men on guard there and then came back, killing Clifford. *Why?* It didn't eat him. *Out of anger?* And the thought was strangely chilling now as Slaughter left the solid concrete of the sidewalk, stepping on the rustling grass and weeds and crunchy gravel of the field.

Slaughter told himself that this was stupid: he was tired, he should be home and asleep by now. But if there were some kind of wild dog coming into town, it

73

would return to where it was successful at its killing, and the next night was as good a time as any to expect it. He was ten steps through the field now, moving just up from the corner in a vague line toward the center and the hollow there and Clifford's house up near the far end of the other block. This route would have been close to the direction Clifford followed, although Slaughter wouldn't know for sure until the two men he'd assigned to this had come here in the light of the morning and investigated. Oh, that's fine, that's really well, he told himself. He understood now just how tired he must be, shuffling through here, marring any tracks which they might find. That's great police work. Like a bad joke. Thinking that the criminal will come back to the crime scene, our investigator scuffs out any evidence which might be left. That's really fine. Just what the hell must you be thinking? Well, I've done the damage now, he told himself, and he was too committed to the notion to go back without some satisfaction. He might just as well keep going.

Which he did reluctantly. Because in spite of his determination, he felt really, unaccountably disturbed now. Not the vague uneasiness which he'd been feeling since he'd come on Markle's body. This was something different, more precise, some visceral reaction to this place and hour. Part of it was no doubt caused by his fatigue, by memories of Clifford's shredded face, by thoughts of what the coroner had called "psychotic" animal behavior. Mere Pavlovian suggestion which he understood and could make compensation for. And part of it was no doubt too the stillness of the night, him all alone here in the silence which by contrast emphasized each brushing of his pant legs through the weeds and grass, each crunching of his boots upon the gravel. He was knee-deep in the grass now, moving slowly, flashlight in his left hand ready to be switched on if he needed it, right hand near the open holster of his gun belt. Slaughter told himself that he was being silly. He had gone through worse than this when he had worked

74

on night shift in Detroit, checking through an unlocked warehouse, chasing someone down a mazelike alley, walking in that grocery store, those two kids. That was quite a while ago, he told himself. You're just not used to this the last few years. It didn't help as well that now a rustling wind had started, blowing through the weeds and tall grass, making sounds as if there were some movement in them. Once he turned, but he saw nothing, fighting back the impulse to switch on his flashlight. Save it till you're absolutely certain, he was thinking. Don't scare off some thing before it's close enough for you to see it.

So he kept on walking farther. He had thought that with the night light from the stars and moon he'd have no trouble seeing. But the silver glow distorted things. Indeed it made them seem much nearer, and it obscured details so that everything seemed blurred together. He glanced toward the stock pens with their shadows and their faintly moving shapes of cattle and the buildings in behind them. He was thinking that he'd better not get too close over there, or some guard might mistake him for a thief and shoot him. He was halfway through the field and couldn't find the hollow. He'd been glancing so much all around that he had angled from his course, and now he didn't know if left or right was where he ought to go. The hollow had been rimmed by long grass, he remembered, and he maybe wouldn't find it even if he stood ten feet away. He told himself he should have kept his eyes toward Clifford's house across there, keeping in a line with it, but now that he considered, there was no way drunken Clifford would have staggered in a straight line anyhow. He would have veered off one way, then the other, so that this was still a replication of what happened, though the hollow was important yet, and Slaughter figured that he'd shifted too much toward the stock pens, moving now the other way, and it was then that he was further conscious of the wind. Or rather absence of it. But the

75

rustling through the grass had still continued, coming nearer.

He turned startled, ready with his flashlight, lurching back to gain some distance, and the tangled strand of broken fence wire must have been there all along for him to see when he first came here, staring down at Clifford. It was snagged against his heels now, and his arms flew out, his head jerked up to face the moon, and he was falling. He was braced to hit the ground, already calculating how he'd have to roll to break his fall, but he kept dropping, surging heavy past the level of the ground, and then his head struck something hard which set off shock waves through his brain and left him sightless for a moment. He was rolling. That was all the motive he retained, just reflex and his training, pure adrenaline which scalded him to educated motion. He was reaching for his gun. He'd lost it. He was in the hollow. Panicked thoughts which he was powerless to order. Christ, the hollow. It had happened just like this to Clifford. He groped for his flashlight, but couldn't find it. He heard rustling coming toward him. Scrambling from the hollow toward the open ground where he at least would have the chance to run, he felt the claws flick down his face, and he was screaming, falling backward, landing breathless on another object which was so hard that it seemed to rupture his right kidney. He was fumbling for it, Jesus, and he saw up there the thing as it was crouching now to leap at him, its fur puffed up to make it even larger, hissing, eyes wild, mouth wide, teeth bare, leaping toward him, but he had the gun from underneath him now. He raised it toward the hissing fury diving toward him, squeezing on the trigger, blinded this time by the muzzle flash, knocked flat by the recoil as the fury blew apart above him, thudding on his stomach, and he didn't think the blood would ever stop its shower upon him.

32

Dunlap wakened. He was fumbling toward the head-board. Then he gradually relaxed. The room was empty. He was reaching for the bottle on the floor. He dimly recollected how he'd stumbled from that alley, lurching down the street. He saw his suitcase and his tape recorder and his camera in one corner, and he'd thought that he had left them in that bar where he'd made trouble. How the hell then did they get here? Had those cowboys come back in the alley with his stuff? Or had he gone back in to get them? He was baffled as he sipped the whiskey, waiting for his head to clear. His jaw hurt, and he knew, without the need to look, that it was bruised. He felt the stabbing in his ribs from where they'd hit and kicked him, and he traced the bones but found no breaks or twisted angles.

He was drinking as he glanced around the room. The sun was slanting toward the window, and the place was small and musty, space enough for one three-quarter bed, a desk and chair, a TV on the desk. The TV had no channel dial. The open window had no screen, and insects now were flying in. The place had been erected back in 1922. He knew that from a plaque which he had seen imbedded in the bar downstairs, as if a hotel so outdated were a fact the town was proud of. Threadworn carpet, creaky bed, a common toilet at the far end of each hall. He'd had to get up in the night to urinate, had made a wrong turn coming back, and almost didn't find his room again, so involuted were the halls, one merging in a T with the others and those others merging yet again with others, like a rabbit's den or some gigantic maze which kept on twisting in-ward. He was fearful what he'd do in case of fire, which considering the tinder walls was overdue for several years now, and he didn't like the thought of jumping toward the alley from the second story.

Plus, he didn't have much strength to do it. He was sick again. He tried to think back to a day when he had not felt sick, and with his lack of recollection, he was doubly fearful. How much longer could he keep on doing this? He'd sat and watched the reruns on the set behind the bar downstairs from ten o'clock until the place had closed. He had no way of telling just how much he drank, except that near the end the barman had looked strangely at him, and the programs were a blur of ads and station breaks. And don't forget the stock reports. Oh my yes, not the stock reports. But out here stock was not the closing points of Xerox, Kodak, or the rest of them. No, stock was cattle, and the market prices came on first at ten and then at twelve and then again at sign-off time. He told himself that he could not have drunk too much if he could recollect all that in detail. No? Well, why then was he shaking? Why was he so sick that breakfast was a thought he couldn't tolerate? He had to have another drink before he dared go down the hall to shave, and then another when he came back, before fumbling with the buttons on his shirt. It scared him. This much he could recollect, a time when he had not required whiskey in the morning just to function. He was picking up his tape recorder and his camera, staring at the whiskey and then vowing that he'd leave it as he shifted past the bed and out the door.

The hall went to the right, then left, then right again, then opened on three sides to show the lobby down there, moose head on the wall—from twenty, thirty years ago, no doubt; the thing looked worn enough for that—gray inlaid tile floor, discolored wooden check-in counter, some old wrinkled man in denim clothes behind the counter. Dunlap drew a breath and instantly regretted it: the must was even worse up here. He asked himself again what he was
78

doing here, and then he started down the steps, went out the door.

The sun was like a white-hot knife that probed behind his eyes. Eight o'clock, and how bad would the day be if the sun was fierce this soon? He didn't want to think about it. Eight o'clock, and that was something else his drinking had affected. Now he hardly slept at all, and when he did . . . He didn't want to think about that either, not that antlered figure which kept coming toward him, each night closer, feline eyes turned staring at him, wolf's tail hanging. He was trembling. Get control, he told himself. The dream began just after you had left here, and you're going to see it end here.

33

It had left the town to reach the mountains, lurching higher. Even with the trees for shelter, it was blinded, and it squinted, head down, as it stumbled through the trees and bushes, clawing at the rocks to scramble higher. It had killed a dog back there and eaten. Now it winced, and it was moaning. Sleep. It needed sleep. But somewhere up above would be the home that it felt calling. What, it didn't know, and where, it had no comprehension. But the snow-capped peaks were like a magnet, and it scrambled higher, moaning.

34

Dunlap, in the back seat, looked at Rettig and the young policeman in the front. They turned in through an open, listing, wooden gate. Then they were on a rutted, weed-grown wagon road, and he heard gunshots, several, one upon the other, louder as the cruiser bumped along the dusty road. He leaned ahead.

"Some trouble?"

But the two policemen didn't answer. They were speeding down a hill, the dry red earth on either side, and he saw buildings in a hollow: first a summer house, that's what he would have called it, three rooms maybe on the inside with a porch in front, all painted white; and then a barn, and it was painted white as well; some kind of shed, and *it* was white, and all three were beside a fenced-in pasture where two horses shied from what disturbed them in a gully.

35

Slaughter stood upon his porch and watched the horses shying. Then he turned to Accum. "No, it was a cat, I said. I blew its goddamn head off."

Accum stared at him. "But I don't understand."

The gunshots sounded from the gully, down behind the barn.

"Some big tom, I mean a *big* tom, fifteen pounds at least, and if I hadn't shot it, I'd have looked like Clifford."

Accum frowned and shook his head. The thing just didn't make much sense. Not only the attack, but Slaughter's fierce reaction. Slaughter looked like hell. Oh sure, he had been working late, and after all, he'd been attacked, but by a cat for God sake, and that hardly was a reason for his eyes to look the way they did. And then it all made sense. That hollow, thinking he would end up next like Clifford. Why, he likely hadn't felt afraid since he had come here from Detroit.

He wasn't used to it. and he was angry that a cat had so unnerved him. Accum hadn't thought that Slaughter would be capable of fear. The thought was strangely new to him. He felt a sympathy, his liking for him even greater.

"Look, you said it was a dog."

"That's right. A dog is what killed Clifford."

"Then you tell me why that cat attacked me."

Over by the gully, they continued shooting.

"I don't know. You'd better let me see that scratch, though."

Slaughter waved the outstretched hand away. "I fixed it up myself." The scratch was long and deep across the cheek, thickly scabbed and ugly. "Old Doc Markle made me keep some anti-tetanus injections out here. Just in case. From when I tried to raise those horses." He was pausing. "Ever have to stick a needle in your butt?"

They started grinning. "No, I'm glad to say I haven't."

"You should try it. Anybody saw me would have thought it was some kind of weird, unnatural behavior."

They were laughing as the gunshots sounded from the gully.

"I was thinking about stitches."

"No, it isn't bad enough for that. I should have gone to see you, but I only wanted to get home."

And they had stopped their laughter. Sure, I understand that too. I get it, Accum thought. You didn't want someone to see you shaking from your fear.

He heard the motor droning close and turned to see the cruiser angling down the red-clay road between the hillocks.

36

Slaughter watched it coming: Rettig, and the new man in the front beside him. As he saw them drawing closer, dust cloud rising, he made out as well another person, this one in the back, a man he saw now, in a gray and wrinkled business suit, a face which even through the dusty windshield seemed about as gray and wrinkled as the suit.

But when the cruiser stopped and they got out, the man hitched up a tape recorder and a camera. Slaughter hadn't seen him since the fall of 1969, but what a difference ten years had produced. The dry and brittle hair as gray as . . .

Slaughter stepped down off the porch and started toward them. "There's some beer inside," he said to Accum. "See you later."

"Wait a minute. I have questions."

"Later." And he kept on walking toward the gray-faced man who had the tape recorder and the camera.

Rettig and the new man didn't even bother looking toward the gully, but the gray-faced man was staring that way toward the gunshots.

"We did everything you told us," Rettig said as Slaughter reached them. "Nothing."

"I expected." Slaughter watched the gray-faced man and put his hand out. "Mr. Dunlap."

"Then you know him?" Rettig said. "He told us—"

"Yes, I know him. Gordon. It's been quite a while."

And Dunlap smiled then. "Nathan." They were shaking.

"I've had several calls about you."

"Parsons?"

"That's right. How'd you get here?"

"On the train."

"That isn't what I meant."

"I know that. Can I see you for a minute?"

"Go ahead."

"That isn't what I meant."

"I guess I know that." Slaughter turned to Rettig. "See if Accum has some questions."

Rettig looked at him a moment. Then he started toward the porch, the new man with him.

Slaughter turned to Dunlap. "What's that bruise there on your face?"

"A minor disagreement. And that scratch on yours?"

"Some trouble with a cat."

And they were silent as the shooting kept on from the gully.

"Nathan, if you wouldn't mind my asking."

"That's just target practice."

Dunlap didn't understand.

"A kind of pattern we got into. Saturdays I have the men I work with out to drink some beer and eat a little chili. At the start, before they drink the beer, though, they go back behind the barn and do some target practice. Some towns like this don't require that, but I insist they shoot two times a month at least. The shift in town today will come out next week, and we alternate like that. You care to see?"

But Dunlap only looked at him, and Slaughter couldn't tell what he was thinking. "Sure."

And that surprised him. "Fair enough."

They started walking toward the barn. Then Slaughter looked, and Dunlap's brow was furrowed.

"Nathan, I don't get it. What about Detroit?"

"Oh, I got tired, I suppose. I wanted something better, much more peaceful."

"Potter's Field?"

"As good a place as any. I have horses. Oh, I know it doesn't look like much, but I've been happy."

They were closer to the barn. "So what's the problem?"

"*That's* the problem."

"Pardon me?"

And they were stopping, gunshots louder.

"Nathan, things are different since I saw you."

"Ten years makes a *lot* of difference."

"No, that . . . listen, I'll be blunt with you. I always was. I've had some kind of breakdown. I don't understand what's happened, but I've lost it, any edge I had. I don't know what I'm doing."

Slaughter stiffened. You, too? he was thinking, but he didn't show reaction. He just watched him. "Tell me how to help you."

"I don't *know*. I mean, it's crazy. Look, I have this dream and— All right, I was here before. December, nineteen seventy-one. There was a compound up there." He was pointing toward the mountains.

"Yes, I heard about it. That's before my time."

"I did a story which was never printed. After that, I started dropping. Yesterday when I met Parsons, I found out there was a murder back then that I didn't know about, and now this fellow Clifford—"

"How'd you learn that?"

"I still do my job. You asked me how I got here. I'm not certain. God, I wish I was. I took a train to reach Seattle. When it stopped here, I had no choice. I was getting off, and I have no idea what I'm doing here. I'm looking for excuses. Do you want to hear the weird part? It's this dream. It's like it's calling me."

And Slaughter didn't show reaction. "What dream?" He was thinking of his own dream.

"Please don't ask me."

"You've been drinking?"

"Plenty."

"Take it easy. Look, I have to check my men. That won't take long, and we can talk some more."

And Dunlap nodded. "I just wish to hell I knew what I was doing."

They were walking past the barn, the gunshots louder, echoing, and then they came around the back, the dirt here hard and brittle, and the five men were in jeans and rolled-up shirt sleeves, spread out by the gully, handguns aimed and shooting at some cans below a ridge beyond the ditch. The ditch was maybe twenty feet across, the cans another five feet farther on, and three men now were stopped, reloading, glancing at where Slaughter came with Dunlap past the barn to reach them.

"How's it going?" Slaughter asked them, and the two who still were shooting turned and grinned at him.

"That beer had better be as cold as you pretend it is."

"I lied. It's even colder."

They kept grinning.

"We could use a few new targets." Slaughter pointed. All the cans across there had more holes than metal, barely held together by the seams that joined them.

"Well, we figured once we blast them till there's nothing left, then we can say we earned the beer."

"A hundred shots per man. No less than that."

"But we don't see you out here shooting."

"I put in my time already."

"Sure you did." And they were grinning.

Slaughter glanced at Dunlap, then at them, and shrugging, he was reaching for his handgun in its holster.

Dunlap stepped back automatically. He stared at it as Slaughter walked up to his men and grinned, his elbow crooked, his handgun pointed toward the sky. He concentrated on the cans across the gully there, then braced himself, his body sideways, feet apart, left hand on his hip, and slowly lowering his right arm, he was lining up the sights. His handgun was a .38 revolver, western-style, chambered for both standard loads and magnums. Ruger made it—checkered grip, a perfect balance for his large hand, single-action so he had to cock it each time. But he felt a cocked gun was more accurate. It made less motion when he squeezed down on the trigger. And the one can over there was flipping now, the gunshot solid, recoil spreading smoothly through his body, and he cocked again and fired, cocked and fired, five times altogether, gun-shots echoing on top of one another as the can went through its clattered antic dance and, with the last hit, fell apart. He'd worked his hand as quickly as the eye could follow, and indeed he knew that he was showing off, that really what his men wanted was to see him do that trick which had them laughing, clapping now, as he shrugged, slipping every empty from the side port of the handgun's cylinder. He pocketed the cartridges.

"You've got rounds to shoot yet," he was saying, pointing toward the half-full cartridge boxes by their feet. "That beer is getting colder." He was glancing at where Dunlap stood beside the barn, and he was walking toward him. "Pick up all your empty cartridges this time."

"Yeah, yeah," they grinned and looked back toward the riddled cans. Then they were shooting once more as he went with Dunlap past the barn to reach the house.

"You're still as good as ever," Dunlap said.

"It's nothing that a little practice doesn't help. I wasn't kidding. I go out to shoot before they get here. Sometimes I shoot with them. Mostly I just sit up on that porch and welcome people. One thing that I've learned since I've been out here. There's a western gentleman inside me trying to display himself."

And he saw Dunlap smile then. That was good. It meant that Dunlap didn't understand how really both-ered Slaughter was, how these men weren't here just for target practice: they were here to talk about this trouble that was on them. He was pushing fresh rounds in his handgun. "What about this dream?"

"I said I didn't want to talk about it."

"Take it easy. In Detroit, we lived through all that shooting. We can manage this." And he was smiling as he stepped up from the crunchy gravel, walking on the hollow-sounding porch, and he was just about to ask if Dunlap wanted any beer when he saw Accum turn to him.

86

"Your man here says it's still down in that hollow. Look, I want to know if that thing bit you."

"No. I thought about it, and I checked. I even took my clothes off back here, and the only mark is where it scratched me."

Dunlap had been glancing once more at the scab on Slaughter's cheek.

Accum was persistent. "Scratched, not bit you?"

"Does this mark look like it bit me? No, I'm certain."

"Well, I want to check that cat, regardless. Cats don't go at people that way."

"Some cats do. When I was in Detroit, I had my share of bites and scratches. Cats gone wild and living in abandoned tenements. You're getting what I mean, though. This is different. Cats might fight back, but they don't come looking to attack you."

And the five of them were silent. Dunlap had been listening with interest. Slaughter turned to him. He noticed that both Rettig and the new man had been looking at him too.

"You're right," he said to Accum. "This man here is Gordon Dunlap. We were friends back in Detroit. He did a story on me once." He turned to Dunlap. "Gordon, we've got something here, but it's not quite the thing I want you telling anyone. Now I could ask you to go in and have a beer, but then you'd think that we were hiding something from you, and you'd only work a little harder to find out about it. So I'm going to let you stay. But understand this. Anything about the compound, that's your business. What we're saying now is strictly off the record." And he waited.

"Sure. I guess you have your reasons."

"You'll know soon enough." He turned toward Accum once again. "I loaded magnums before going in that field. I told you, when I shot the cat, I blew its goddamn head apart. I'm no pathologist, but I'm aware of this much. If you want to check for rabies in some animal, you run some tests on portions of its brain."

"That's more or less correct."

"Well, brains, hell I can give you all the brains you want. They're scattered, bits and pieces, all across that lousy field. But they'll be so contaminated, you won't have a use for them." And he was staring. Get control, he told himself. The shooting had been helpful, but this subject had been raised again, and he was terrified once more.

He turned to Dunlap. "There. We've said it. Now you understand. If that word ever gets through town, there'll be a full-scale riot."

Dunlap's face was ashen. "That's what happened to this fellow Clifford?"

Slaughter studied him. "You do your job. I'll give you that. No, we're not sure about him. We've been edging round this subject since last night." He turned toward Accum once again. "You're sure it was a dog that killed him, not a cat?"

"I told you."

"Swell." And Slaughter stared down at the floor. "I need a beer." He looked around.

"Sure," Dunlap told him. "I'll take one."

And Rettig: "Me as well."

"I'll bring a cooler," Slaughter said, and he was going in the house.

37

Christ, what's the matter with you? he thought trembling once the door was closed. You're damn near cracking up. A cat attacks you, and it's like you never used a gun before. What's happening to you?

I'm just not used to this.

You're weak and soft is more the truth. This easy life, you really fell for it. Hell, life's so easy that you lose your nerve the minute that there's trouble.

No, that isn't true. I do my job. I'm good at it.

But you know that you're lying. You can go through years of doing what you think must be your best. But then you get in some real trouble, and you understand that you were coasting, and you didn't even know it.

Hell, I don't know why I even bother trying.

Sure you do. That emptiness inside. That grocery store. You want to show them.

And that purely was the truth.

He stood inside his small neat kitchen, staring at two coolers which beneath their lids were filled with ice and beer, and he was thinking that he'd open one can right away. But that would be a public weakness, one can open and in sight as he brought out the cooler for the others. Maybe not in their eyes weakness. But in his. And he was lifting up the cooler, passing by the sofa in the living room, and fumbling with the handle on the door.

They didn't even look at him, just concentrated on the cooler as he opened it, the glinting liquid-slippery ice, the cans of Bud. They made a ritual, all snapping tabs at once and raising beers as if in toast, then sipping.

"Fine then, what do you suggest?" he said to Accum, and the beer was cool and golden in his throat. He hoped it would relax him.

"Well, no matter what you say, I want to see that cat. I'd tell your men to keep an eye out for strange animals. I'll check the hospital for anyone who comes in bitten." Accum stared down at his beer. "You see, there's not a lot that we can do until we have another incident."

"That's *if*." And Rettig hadn't spoken in some time, and they were looking at him.

"Right. That's not until but if. Let's hope at least." The beer was cool in Slaughter's stomach.

"Don't wait for a dog or cat that's foaming at the mouth. A symptom like that shows up late," Accum
89

told them. "What we're looking for is some attack without a reason. Totally irrational aggression."

Something clicked in Slaughter's mind. "That's funny."

"What?"

"You said the same about those dogs up in the hills."

And everyone was silent.

Too much so, he realized. It wasn't only them but everything around them. Sure. The men had stopped their shooting. They were walking past the barn now, laughing, holstering their weapons as they joked among themselves and came near, rubbing hands together as they stepped up for a beer.

"Who died?" the one man said.

"It's nothing. We've just got a little problem."

"We picked up the empty casings."

"Good. Reload them. We might need them."

And they paused where they were reaching for the beer.

"I have to check my horses. Take a walk. I'll tell you all about it."

He was stepping from the porch. "There isn't much to tell," he heard, and saw where Rettig had moved back a little, talking now with Dunlap.

Rettig evidently saw how Slaughter looked at him.

"You're sure it's all right if I talk to him about the compound?"

"I don't care." You're getting jumpy, Slaughter told himself, and he was walking with the other men to reach the horses.

38

Rettig watched them go. Despite permission to discuss this, he was nonetheless reluctant. He remembered yet the secrecy with which the case had been conducted. There had been such trouble in the town, such bad publicity that winter, that the council had arranged for secret sessions to discuss this new development. Parsons had been mayor then, as he still was, and the general agreement had been to keep news about the murder quiet. Otherwise those hippies might come back, and those reporters, and the trouble might begin again. The trial had been a quiet one, the matter kept within the valley, with some understanding from the nearby towns beyond the mountains, and the valley had just gone back to being normal. Even though the state police had jurisdiction in the case, and they were separate from the town, they'd nonetheless cooperated with the town, realizing that the valley was related to the town, and Rettig, who had been a trooper back then, had been warned to keep his mouth shut. Oh, no one had ever come right out and said that, but the implication had been clear, and he was very careful. It was seven years now since he'd really thought about the case, but he remembered how things were back then, and it was hard for him to break his habit. "Really. Not too much. You figured most of it already. I went up and searched the place."

"The red Corvette. You found it?" Dunlap asked him.

"What?"

"The red Corvette. The classic 1959 that Quiller drove."

"I heard about that. No, I never found it. Oh, I found a van and then a pickup truck. But that was all. No red Corvette. Believe me, I'd remember."

"What the hell is going on?"

And Rettig looked at him.

"I've done some checking, and as far as I can tell, he never sold it. But I know he took it up there. Tell me what he did with it."

"Who knows? I'm telling you just what I saw. If I'd been looking for that car, I might have found it. But I had my mind on searching for the boy."

"You found him?"

"In a while. It took me *quite* a while. I checked the compound and the forest. If I hadn't stopped to take a leak, I maybe never would have found him even then. But I went over by an outhouse, and I found him in a slit trench they were digging for another one. He sure was dirty. I remember that. And scared, although he never said what happened to him in the compound. Mostly he was scared about his father. Even when I brought the boy down to the cruisers, he refused to get in with his father. We were forced to drive them separately."

"And what did Quiller have to say?"

"Excuse me?"

"Quiller."

Rettig shrugged. "Nobody ever saw him."

"What? You searched the compound, and you never saw him?"

"No one did."

"Well, where could he have hidden? Why would he have hidden in the first place?"

"Don't ask me. He might have been out in the forest. I don't see the difference that it makes."

"No, I don't either," Dunlap told him, frowning, watching how the others still were looking at him. "But I wish I understood this."

39

"Warren!"

He was screaming. She came running from the living room to reach the kitchen, staring out the screen door, and she saw him racing through the backyard toward her.

"Warren!"

He was clutching at his hand. She saw the blood, the mangled flesh, and she was pushing at the screen door, rushing out to meet him.

He kept screaming.

"Warren! Tell me what it is that happened!"

She was holding him, the blood across her sleeve now; felt his frantic tears drop off his cheek to wet her blouse.

He just kept screaming.

"Warren! Please! You've got to—"

"It's the glass!"

"But—"

"Broken glass!"

"You've got to show me!"

She was staring at him, at the blood. She wasn't certain what to do. She knew she had to stop the blood. But what had caused it? How bad was the cut?

She tried to lead him. "Show me, Warren."

He was pointing toward the backyard. She was staring past the backyard toward the metal barrel in the old man's yard across the lane. She saw the blood across the rim, and she was running. She was staring so hard at the metal barrel that she didn't see the toy truck by the bushes, and she tumbled, sprawling on the gravel of the lane, her hands gouged bloody by the stones as she lurched quickly to her feet and stumbled toward the barrel.

"Oh, my God, the blood."

It covered everything in there, the rusty cans, the broken glass, the refuse from the garbage fires the old man set before the town refused permission. Warren must have climbed up on this cinder block and reached in there for something, but he lost his balance, and he cut himself.

She swung around to see him. He was clutching at his hand, running toward the back door, and she called to him, but he was in the house already. She was running toward him, through the lane and past the bushes, back door getting larger as she reached it, fumbling at the handle, charging in. She saw the blood across the floor, and she was racing down the hallway toward the bathroom, but he wasn't in there. Where? She doubled back. He sat there in his bedroom, crying, blood across the sheets. She hurried toward him. Never mind the sheets. She grabbed one, wrapping it around his hand and guiding him to reach the bathroom.

"No!"

"I have to wash it, have to see how bad it is."

"Don't touch it!"

He was crying as she freed the bloody sheet and pushed his hand down in the sink. She turned the tap on.

He was screaming once again.

Too hot. She turned the other tap, and now the water felt lukewarm, and she was brushing at the bleeding flesh. She saw the wound, but blood kept squeezing out, and she was brushing at it, freeing all the dirt and darkened clots, and Lord, the hand was mangled. Deep and wide and jagged. Oh, my baby, she was thinking as she felt his weight against her, and she knew before she looked that he had fainted.

40

He smelled something strange. He didn't want to be here, and he tried to slip back in the darkness, but the smell was even stronger, and he couldn't keep from blinking, jerking back as light was all around him, and he saw the strange man in the white coat leaning close. He started crying.

"Warren, it's all right."

His mother's voice, and he was turning toward it. There. His father close beside her. They looked angry.

"Mommy, I—"

"It's all right, Warren. Please don't be afraid. You're with a doctor."

Back now to the man, his white coat flecked with red spots down his arm. The man was holding something like a plastic pill which he had broken open, and the strange smell seemed to come from it. Warren kept on crying. This man was much younger, thinner, than the doctor whom he always went to, and the freckles on his face looked like the blood specks on the white coat, and he couldn't stop from crying.

"Ssshhh, it's all right, son. We're here now. You're just fine."

And Warren slowly understood then that they had him on a table, that his body had been covered with a white sheet, that his hand felt numb and awkward. He was raising it. The hand was like a white club, bandaged so he couldn't even see or move his fingers.

"He's still suffering from shock. He'll take a while to get adjusted," he could hear the doctor saying.

Someone dried his eyes. He looked. His mother. She was smiling. So she wasn't angry, after all. He wondered how he got here.

"Warren, can you tell us how it happened?"

He was turning toward the doctor, trying to remember what the plan was.

"Yes, the glass," he told them slowly.

"In the barrel?"

"Yes, I cut myself."

His father clenched his fist. "I'm going to sue that old man—"

"Harry. Please, not here," his mother said.

So he had got away with it. He let them go on talking.

"Warren, let me tell you what I did for you," the doctor said. "You have to make sure that you keep the bandage on. I sewed you up. I gave you stitches. Do you understand that?"

"Yes, like Mommy when she makes a dress."

And they were smiling just a little.

"Something like that. You were cut too deep to let the wound heal on its own. I took some string like this, except it isn't a string. It's more like what we used to call a piece of catgut, and I sewed the cut together."

"Will the string stay in there?"

"No. A week or so from now, I'll take the stitches out, and you'll be like before. Except you'll maybe have a scar"—and now the doctor looked once at his mother and his father—"but you've a lot of growing yet to do, and most of it will disappear. Now what you've got to understand is that you can't put much weight on your hand. If you try to pick up heavy things or make a fist or anything like that, you'll risk the chance of pulling out the stitches too soon. Take things easy. Let your mother or your father do the lifting for you."

"Will they make my bed for me?"

"You bet we will," his father said. "And I'll still pay your full allowance."

Warren started grinning then. Oh yes, he'd got away with it, and he was wiping at his tears, awkward with his bandaged hand, trying to sit up.

"Here, let me help you."

Mother, and she had him sitting on the table edge.

"He's going to be all right, I think," the doctor said. "Take him home. Here are pills for when the local anesthetic wears off. Call me if there's any trouble. But I think that all you'll have to do is bring him in a week from Monday."

"What about the bandage?"

"Change it every night. The first few times you ought to soak the bandage before it's removed. I don't want any dried blood tearing at those stitches."

"Dressing?"

"Anything you have around the house. First-aid cream is fine. I gave him anti-tetanus. I don't see any problems coming up."

"Fine then. Thank you."

Father: "Really."

"I'm just pleased you got him here so quickly. He was bleeding quite a lot."

More talk, but Warren didn't listen. He was looking at the room, at all the cabinets and shiny metal things, and while he didn't want to think about it, he was dizzy. Once he almost toppled forward off the table.

"Here, young man. I think we'd better get you home."

In spite of what was now an itching, burning pain along his hand, he couldn't stop from feeling happy. He had got away with it. He thanked the doctor as his mother told him, even raised his good hand, shaking with the man, and then they walked out through the door, and this was not the doctor's office which he always went to. They were in a hallway, and he saw the nurses, saw the old man in a wheelchair, and he marveled that they'd brought him to the hospital. He'd known that he was hurt bad, but not *that* bad. They were going out through doors that hissed and swung ahead, the nurses back there smiling at him, and they started walking toward the car.

His father held his good hand. Why, his father wasn't angry that his mother had to call him here from work. He guessed that running in the bedroom had been better than he'd planned. He hadn't thought to do it until he had started running toward the bathroom. All night long, he'd tried to figure how to hide the bite. His hand was swollen, jagged. He'd been wincing from the pain. At breakfast time, his mother had come in to wake him, but he'd snuggled in the sheets as if he wanted to keep sleeping. He had stayed there till he knew that she would surely come to wake him. So he'd listened till he heard her in the living room, and he had managed then to dress himself. The pain had been so bad that he was shaking. He had slipped and got some blood across his sleeve. But he had figured what to do by that time, and he'd snuck outside to reach the barrel over there. The worst part had been leaning in to let some blood drip on the glass. When he had pulled the bloody rag off, he had seen the swollen throbbing ugly bite, caked with dirty blood. He'd shivered, touched the hand against a broken bottle. That had been his plan, at least. But he had lost his balance, and the wound had burst, not from the glass but from the pressure. He had never felt such shrieking pain.

He couldn't stop his screaming.

41

"Tell me how you got here."

"In my car."

And Dunlap laughed then. They were driving down the highway toward the town, and Dunlap looked at him. "No. Really."

"It's not something that I care to talk about."

"You sound like me." And Dunlap saw how Slaughter glanced at him.

"Your hands are shaking."

"It's a habit."

"Need a drink?"

"A couple."

"You should have a bottle with you for emergencies."

"I left one in my room. I figured I'd be brave."

"That bad?"

"It's worse than that. I wasn't kidding."

"What about your dream?"

"You tell me how you got here."

Slaughter looked at him. His eyes were strange, and he was thinking. "Something happened to me. I just lost my nerve."

And Dunlap knew how hard it was for Slaughter to admit that.

"I'm depending on your friendship."

"Yes, I know that."

"I don't care to tell you what exactly, but I never was the same again. My wife divorced me."

"You were cheating?"

"No, I never had that inclination."

"She just couldn't take it?"

"That's right."

"I suspect my wife will soon divorce me too."

"Same reason?"

"That's right."

"Drinking?"

"Partly."

"Then I left the force. I sat down one night at my kitchen table, and I asked myself where I would rather be."

"And you chose *here?*"

"Just wait a second. I spread out a map. I had this daydream about mountains. Horses running free. I'd never seen them, never been around them. But they represented all the things I wanted. I checked through the mountain states. I sorted through them, which states were synonymous with horses."

"And you settled on Wyoming."

"I just closed my eyes and put my finger down."

"And Potter's Field?"

"I know a lot of people who decided on a place for lots worse reasons."

"I'm not questioning."

"I know that. So I left the next day, and I loved it. Oh, I had some hard times at the start. I tried my hand at raising horses, and I made a mess of it. The next thing I was in police work again. But life here is exactly what I want to make of it. Things aren't so complicated that I have to give in. I have freedom. Look, what happened to you?"

"Oh, a person has ambitions, I suppose. You want to prove how really good you are, and I just never lived up to my expectations."

"Or you maybe liked the booze so much that it distracted."

Dunlap shrugged. "The chicken or the egg. What difference does it make? I ended here. No matter how it happened, I know where it got me. Nowhere. Nothing personal."

"Well, why not just give in then? Maybe settle in a place like this?"

And Dunlap started laughing.

"No, I meant it," Slaughter told him. "Things could be a whole lot worse. Sometimes we end up exactly where we should be."

"Or deserve to be. It's too much, Nathan, showing up together once again. I'm glad to see you, but I don't like what I'm feeling."

42

It was sniffing at the shoe. It scurried back to settle on its haunches, puzzled by the odd sensation in its throat. The choking spasm passed, and it was staring at the shoe. It waited, almost sniffed the shoe again, then made its choice, and scuttled toward the pile of clothing in one corner. Blue and stiff, yet muddy, damp just like the shoe. And once again it had that sharp constriction in its throat—which made it angry, and it cuffed out at the clothing. Then it snarled.

Over to one side, another kind of shoe, this one dark and scuffed, light spots showing through the surface, a faint odor, partly sweat, and partly from the animal the hide had once belonged to. It was sniffing closer. Then it bit the leather, and it shook its head, the shoe loose in its mouth so that the shoe flopped one way, then another. But the clothes that hung down brushed against its head, and that annoyed it, so it pawed up at the clothing, snagged against a pocket, pulling, and some clothes dropped down upon it. Muffled, frightened, it was fumbling to get out from under, snarling, pawing, and the clothes dropped free. Then it was nosing. Soap and chemicals, and it was barking. As it bit hard in the cloth and held the garment, tearing, it heard noises coming down the hallway out there. It turned, staring. But the door was closed. The noises stopped. It went back to the garment, snarling, tearing.

Something rattled. It was facing toward the door. The handle moved. It stiffened, garment hanging from its teeth. The handle kept on moving. Then the door came open, and she stepped in. Garment dropping from its mouth, it bared its teeth and snarled at her.

She breathed in sharply. "Warren?"

And it sprang at her. She stumbled back. Her elbow hit the door. The door swung shut behind her, and she fell against the door jamb, fumbling with the handle, as it sprang at her again. She scrambled toward the dresser to avoid it.

"Warren!"

But it only snarled and kept on coming.

"Warren!"

She was kicking at it, throwing pictures off the dresser, dodging toward the bed now as it leaped, and she was climbing on the bed and screaming. When it leaped the final time, it caught her not quite balanced on the bed so that they both went crashing off the other side, her back hard on the floor as it came clawing at her throat. It felt the blood pour down upon its lips, salt taste in its mouth, and gagged. It pawed to clear the salt taste, angered by the gagging, slashed its teeth down toward her face, but in that moment's hesitation, she had gripped the table near the bed and scrambled from the floor to kick at it. The shoe came toward its face, but there was time to dodge, and now it sank its teeth hard in her leg above her shoe. She wailed and kicked to free the leg, but it was growling, biting, and it felt the blood spurt in its mouth, that same salt taste. It gagged again as, shouting, she was twisting with her leg and jerking free. Something hard smashed on its shoulder, glass and lampshade falling past. The pain surged through its shoulder. Whining, it was stunned another moment. But she wasn't there before it any longer. She was stumbling past it toward the door, and it was turning, snarling, leaping as she reached the door and grabbed the handle, pulling, squeezing out to reach the hallway.

It banged up against the door and clawed to move the handle. She was out there, screaming. But the handle wouldn't move. It heard her out there screaming, dimly understood that she was gripping at the handle, pulling at the door, and knew that there was no way to her. More than that, it sensed the danger. Others would be coming. They would trap it. Have to get away. It swung to find an exit, saw the open window, screen, then porch and open air, and it was charging forward, leaping, slamming at the screen. The mesh pressed, cutting at its face. The screen gave way, and it was falling through, the porch now rising up to meet it. Darkness. Pain. It shook its head, the salt taste flooding in its mouth. Then it could see again, and spitting, gagging, it was vaulting past the railing toward the bushes.

"Warren!" it heard someone shouting.

102

43

Slaughter heard as he came driving toward the outskirts. He was reaching for the microphone. "I've got it, Marge." He flicked the siren and the flasher, staring now at Dunlap. "Well, that drink will have to wait." He pressed hard on the pedal, racing past the houses, swerving on a side street, people staring, as the siren wailed and he was concentrating on the street before him. He was veering just in time to miss a young boy in a wagon. Sure, if you're not careful, you'll hit one kid, rushing to find out about another. Slow down. There's no point in racing if you never get there.

But he couldn't force himself to slow. His hands were shaking as he strained to watch for people stepping from a corner or from cars parked at the side. He roared on past a stop sign, one car coming at him from the other way, then swung around another corner as he saw the people up there and the cars along the street and one tall woman standing, crying, other women grouped around her.

They were turning toward the cruiser. He was reaching down to cut the siren and the flasher. Other people now were crossing toward the house, and he at last was forced to slow. He pulled up by a car before the house, double-parking, switching off the engine, reaching for his hat. A plumber's truck was coming toward him. It was stopping as he slipped out from the cruiser, rushing toward the lawn. He glanced once toward the truck and saw a tall man jump out, running toward the group of women, and he guessed this was the husband as they both came to the women in one instant. They were pushing through. He vaguely had the sense of Dunlap just behind him.

She was clinging to her husband.

"Peg, what happened?"

"He attacked me."

"Who? And that was Slaughter, stepping closer.

She kept sobbing. "Warren did." She gasped for breath.

And Slaughter had a name at least.

"What happened to your leg?"

They stared down at the blood that oozed along her leg across her shoe.

"He bit me."

"Who?" her husband said.

"I'm telling you. I couldn't keep away from him."

"Where is he?" Slaughter said.

"The window. He was crawling like some animal."

And Slaughter started running toward the house. It was a single-story building with a porch along the front and down one side. He guessed that Warren was the boy he'd heard about when Marge had called, and he was thinking that he'd better look in through the windows rather than go in the house and risk the chance of something coming at him. He was past the aspen in the front yard, running up the stairs and on the porch. The porch was rumbling under him as he looked first in at the living room and, seeing nothing, ran along the side. Another window toward the living room, but he did not look through it. He was stopping, staring at a broken screen that hung out from another window. Then he drew his gun—a gun against a little boy?—and swallowed, looking in at what had been a bedroom. But the place was wrecked, and he could see the blood, both on the floor in there and on the porch out here, turning toward where it was on the railing just above the broken bushes at the side. He stared off toward the gravel lane back there, and he was running toward the front again.

The woman had continued sobbing as her husband held her. People stood back from them, watching, talking to each other.

"Did he break out through the bedroom window?" Slaughter asked her.

104

She was nodding, gasping for more breath.

"He ran down toward that lane in back?"

"I didn't see. I only heard the noise, and when I looked in, he was gone. What made him do it?"

"I don't know yet."

"I don't understand why he would bite me." She was sobbing uncontrollably again as Slaughter thought and then ran toward the cruiser.

"Marge, we've got a situation here. That young boy had some kind of breakdown. He attacked his mother, and he's running loose now. I want everybody looking for him."

"But we've had too many calls already."

"I don't care. Just get them. It's the same address that you gave me. And one thing more. Get Accum."

"Someone's dead?"

"Just get him. There's no time to talk about it. I'll call back in fifteen minutes."

He was hanging up the microphone. He hadn't thought to ask the mother, but he knew the answer even so, although he had to check for certain, and he slipped out from the cruiser, staring once at Dunlap who was near him, and then running toward the woman yet again.

She still was clinging to her husband.

"Mrs. Standish." He had seen the name up on the mailbox. "Mrs. Standish, look, I know that this is hard for you, but please, I need to ask some questions."

She was slowly turning to him.

This would bring the trouble in the open, but he had to ask the question. He was glancing at the people near him, turning so his back was to them.

"Did your son complain about an animal that maybe got too rough with him? A dog that bit him, or a cat? Anything like that?"

They stared at him.

"But I don't understand," the woman said.

"No bites at all," the husband said. "We told him not to play with animals he didn't know."

"He cut himself," the woman said, and Slaughter looked at her.

"What is it?" she was saying.

"I don't know. Just tell me how he cut himself."

"Some broken glass," her husband said. "A barrel in the lane back there."

And Slaughter now was puzzled. He'd been certain that the boy was bitten. "Several weeks ago. Think back. Did anything seem strange to you?"

"This morning."

"What?"

"He cut himself this morning. Why a dog bite? Why is that important?"

Slaughter couldn't bring himself to say it. "We've had trouble with those wild dogs in the hills. It's nothing. Look, I need a picture of your son. To help my men identify him."

He was hoping that he'd changed the subject, and they looked at him and slowly nodded. They were walking toward the house, Slaughter just behind them, and he really didn't understand now. If the boy had not been bitten, why had he behaved the way he did? Could be that what he had said to Marge was true. The boy just had a breakdown. Maybe they mistreated him. Maybe he fought back and ran from home. The only way to know was find the boy, and as the couple went inside the house before him, Slaughter turned to stare out toward the sun, which now was almost at the western mountains. Dusk would be here soon, then night, and how on earth they'd find the boy when it was dark, he didn't know.

He glanced in at the living room. The place was absolutely clean and ordered. Surely anyone who kept a home this well was not the type to beat a child. But he'd been fooled that way back in Detroit, and he was wishing that his men were here so they could set out, looking for the boy.

The husband came back with the picture. Blond and bright-faced, blue eyes, in his Sunday suit. The boy was much like Slaughter's son had been at this age, and he had some trouble looking at the picture. God, the boy must be in terror out there. Slaughter couldn't show his feelings, though. He simply told him, "Thank you. I'll return it."

"Listen, my wife's too upset to come back out and talk about this. Find him, will you?"

Slaughter heard the sirens, turning as two cruisers pulled up in the street out there. "We'll have him back. I promise." Then he paused. "I think your wife should see a doctor."

"She'll be all right once she rests a little."

"No, I mean her leg. A human bite. It's probably infected."

"I'll take care to clean it."

"See a doctor," Slaughter told him. "I'll check back to ask about it. Look, I have to go."

And he was stepping from the porch, the picture in his hand, policemen coming toward him.

"This is who we're looking for," he told them. "Warren is his name, and it's my guess he's scared. But stay away from him. He's just a kid, but he attacked his mother, and I don't want any of you hurt."

They frowned at him, then at the picture.

"You two check the streets down this way. You two check the other way. I'll take the lane in back. Remember. Don't get careless just because he's little. I don't know what's happened here, but something isn't right."

And he was staring at them. Then he turned to face the people on the lawn. "Everything's okay now. We'll take care of things. I want you all to go back to your homes."

But they just stood and looked at him.

"You're only in the way here."

He was walking toward them, gesturing for them to leave, and slowly they were breaking up and going.

"You'll know soon enough what happens here. Just go back to your homes."

And as they drifted toward the houses, he was turning toward his men. He saw them getting in their cars, and he was all alone out here, except for Dunlap, who was staring at him.

"There's no time to take you to your room."

"I hoped there wasn't."

Slaughter nodded.

"If he wasn't bitten."

"Yes, I know. It doesn't make much sense." And they were shutting both their doors, and he was driving.

44

He had heard a noise down in there and had seen a dog run from the hollow, glancing furtively at him while, ears back, tail low, it now loped away. He saw a bloody strand of sinew hanging from its mouth, and though he'd have to check the textbooks in his office, he was certain that he'd read somewhere that rabies could be passed on from the meat of tainted animals. He didn't have a gun, wouldn't know how to use it even if he had one, but if Slaughter had been here, he would have asked the man to shoot the dog.

Either that or trap it. But that second way was risky, and the dog might be too clever for them. Better just to shoot it. Never mind who owned it. Never mind that he himself would want a living animal to run some tests on. That dog was a danger. It was loping toward the cattle pens, and he was bothered by the damage that the dog could do if rabies were indeed the problem here. Oh, this soon it would not develop symptoms, bite the cattle, but it certainly could leave the virus, maybe drink from where the cattle drank, and they would then contract it. He was watching as the dog now disappeared among the bushes by the cattle pens, watching as the cattle shifted slightly, brown shapes in a group across there, and he licked his lips and looked up at the summer sun.

Noon, and he was thirsty, worn down by the heat. He'd left his suit coat in the car, had pulled his tie and fumbled with his top shirt button. Now he rolled his sleeves up, and he walked down in the hollow. Every sound he made was vivid to him, dry sand crunching underneath his shoes—he never wore the cowboy boots so many of the townsfolk wore, his suits still those that he had owned back in the East—and he was positive that he would waste his time by running tests on what was in a heap before him. There were only bits and hints of brain, and worse, they were contaminated, fly eggs on them now, corruption setting in. The cat had been a large one, black, a massive tom. He could understand why Slaughter hadn't seen it, had been startled when it suddenly came leaping at him, but he wished that Slaughter hadn't killed it or at least had shot it somewhere else besides the head. Well, there was no way to correct that. Certainly he couldn't leave it here. In case it was contagious, he would have to seal it in a bag and then destroy it.

He was thorough. Putting on a lab coat, rubber gloves, a face mask, he was using heavy forceps to drop pieces in the open plastic bag he held. The process took a half an hour. When he shoved the carcass in the plastic sack, he put the forceps in there too. He didn't trust the dried blood in the sand and had to go back to the car to get the shovel that he always carried in the trunk, the bag of lye, and fifteen minutes after that, he'd finished, sand scooped in the sack, the hollow pale with sprinkled lye. He tied the plastic sack and put it in another sack and then inside the trunk. He put the bag of lye, the shovel, and his lab coat and his face mask in another, careful with the gloves he took off, shoving them inside. He locked the trunk, and didn't know another way he could have done it.

He was conscious suddenly of silence. No wind, no

109

cars going by or people talking, no sound over at the cattle pens. Well, Saturday, he thought, there wouldn't be much doing. But he had the odd sensation he was not alone. Of course, he thought. My coat and rubber gloves and face mask in that hollow. I'd have seemed like I was from another planet. Sure, the neighborhood is inside, staring past the blinds at me. But when he looked, he saw no indication, and he did his best to stop the premonition in him, getting in his car and driving off.

He headed toward the hospital, glancing in his rear-view mirror where he saw two men come laughing from the Railhead bar. He saw a woman coming from her house across the street and getting in her car. He thought he saw, reflected dimly, workers from the stock pens walking down the street behind him. It appeared as if the world resumed its motion once he left that place, and he was thinking he should get control of his imagination. Keep your mind in order.

Because really this was something that engaged him. If he didn't dare consider all the trouble that was maybe on the verge of breaking out, he found the problem in the abstract quite attractive. He was up the way he once had been in Philadelphia. A riddle to be solved. A secret ready for him to discover. He was driving, glancing at a cat that perched in royal feline splendor on a porch rail. He was passing one young boy who walked a cocker spaniel. And because the day was hot, he leaned his elbow out the open window, arm hairs shifting in the wind the motion of the car made. He was almost startled by the high that he was feeling. Ten blocks later, he was turning up the driveway toward the parking stalls behind the hospital. He waved to one man from the children's ward who drove out past him toward the street. He reached the back and pulled in at his space, getting out, his key in hand to open up the trunk, when something slowed him and then stopped him.

It was something that he'd grown so used to that
110

he'd long since stopped attending to it. Except last night when he and Slaughter had been talking in the office, and he'd noticed it, but Slaughter had first turned to it, unconsciously reminding him, and anyway the thing had been so much in keeping with their conversation that of course he would have noticed then, but normally it simply blended with the background, and it wasn't worth consideration. Now when everything which he'd been mulling through distracted him, the sound had changed, had drawn attention to itself.

He paused, his head turned, hand outstretched to reach the trunk. Even when he shifted his entire body toward the trees back there, his hand was yet outstretched and stiff until he noticed it and dropped it slowly to his side. He felt his muscles tighten, almost couldn't make them work as he walked squinting toward the trees. In all the years he'd worked here, he had never gone back in them, never once been curious. There was a dry stream bed, he knew, which in the spring was filled with rushing snowmelt from the mountains. But a flood was not a thing to walk near, and he'd always watched it from the distance of his parking space. The trees here all had leaves, their branches open in the early spring, and there had been no trouble seeing. But in June now, everything was like a jungle back there, trees thick, drooping, bushes full and vine-enshrouded, not to mention that there was a rusty fence.

He had a fear of snakes, of things that crawled he couldn't see, but he was thinking only of the sound beyond the trees now as he reached the fence and, glancing at the thick high grass beyond it, gripped the sagging post to balance for a foothold on the wire. The post continued sagging as he gripped it, and his weight kept pressing, and the post snapped softly, weakly, toppling toward the ground where it hung bobbing in the wires.

He looked down at the ants, a hundred of them, next a thousand. They were scurrying to flee the ruptured

111

nest inside the post gate, lucent rice-shaped eggs gripped by their pincers, rushing off in all directions. He lurched back, revolted. All those ugly crawling things. His skin began to itch. His mouth went sour. He was conscious of the irony that he could look at burned and mutilated corpses, maggots on them, and be only occupied by how much damage had occurred within the lungs, and yet he couldn't bear to see these insects and their crazy panicked scurrying below him. Well, he thought, it had to be suggestion, the surprise. In the morgue, he had control, but here the situation governed him, and as the sound beyond the trees came even stronger now, he made himself go near the fence. He stepped across the sagging fallen wires, avoiding where the ants were, staring at them even as he worked around them toward the trees.

He felt the bushes clutch against his pants, and he was turning forward, stooping underneath a tree branch, soon encircled by the trees. The ground was sloping, long grass, vines that clung hard to his pant cuffs. Everything was close and dark and humid. Then the trees gave out, and he was looking at the stream bed. It was deep between the banks, dry, with sand, and here and there a rock or water-polished piece of driftwood. He saw tiny tracks of animals distinct upon the sand. He glanced along one track and saw some movement ten feet to his right along the bank—a chipmunk up on hind legs staring at him, in an instant darting in a hole beside a tree root. Then the chipmunk poked its head out, blinking at him.

He glanced toward the stream bed once more, swallowed, and with one leg cautiously before him, he eased down the loose earth of the bank. The sand down there was soft beneath him, and he didn't like that feeling, didn't like the torn, half-buried tire he saw wedged among the silt and rocks down where the stream bent to his right. He was eager to get up there on the other side, stepping sideways on the loose earth of the other bank, edging slowly up, then listing off his balance,
112

clutching at a tree root up there, but the clutching was instinctive, and abruptly he released his grip, scrambling upward, dropping to his knees once but yet clawing upward.

Then he reached the level, and he stood there, breathing, glancing all around. He brushed the dirt from both his pant legs, staring at his hands. The noise was even stronger, though, and slightly to his left, not straight ahead. He angled toward it, stooping past more trees, avoiding bushes, and abruptly he was free of them, the sun stark on him, open air before him, just the houses past the backyards here, the white fence all along this back end of the houses.

He was reaching out to climb the wooden fence when he thought better. Down there to his left, the sound was even closer, stronger. From that backyard two lawns down. He walked along the fence, and then he saw it, tangled in its chain, the doghouse scratched and bitten, splinters on the ground and blood spots on the lawn, an Irish setter, and the sound it made was chilling. Not a growl exactly, not a bark. Much lower, almost speaking, deep within its throat, long and drawn out, suddenly a sequence of quick choking, then that drawl-like laryngitic moaning. He was staring at the bloody lips, the froth that dripped in great gobs from the corners, and as it stopped biting at the chain and went back to the bone-revealing sore that it was chewing on one hind leg, he was gripping the fence and looking at the unmown grass here, gasping to control the churning in his stomach. He was staring at what he could only call the face of evil. Later he would recollect how those peculiar words occurred to him. He'd judge and weigh them, hoping to condemn their wild emotion, but he knew that they were fitting. He had never seen such open, brutal, insane evil, and his instinct was to flee from here, to clear the image from his sight.

Instead, he rushed along the fence until he faced another backyard, climbing over, straining to see every

113

portion of this yard in case there maybe was a dog in here as well, but there was nothing, just a tiny plastic wading pool, and he ran past it, hurrying along the side until he reached the sidewalk in the front, and then he swung across the next yard toward the front door of the house whose dog was baying even more grotesquely.

If he'd been the man he claimed to be, he would have known what next would happen, would have paid attention to the weed-choked lawn, the untrimmed bushes, would have understood the owner here. But he was taken up with urgency. He gripped the wobbly railing, charging up the stairs. He pressed the doorbell, but the television blared out from the open window so he couldn't hear the doorbell. He couldn't even hear the dog now, and he pressed the button once again, staring through the screen door past the open wooden door in there and toward the shadowed living room. He realized the doorbell wasn't working. As a crowd cheered in there, he was banging on the screen door. He was shouting, "Anybody home?", banging so hard that the wood was trembling, and a shadow moved in there, pale against the murky sofa, someone coming to the door.

The man was husky, naked to the waist, a can of beer in one hand, face unshaven. "Yeah, what is it?"

"Look, your dog—"

"I know. She won't stop barking."

"She needs treatment."

"What? I told the neighbors I was working on that. Why, I even got a special collar."

"I don't—"

"One with batteries. The kind that sends a shock to stop her barking."

Accum gaped.

"Just who are you?"

"The coroner."

"You live around here?"

"No, I—"

114

"Well, then, mind your own damn business."

There was no way he was going to make him understand. He gripped the door to pull it open, heading in there.

"Hey now, wait a minute."

"Got to use your phone."

"The store down on the corner."

"There's no time."

The crowd was cheering on the television. As he squirmed to get around the man, he saw beyond the sofa where the television showed two boxers slugging at each other in the middle of the ring.

"I'm losing patience."

"Rabies."

"Don't be nuts. She had her shots. The collar makes her act that way."

"I can't afford to take the chance."

The two men now were struggling toward the middle of the room.

"I have to phone a vet."

"If you're not out of here, you're going to have to phone an ambulance."

But Accum managed to slip past him, dodging toward the phone which he had seen beside the sofa.

"Now you stop right there."

But he was dialing.

"Okay, buddy, don't forget I warned you."

As the woman's voice came on the phone to tell him "Animal Associates," Accum turned in time to see the hand that held the beer can lunging toward him. He was vaguely conscious of the other hand that set him up and held him steady. But the blow that split his face and shocked him backward he was never conscious of at all. He had a sense of someone moaning, and he wondered through the spinning darkness what that murky cheering was.

45

It crouched behind the deer cage, watching as the brown and white police car reached the lane end, stopped a moment, and then drove up toward the swimming pool. The thought of water made it gag again, and when it crawled out from its cover to be certain that the car continued moving, it saw people diving from the high board, bursting in the water, splashing, and it had to turn away to keep from retching. There were people over by the swings and slides, children and a mother. They were laughing. There were people, one man and a woman, coming toward the deer cage. In the cage, the deer had long since shifted toward the side away from it. They stared at it, their withers rippling nervously, and it was bothered by them just as much as by the people coming near. Those antlers— and it wanted only to be on its own, to hole up somewhere safe, to stop the spasms racking through it. Finally the people reached the deer cage, and it scurried through the bushes up the slope. It dimly recollected that a walkway angled up the slope above there, and it reached the walkway, wooden steps that cut up high across the slope. It started running. In the sunlight, it was pawing at its eyes and squinting. Once it stumbled, falling, and it scrambled on all fours now, rasping, whining, bleeding through the bandage on its hand. It reached the top, and it could see the mansion over there. Its mother once had brought it here to see the place, a big tall old-time house with many rooms and stairways, and it yet retained the image of those darkened corners, all those sheltered crannies it could hide in. Squinting far around, glancing toward the park down there, the people, it was turning toward the mansion once again. It saw the trees that grew around the
116

place, the bushes, and the gravel drive that led up to the front steps. Now it saw the car parked in the front, and it was ducking toward the bushes, shifting closer. All those darkened rooms. The front door suddenly came open, and it paused among the bushes. Then a man came out, and he was talking to a woman. They had boxes in their hands.

"The afternoon's been slow. I don't think anyone will come up now."

"Well, I've got guests. I can't stay any longer."

They had closed the door. The man reached up to put a key inside the lock.

"I didn't tell you. Eva phoned. She couldn't find her key."

"Well, she can get mine in the morning."

"No, she wants to do her work today. She can't come in tomorrow."

"But if vandals—"

"Just ten minutes. I expected her before this."

"It was your idea."

"What a gentleman."

And they were laughing as they started down the stairs.

It crouched behind the bushes, watching as they put the boxes in the car.

"I'll drive you home."

"No, that's all right. I need the walk. So when's your next shift?"

"Not for two weeks. Sunday afternoon."

"They've got me chairing meetings."

"Well, I'll see you."

He was nodding, walking down the gravel driveway, and the woman now was getting in her car and driving past the man. She blared her horn. The man was waving, and soon both the man and car were out of sight.

It waited just a while, regardless. Then it crept out from the bushes, running toward the porch. It huddled by the steps and looked around, then scampered up the steps and turned the knob, and it was in there.

117

Very quiet, dark and musty. It remembered now the long wide hallway, bigger than the living room at home, and there were tables, stacks of papers to one side here, and a box where people put their money in.

Its mother had, at any rate. She had explained about historical societies, and how an old house like this had to be preserved for people to appreciate the way things used to be. It hadn't understood the words exactly, but it sort of had the sense that this old place was special, and it hadn't liked the must back then, but now it did.

The hall was shadowed, rooms on both sides, old-time furniture in there with guns up on the wall and maps and oval photographs. It listened, but there wasn't any movement in the house, and it was creeping forward. Now it saw a large room with the longest table it had ever seen, huge-backed chairs beside it, plates and glasses set out, knives and forks and more spoons than it understood, as if a party soon would happen, people eating. There were ghosts here, it was sure, but oddly, that was comforting. The staircase wound up toward the second floor, a caged-in elevator to the side. Its mother had explained about the elevator, how the elevator, how the platform rose without an engine. You just pulled down on the rope that dangled in there, and a pulley then would turn to raise you. But the cage had boards across the front, and anyway it never would have stepped inside there. All those bars. The place was too much like a trap.

It walked a little farther, pausing as the floor creaked. No, it made that noise itself. There wasn't anybody in here, and it wondered where to go. Up the stairs or toward the cellar. No, the cellar would be like a trap as well, and so, boards creaking, it was inching up the stairs.

And stopping as the front door swung in. And it turned, the daylight out there strong and painful, staring at the man who stood within the open doorway. This man had just left. He'd walked until he'd disappeared along the gravel driveway. That was why there
118

hadn't been a warning, why there hadn't been a car sound to alarm it, and it hissed now as the man came forward toward it.

"Yeah, that's just what I expected. Leave the door unlocked, she says. God dammit, kid, get out of here."

It kept on hissing.

"What's your name? I'm mad enough to call the cops."

It growled then, and the man stopped, frowning.

"None of that damn stuff. You get your ass on down here."

One more step. The man was at the bottom of the stairs. He reached, and it was leaping, body arcing down the stairs to jolt the man and send him sprawling.

"Hey, God dammit." But the man apparently expected that it next would try to scramble past him toward the open door. The man lunged to the side to block it, neck uncovered, and it dove in straight below the chin.

"My Jesus."

They were struggling. Now it felt the blood spurt in its mouth. It gagged again. The taste was not unpleasant, even in a way compelling, though the choking was an agony. It chewed and swallowed, gagging.

And abruptly couldn't breathe.

The man was squeezing at its throat. It felt the pressure in its chest. It squirmed. It twisted.

"Goddamn kid."

Then teeth free, it was snarling at the hands around its throat. It tried to bite the hands but only nipped the acrid cigarette-vile suit coat sleeves, and suddenly one leg was underneath it, pushing, as it flew high to one side, its body cracking on the hardwood floor and rolling sharp against a table.

Even so, its instinct now was automatic. Turning, it was scrambling on all fours and braced to spring again. The man was rolling, coming to his feet. They stared at one another.

Then the man looked at the blood across his clothes.

He touched his neck. "My God!" He understood now, hands up, stumbling backward.

And it leaped, but not enough to drop the man, just knock him farther backward. "Oh, my God!" the man kept saying. And the open door was suddenly behind the man. The man was out there, kicking as it leaped again. Its shoulder took the kick. The jolt spread through its body. It was falling, landing on that shoulder. It was crawling back and snarling.

Snarling not just toward the man but toward the car sound coming up the lane now. It was squinting past the man toward where the car was coming into view. A different car. A different woman driving. It was snarling, crawling farther toward the stairs. Its shoulder wasn't working. It was listing, snarling, at the stairs now. As it heard the car door out there coming open, as the man turned glancing quickly out there, it was mustering the little strength it yet retained and scuttling up the stairs. The stairs kept winding. They kept going round and round. It reached the second floor and, out of sight from down there, huddled, tensing.

"Mr. Cody!"

It heard rushing footsteps on the outside stairs.

"Good Lord! Your throat! The—Mr. Cody!"

"Never mind me. Get in there and call the cops, an ambulance."

It heard the body slumping down the doorjamb, heard the rasping.

"Watch for *some* kid, *some*thing, on the stairs."

It swung to face the hallway.

46

It was higher in the mountains. Once a pack of dogs had come for it, but it had snarled, and they had stopped then, sniffing toward it, ears low, edging backward. It had feinted toward them, and they'd scattered, fleeing toward the bushes. It had seen their tails between their legs, their frightened backward glances, and it glared a moment in its triumph. Then it scanned the forest toward the mountains, spellbound by the snow up there, whatever called it, lurching higher.

47

Willie heard the scratching. It was coming from his cellar door. He'd been out drinking with his brother all night. They had found two girls and come back here to his place. Now when he had wakened, they were nowhere to be seen. The place was littered, beer cans, liquor bottles, cushions on the floor, and cigarette burns in the carpet. There were french fires on the table from two nights ago, and he was laughing to himself at what his wife would say if she were back here. Then he reached inside the fridge to get an Oly, and he heard the scratching that was shredding at his cellar door. At first he thought it was an animal, but all the windows down there were nailed shut. There wasn't any outside door. He got it then. His brother. Sure, they went down there and, when he woke up, guessed that they would scare him. He was grinning as he opened the door, and she was waiting.

"Hi ya, sweetie."

But her smile was strange, and blood was dripping from her lips. He frowned. She started toward him, and his first thought was that she had hurt herself, his second that his only weapon was the beer can. Willie never had a third. The sharp long nails which last night he'd admired ripped his throat and scratched his eyes. He fell against the sink and cracked his head. He heard her fumbling in the knife drawer.

48

"Look, you've got to help me."

Accum blinked up at the shirtless man. The television news was droning.

"I don't—"

"Hey, you didn't give me any choice. I didn't mean to hit you that hard."

And the afternoon came back to him. His head hurt when he moved it, and his lips and nose felt like another person's. When he touched them, they were senseless, swollen, but he felt the blood, and he was groaning.

"Look. My dog. You've got to help me."

"What's the matter?"

"She's not moving. She just lies there, staring at me."

"Jesus, stay away from her."

"I am. My God, if only I had listened. Can I get it if she licked me?"

He was struggling to sit up now. "When?"

"This morning. She was acting fine then."

"Wash your hands! I hope you didn't touch your mouth. You don't have any cuts she might have licked?"

"I can't remember."

"What?"

"I don't have any cuts. I don't remember if I touched my mouth."

"I told you, wash your hands." The effort of the conversation made him dizzy. He was slumping back. "Use disinfectant. Gargle. Mouthwash. Change your clothes." And he was gripping at the sofa arm to brace himself and stand. He fell back. Then he drew a breath and made it to his feet. The blood was all across his tie and shirt. That made him angry, and that helped him. "Hurry up and wash your hands." Then suddenly he thought about the hand that split his lip and smashed his nose. He bolted down the hallway, shoving past the man who now was in the bathroom. "Get away. I've got to wash my face."

He splashed it, soaped his hands and scrubbed his face, scrubbed until the pain began, and yet he kept on scrubbing. He was peering at the blood that mingled with the soap upon his hands and dripped among the swirling water in the sink. He kept on scrubbing. Then he grabbed a towel and scoured until the porous cloth was bloody.

"Rubbing alcohol!" he ordered, fumbling in the cabinet behind the mirror, but he couldn't find it. "Alcohol!" he shouted, and the man was pulling at the door below the sink. They saw the bottle at the same time. Accum grabbed it, twisting at the cap and splashing. But he needed more. He leaned his face down sideways toward the sink. He poured. The hot sweet alcohol was flooding, burning. He was snorting. Then the effort took its toll, and he was sinking to his knees.

"My God, you're just as crazy as that dog out there."

"You hardly know the half of it. Just wash your hands and face and gargle as I told you."

He was slowly coming to his feet. The man was at the sink, swabbing soap around his hands. Accum stared, and he was angry. Lord, I might need shots. Then he was stumbling from the bathroom, down the hallway toward the kitchen. Out there, through the window, he now saw the dog stretched out, the blood and foam around her mouth, slack-jawed, staring off at nothing.

That was all he needed. He was groping from the kitchen toward the phone.

He had to concentrate to dial. The buzzer kept on sounding. No one answered. What's the matter with them? Saturday. He peered down at his watch. Of course, they won't be there now. He was flipping through the phone book. Vets. And then he had it, dialing.

This time someone answered.

"Dr. Owens."

"Yes, who's calling, please?"

"The coroner."

"I'm sorry. He's not home right now. I'll have him call.... No, wait a second. He's just coming in."

"Yes, Dr. Owens here."

"It's Accum. There's a dog I think has rabies."

"You're quite certain?"

"No. I told you I just think that's what it is. The dog has got some kind of collar that sends shocks to stop her barking. Hell, this could be heat exhaustion or distemper. I don't know. You'd better get on over here."

49

The blind man paused where he was making tea. His dog was growling once again. He hadn't heard her growl like this since they had gone out walking two nights earlier, and suddenly he was afraid. Somebody must have come in while he took her to the park. He started backing toward the cupboards.

"Someone there?"

The dog kept growling.

He was holding up his hands. "Please, I'm an old man. Steal, but just don't hurt me."

She was close now to defend him, and he waited for the gunshot or the hatchet as he understood that there was no one else, that she was growling just at him, and he was praying.

50

Dunlap gripped the dashboard as the cruiser swerved too sharply around the corner, skidding past the swimming pool and up the tree-lined gravel driveway.

He was watching now as Slaughter grabbed the microphone. "It's Nathan, Marge. I'm almost there. Make sure you send those other units. What about the ambulance?"

"It's on its way."

"I hope so."

Dunlap looked down past the trees and toward the park spread out below him. When he glanced ahead, the road was curving, and abruptly he could see beyond the trees up to the hilltop, wide three-story mansion up there, last rays of the sunlight glinting off the windows, driveway curving past the front porch, columns with a roof above the driveway.

Slaughter skidded. Dust cloud settling, Dunlap got out quickly, Slaughter putting on his hat and hurrying before him through the dusk. They reached the front stairs, footsteps scratching on the stone.

The two policemen turned to them.

"The kid is on the second level."

"Or the third. You're sure he's even up there?"

"Ask these people."

Dunlap looked and had to turn away. A man was

slumped inside the front door, shirt and suit a mass of blood, his throat ripped open, his hands clutched at his his wound.

"The ambulance," a woman blurted.

"On its way. You're sure he's up there?"

"Mr. Cody—this is Mr. Cody—said the boy ran up the stairs as I stopped in the driveway."

"That's your car?"

She nodded.

"Better move it. There's a lot of traffic coming up here."

Even as he said that, they were turning toward a cruiser speeding up the gravel driveway. Just behind it, siren wailing, came the ambulance.

"We'd better move him. Can you walk?"

The man was nodding, struggling weakly to get off the floor.

"Here, let me help you." Slaughter faced the two policemen. "Watch those stairs." He held the man and walked with him across the stone porch down the stairs. The two attendants from the ambulance were running toward him. Officers were running from the other cruiser.

Now the woman came down helping.

"Is there any way to get down from the second story?"

"There's a roof above the servants' quarters in the back. I don't know how he'd jump down and not hurt himself."

"The trees around the house."

"I never thought—I just don't know."

"The back," he told the two policemen running toward him. "Make sure no one leaves the building. It's the kid we're looking for."

"The kid?"

"Just make sure no one leaves. Be careful of the roof above the servants' quarters."

Slaughter gave the wounded man to the attendants. They were staring at the blood across his own hands
126

and his shirt. "A young boy bit him. That's right, isn't it?" he asked the woman.

They were staring as she nodded.

"Bit me," Dunlap heard the injured man repeating, voice distorted, barking. Added to what he'd been feeling, he was fearful that the jagged throat would do the job and make him sick. He had to glance away again.

More sirens, two police cars skidding up the gravel driveway, dust cloud rising all around them. Slaughter was already walking toward them.

Dunlap stood there in the middle of it all. His hands were shaking. He was sweating for a drink, and brother, did he need one. There were times when he suspected he would scream. That's just dramatics. You were looking for a story. Now you've got one. He was not yet certain what was going on here, but whatever, it was getting worse, and if he screwed this story up as he had screwed up many others, simply out of weakness, there was no one he could blame except himself. You'll get your drink. Just keep control. This thing tonight is almost finished.

Is it? Maybe it's just getting started, and he saw the two attendants put the injured man in back. The woman was inside her car and moving it. Slaughter stood between the cruisers, talking to the officers who'd just arrived.

He turned to face the mansion, squinting through the dusk toward what he guessed were two policemen in there. This was all too much. He didn't know if he could stand it. He was shaking even worse. He started walking toward the woman who was getting from her car where she had moved it to the side.

"What *is* this place?"

"The Baynard mansion."

"What?"

And Dunlap learned then about Baynard who had been the richest man around here. Back in 1890. "He had cattle all across the valley, and he built this place up here to suit a southern woman he had married."

127

There was something automatic in the way she said it, as if she had said it many times before. He watched with wonder as in bits and pieces she explained how Baynard had brought from the South the wood, the furniture, the bushes, everything to make his wife feel more at home. And then his wife had gone back South one summer where she died, either that, or else she'd left him, and he lied about her dying.

"No one knows. We've tried to find the record of her death. We never managed. She had reasons if she left him. He was hardly ever home, gone on business, working as a senator. Plus, there were rumors about certain kinds of parties on the third floor. But he said she'd died, and everyone agreed to that, and he came back and never left the house again."

He learned how people said that Baynard wandered through the house for days on end. The cause of death was claimed to be a heart attack, but everyone suspected he just drank himself to death. And one thing more—the rumors that he killed her, that she told him she was leaving, and an overbearing man like him, he flew in such a rage that she was dead before he even knew he'd struck her. Then he hid the body, and he wasted in his grief. At last he killed himself, and members of the family hushed it up.

"But those are rumors. No one ever proved it, though in recent years they looked for her. They never were successful, though."

"But back in 1890—how come *you* know all about this?"

"I'm a member of the Potter's Field Historical Society."

"I still don't understand."

And she explained then: "No one lives here. Baynard had two children. They grew up to manage the estate. Then *they* had children, and this new set gave the mansion to the county to avoid the taxes. They're not wealthy anymore. They live in houses down the hill beside the swimming pool. We've fixed this place up just the way it used to be. The plumbing's from the 1890s. We don't have the power on. To get around at night, you have to use some candles or a lantern."

Oh, that's swell, he thought. The only thing that's missing is a thunderstorm.

Well, there would be no storm, but sundown would do fine. He saw the orange distorted disc where it was almost down behind the western mountains. Soon the grounds would be completely dark, except for flashlights, headlights, maybe even candles, lanterns as this woman suggested, and the search up through the mansion for the little boy. He felt his scalp begin to tighten as the woman said behind him, "Whose child is it?"

"I don't know."

Exhausted, he walked toward where Slaughter spoke to the policemen.

"We need nets," he heard as he came closer.

"Nets?"

And Dunlap saw that it was Rettig, standing with the young policeman he had gone to Slaughter's with this morning. That seemed several days ago.

"You heard me. Nets. You think that we should club him, do you? Shoot him maybe?"

"I don't know where nets are."

"Try a sporting store, that zoo down in the park. Rettig, you're in charge of that. The rest of you, I want you watching both sides of the mansion. Let's get moving."

They were staring hard at Slaughter. Then they started running toward the mansion.

"Hold it," Slaughter told them.

And they turned to face him.

"Give your keys to this man here. I want your headlights on the building."

They were glancing now at Dunlap, who had not expected this. Instinctively, he held his hand out. Then he had a set of car keys. He was looking at them, metal stiff and warm yet from the pocket they had been in. Mindless, he expected more, but then he realized that

129

Rettig would take one car. These keys fit another. Slaughter's was the third car, and the fourth and fifth ones had been driven by the other officers who watched the mansion.

Still uncertain, he was waiting as these three policemen started toward the mansion once again. They separated, two and one, to watch the sides, as Slaughter shoved a ring of keys at him.

"You understand?"

"I think so. I'll spread all the cars out so they're pointed toward the windows."

"Run the engines. I don't want the batteries to die. And use the searchlights by the sideview mirrors."

"What about the woman's car?"

"You've got the right idea."

Dunlap nodded, running toward the cruisers. Slaughter's car he recognized, and Rettig now was speeding down the gravel driveway, siren wailing. He went toward the car beside where Rettig had been parked, and got in, fumbling for a key to fit, and started up the engine. In a while he understood that someone else could just as easily have done this, but the tactic was a way for Slaughter to distract him.

And it helped. There wasn't any doubt about that. Breathing quickly, taken up with interest, he adjusted to the burning in his stomach. He was glad to be in motion, driving toward the mansion, aiming straight ahead and stopping where he judged the headlights would be most effective. He groped down to turn them on. He found the switch upon the searchlight, and he flicked it, and this right side of the mansion, almost to the second story, was now bright against the dusk.

He got out running to reach Slaughter's car and did the same, though this time aiming toward the left side of the mansion, and the place was lit up there as well. The woman had been watching, and she didn't need to have somebody tell her. She was getting in her car to move it once again, aiming toward the front door, and the sun was down below the mountains now, the park a murky gray below him, but the windows here reflected all the headlights, and the people wouldn't have to stumble in the darkness.

Dunlap heard another car. He thought it was a cruiser, but the siren was wailing, and he didn't see the silhouette of dome lights. As it stopped where he was watching, he could see the man and woman. Oh, dear God, no.

They were getting out. "Where's Slaughter?"

"I'm not certain."

Just then Slaughter came out from the mansion, standing on the porch, the glare of headlights on him, staring at them. He abruptly started toward them.

They were rushing.

"Look, you shouldn't be here." Dunlap saw that he was angry. "How'd you know?"

"We have a neighbor with a CB. Have you found him?"

Slaughter pointed toward the upper stories.

"That's as much as I've been told. I'm asking you to go back home and wait to hear."

There wasn't anything to answer. Dunlap thought that Slaughter, standing in the headlights' glare, seemed to age a dozen years, cheeks now sagging, dark lines underneath his eyes. Christ, Slaughter wasn't angry. He was frightened.

"Why would he be hiding? Let me go up there and talk to him," the woman said.

"No, I don't think so." Slaughter scraped his boot sole in the dust. "I think that you should let me handle this."

"You heard my wife. She's going up there."

"I can't let you."

"That's what you think."

They were rushing forward. Slaughter stepped ahead to cut them off.

"Those headlights, these police cars. Hell, you've scared him half to death," the husband said.

"I'm trying not to tell you, but you evidently haven't

131

heard the rest. You son attacked again. A man this time. The man is nearly dead."

The wife was frozen, mouth half open. "Oh, my God." The husband gasped.

"The victim's in that ambulance. Go take a look, and then you'll know why I can't let you."

They were turning toward where Slaughter pointed as the two attendants stepped out from the back and shut the doors.

"We've done our best," the one man shouted.

Slaughter nodded as the two men rushed to get inside the front. The siren started as the engine roared, the lights went on, and they were swerving in a circle, speeding down the gravel driveway.

Dunlap watched until he couldn't see it anymore. He turned and saw the woman crying.

"Please. I think that you should leave here," Slaughter said.

"I want to stay."

And Slaughter raised his arms. He let them flop down loose against his sides. "At least stay in the car. The best thing you can do is turn your headlights on the house. And please, don't get out in our way. We've got too much to do. I promise that we'll watch out for his safety."

She was sobbing as her husband held her. They were nodding, moving weakly toward the car.

And then they heard it. Everybody did. They all were turning, mother, father, Slaughter, the policemen by the house, staring toward the upper levels.

Deep inside, above there, which floor wasn't certain, something, someone started howling. It was like a coyote or a dog, a wolf up in the mountains, worse though, mournful, hoarse and hollow, rising, baying, howling, then diminishing, then rising again.

It went on two more times like that, chilling, echoing from somewhere deep above there. Dunlap felt his backbone shiver. Then it ended, and the night, except for idling engines, finally was quiet.

132

"What the hell was that?" a man said faintly from the side.

"I'm not sure I want to know," another said.

And Slaughter, Dunlap close beside him, started racing toward the front door of the mansion.

51

It was gripping at the body's ankles, dragging him across the kitchen. On the stairs, the head kept bumping. Then it reached the cellar floor, and it was grateful for the darkness. Breathing in the must, it pulled the body toward the others in the corner, one man and a woman, stretched beside each other, and it set this new man by the woman. It was breathing in the blood smell from them, staring at the ravaged necks and faces, at the knife which yet protruded from the stomach of this second man. It snarled then without reason, and it wiped its hands upon its dress. Yes, this was better. There was no need to go out now, and the night would soon be on it. Feeling dizzy, it was slumping in the corner by this second man. It dipped its finger in the blood there, licking, and it absently was scratching at the burning, itching arm where yesterday its cat had bitten.

52

Accum gripped the rear door of the clinic, stepping in the lab. He saw the dog up on the table, plastic sheet beneath it, Owens there beside it in his lab suit and his face mask.

Owens turned to him. He didn't even greet him, only said, "The dog was dead before I got it in here."

Accum stared at him.

"But hell, I saw it in the active stage. A couple hours later, and it's dead? Paralysis should take a good deal longer."

"Maybe. I agree with you. This could be something else. You'll find a coat and face mask in that locker over there."

He went across to get them, found a pair of rubber gloves. He put them on, and he was conscious of the buzzing lights up in the ceiling as he walked back to the table.

"First, let's get this collar off." And Owens fumbled to unsnap it, staring at the battery attachment. "What I'd like to do to that guy." He was setting it aside. "You ought to meet some people who come in here, wanting us to make their dog mute, cut its voice box out, its vocal cords. I'd like to cut on them. At least they wouldn't talk so much then." Owens' face was red above his mask. He shook his head. "Well, let's get to it. You're the legend in this sort of thing. Do you cut, or shall I?"

"No. Thanks for asking, but you know your business. I'm just here to help."

"I need that scalpel."

Four quick strokes, and Owens peeled the scalp off. Then the drill. He flicked the switch. The bit was whirring, grinding four holes, widely spaced to form the corners of a square. And then the saw. He used it neatly, motor buzzing as he cut from one hole to another, swiftly, gently, not too deeply. Then the job was done, and he was prying at the skull bone.

"Well, the brain is swollen and discolored. You can see that slight pink color. Indications. On the other hand, distemper sometimes looks like that. I need to take the brain out and dissect it."

Accum handed him the scalpel, then the forceps, and the brain was in a glass dish on the table.

"Ammon's horn."

"That's right." And Owens cut the portion that he wanted. "You can do the slides."

"You want them pressed or done in sections?"

"No, the sections take too long. Just do impressions. What we're looking for will show up just as well."

So Accum simply pressed a bit of tissue on the slide and smeared it evenly, then looked around.

"It's over by the cabinet."

The microscope was in a wooden case, a jar of Seller's stain beside it. Accum put some stain across the specimen to make what he was looking for stand out in contrast. He arranged the slide and peered down through the lenses.

"Can you see them? Negri bodies."

Accum kept on peering.

"What's the matter? You should see them."

Accum turned to him and shook his head. "I think you'd better look."

"You mean you didn't see them, and we have to do the other tests?"

"I mean that you should take a look."

Now Owens frowned as he peered through the lenses.

What they'd looked for was some evidence of Negri bodies. These were tiny, round, and sometimes oval structures in the protoplasm of the nerve cells in that portion of the brain called Ammon's horn. In current theories, they were either rabies virus particles, or else degenerative matter from the cells affected by the virus. Maybe both. But seeing them was certain proof that rabies was at work here.

"I don't get it. Something's wrong. They shouldn't look like that."

But Accum knew. He watched as Owens peered down through the lenses once again. Because the things he'd

135

seen were neither round nor oval. They were oblong with an indentation on one side.

"They look like goddamn peanuts," Owens said. "What's going on here?"

"Some related virus?"

"What? You tell me what."

"I just don't know."

"You bet you don't, and I don't either. Rabies is a thing I made sure that I'd recognize, and you can bet there's nothing in the books about these things we're looking at."

"We'll have to do the antibody test."

"It takes a couple hours, and the mouse test takes at least a week. I want to know what this thing is."

"We have to guess for now its rabies. Or a virus that has all its symptoms."

"Which is fine if no one were exposed to it. But what about the owner? And yourself? If this were rabies, then you'd have to take the serum shots, but we don't know if they'd be any good."

They stared at one another. Accum touched his mask, the swollen lip beneath it. He'd forgotten, or more truthfully, he'd tried to keep from thinking of those shots. "I'll take them anyway."

"But what if they don't work well with the virus? What if there's a bad reaction?"

"Hell, if I've already got it, I'll be dead soon anyway. What difference does it make?"

It almost sounded comic, although neither of them laughed. But if he had pretended to forget about his danger, there was something else he knew he really had forgotten. Something that the owner first had told him, that he'd let slip by in the excitement, something that the rabies shots reminded him about.

"He said his dog had been inoculated."

"What?"

"The owner. He first told me that the dog received her shots. I just remembered."

"What's his name?"

He told him.

"We're the only clinic, so his file will have to be here. Try some other slides. Make sure we didn't do them wrong. I'll come back in a minute."

Accum did what he was told. His legs were shaking as he stumbled toward the microscope. He peered at all the slides, and each one was the same, and he was really scared now.

Owens pushed the door more strongly than he had to, tensing Accum.

"He was right. That dog is five years old. She had her puppy shots, her boosters every year."

"Well, could the boosters be the cause of this? Contamination in the vaccine?"

"I don't know, but sure as hell I'm going to learn."

"Even if the vaccine were prepared correctly, could the dog have been so weak that it caught rabies from the vaccine?"

"In the case of rabies, maybe. With a weak dog. One chance in a hundred thousand. But I don't know how that vaccine would produce the thing we're looking at."

"One chance might be all this thing would need."

And they were frowning at each other.

"Look, I've got to make a call."

He grabbed the phone and dialed. Marge was answering.

"I've got to talk to Nathan."

"He's been looking for you."

"What?"

And she was telling him, and he was feeling even sicker.

"On my way."

He hung up, turning now to Owens. "Run the antibody test, the fluoroscope. I'll get back just as soon as I can manage."

"But what is it?"

There was no time to explain. He ripped the coat

137

and gloves and face mask off. He pulled the door to meet the darkness.

53

It was howling in there.
"What's the matter?"
They were grouped along the sidewalk, neighbors staring at the house.
"It's been like that for several hours."
"Can't somebody stop it?"
"What about the old man. It's his dog."
"He's blind."
"That's what I mean. He must have hurt himself."
They started up the sidewalk.
"Hell, I only see him on the street."
"Well, someone's got to do it."
He was frowning, sighing, climbing up the steps. He didn't like the howling in there, fearful that the old man maybe died, that—
He was knocking on the door. The howling stopped. He glanced back at his neighbors.
"Go on. Knock again."
He did, but no one answered.
"Anybody home?"
He tried the door, and it was locked. He went along the porch to peer in through a window, and the dog came through the window at him.

54

"*Jesus. Lord,* I wish that thing would stop."

The men were standing in the headlights, net spread out before them as the howling kept on from the upper stories.

"What if he attacks us?"

"Just don't hurt him," Slaughter told them. "Keep the net between you and the boy. We'll get him tangled in it. After that, we shouldn't have much problem."

Slaughter looked at Dunlap, hoping Dunlap understood how clear and cautious every order had been. If this thing turned sour, he was not prepared to read about brutality. He wanted all his men to know without a doubt that they were only to restrain the boy. He squinted from the headlights angled toward the porch. He saw the mother and the father, and they still weren't in their car. He saw the woman from the Potter's Field Historical Society, the other cruisers that had reached here not too long ago, the headlights of another cruiser speeding up the gravel driveway.

"Well, we've got enough men. Let's get to it."

But the headlights weren't another cruiser. Slaughter recognized the car. He told them, "Wait a second," as he stepped down off the porch, as Accum got out rushing toward him.

"Where have *you* been? I've been looking—" Slaughter saw the blood across his shirt, the mangled lips. "What happened to your face?"

"It's not important." Accum drew a breath. "There

139

isn't any time. I know this thing's a virus, but I'm not sure if it's rabies."

"Is it just as bad?"

"It's maybe worse." He drew another breath. "It seems to work much faster. There's a dog that passed through one stage of the virus sooner than it should have. We're still doing tests."

"Well, what about this boy up there?"

And Accum winced as he heard howling from the upper stories. "That's a boy who's doing that?" His face was twisted with the shock of disbelief.

"I have to think it is. There could be some stray dog up there, but we don't have a reason to believe that."

"Back in med school... But the other symptoms weren't the same as this. A man with rabies might get vicious, even bark and snap at someone."

"Bark?"

"It kills the nervous system. All the muscles in the neck constrict. The victim tries to talk, but every word comes out like barking."

"This is *howling.*"

"That's exactly what I mean. The symptoms aren't the same. That sounds more like an animal. Besides, I never heard of anyone with rabies who had actually attacked someone. Oh, I read cases in the books but never met a doctor who had actually been witness to it."

"But the parents claim the boy was never bitten."

"Sure, and I just saw a dog that had its shots, and now it's dead back at the vet's."

The howling once again had started. They were turning toward the almost full moon that was rising, shining toward the hill and on the house.

"The moon. I should have realized."

"You've lost me."

"Well, that symptom is at least consistent. Rabid victims are enraged by light. Their eyes are sensitive. They seek out darkness. When the moon comes out, they start reacting to it."

140

"Howling?"

"Rabid dogs will, and in this case one small boy."

"They say he cut his hand on glass this morning."

"That's too soon. It takes at least a week before the rabies virus starts to work. But if this thing is quicker than the normal virus, if the glass were licked by anything contaminated, that would be enough to do it. When you catch him, I want to see that cut."

The howls were rising.

"It's like something, someone crazy," Slaughter told him.

"Lunacy, they used to call it. Madness from the moon."

And Slaughter didn't want to talk about this anymore. "I have to go in after him." He paused. Then he was starting toward his men up on the porch.

"I'll bring my bag."

"We'll need it," Slaughter called back, and he hurried up the stone steps to his men. "Is everybody ready?"

They were tense and nodding.

"Keep your gloves on. Rettig, you can hold the net at that end. You three hold it at the other end and in the middle. Just remember. No one hurt him."

Slaughter turned to Dunlap once again to see that he had heard, and they were starting in.

But Dunlap was behind him.

"You stay out."

"I want to see."

"I don't have time to keep you safe from trouble."

"I'll be careful."

"You're damn right you will. You'll stay there on the porch."

And Dunlap stared at him. They waited in the headlights. Slaughter suddenly was mindful of their friendship.

"Fine, I'll take a chance on you. The first time you get in the way, you'll find your ass out on the porch."

"That's all I'm asking."

Slaughter studied him. He turned toward Accum, who was coming with his bag. "You'll need these gloves."

"Hey, I will too."

"You won't be close enough to need them."

They were moving through the big wide hallway toward the curving staircase. Men were spread out at the bottom, net before them.

"Ready with your flashlights?"

They were nodding, turning on the flashlights, beams now arcing up the stairs. Slaughter heard their breathing, smelled their sweat.

What kind of outfit runs this place that they don't leave the power on? he thought. He didn't have an answer. "Then let's do it."

Footsteps shuffling, scraping, they were starting, net spread out before them, up the stairs.

55

It waited. It had scurried to the final landing. Now it heard their footsteps and their whispers, saw their sweeping flashlight beams. They yet were quite a distance down there, but in time they would be up here, and it hissed once as it swung in search of cover. But it saw no rooms behind it, just this one big open space that stretched from end to end. It didn't understand, although it did retain a far-off recollection of its mother who'd explained this. There were slight projections from each corner, spaces in behind, but these would be too obvious. It needed something else. And then it saw what it was looking for. A perfect hiding place and one it could attack from if it had to. It was scurrying to reach the place, and all the while, it kept on glancing at the glow that swept in through the window, cold and

142

pale across the floor. It started howling, couldn't stop itself, was powerless to fight the urge, just crouched there, head up, howling long and high, its throat constricted painfully, and then the urge had been relieved, and it was scurrying. The darkness in this hiding place was wonderful, the blackness soothing and secure. It closed its eyes to rest them after squinting at that cold pale glow that spilled in through the windows. It was breathing quickly, nervous even though the hiding place was comforting. It licked its lips, the scabs of blood that clung in specks against its mouth. That salt taste which it now had grown accustomed to and even had begun to crave. The salt taste had been liquid, and that recollection made it gag again. It started howling.

56

They were stopped down on the second landing.

"It's up on the third floor."

"Maybe," Slaughter told them.

"But you heard it howling."

"We don't know if there's a dog in here as well. I say we do this as we planned it. Gordon, you're so eager. Shine that flashlight up the stairs. Don't wait to yell if you see movement."

"Oh, don't worry. If there's anything, I'll yell my goddamn head off."

Slaughter studied him. "You wish you hadn't come now?"

"Wouldn't miss it."

"You must want that story bad."

"You just have no idea."

Slaughter saw the way the flashlight beam was shaking.

"Booze or nerves?"

"I couldn't tell you."

Slaughter took the light away from him. "I'm sorry. This is too important. Better take this." And he gave the light to Accum. "Do it just the way I told him. No hard feelings?"

Dunlap shrugged, and Slaughter didn't have the time to reassure him. He ignored him, turning to his men. "Okay, we work along this hall and check the rooms. I don't expect to find him on this level, but I can't depend on any expectation."

So, the net spread out before them, they were moving through the darkness. When they reached the first doors on each side, they stopped and looked at Slaughter.

"Try the left side. I'll stay here and watch the other."

Breathing hoarsely, they went slowly in. But there was nothing. They shone flashlights in the corners and the closets, just an old-time bedroom with a canopy above the bed, a net that came down shutting out mosquitoes. They looked underneath the bed, and then they came out, checking all the other rooms along the hallway. Other beds, a playroom, and a study, all rigged out as if a hundred years ago, maps and photographs and guns up on the walls, a chair that looked as if old Baynard had just risen from it, but nobody in there, and they came out, staring down the hall toward Accum waiting, flashlight angled up the stairs.

"I guess we know he's up there," Slaughter said.

They faced the stairs, and net spread out, they started up. Their flashlight beams were making crazy angles on the walls and ceiling. They were shuffling as if any moment they expected some small figure to come hurtling toward them, but instead they reached the final landing, and they swung their beams across the big, third-story room.

"Well, I don't get it," Slaughter said. "What *is* this place?" His voice was echoing.

"You've never been here?" Rettig asked him.

"Always meant to. Never took the time."

144

"The ballroom," Rettig told him. "Baynard's wife was southern, and she didn't like the people out here. She was used to parties, dances, fancy dinners. Baynard built this place to suit her, and the ballroom was his special effort. Once a month at least he had a celebration. Ranchers, those with money, used to come from miles around, better people from the town, congressmen and senators. He paid their way. They'd come up from the railroad in the padded carriages he sent for them. He even brought an orchestra from Denver. They would dance and eat and—"

"What's the matter?" Slaughter asked him.

In the dark, the flashlights angling through the ballroom, Slaughter felt his stomach burning.

"Well, I used to hear about it from my father's father, but I never knew if it was true or not. He said the parties sometimes got a little out of hand."

"I don't know what you mean."

Rettig's words were hollow. "You can see the way the balcony juts out from that end. Well, the orchestra played up there. With that solid wooden railing, the musicians couldn't see too much of what went on below them. In the corners and the sides there, you can see the slight partitions that come out."

"They're triangles."

"That's right. You see those padded benches on the sides."

"Well, what about them?"

"Rumors, I suppose. My father's father said that wives were swapped up here, that people went with different partners in around the back of those things. He said there were secret doors that you could go in for some privacy."

"He knew that for a fact?"

"He never was invited. No one ever found a secret door."

"Then that's just rumors, like you said. I mean, a thing like that, somebody would have told."

"And maybe not have been invited anymore."

145

"But Baynard's wife. Why would she have gone along with this? You said that she was from society."

"I didn't mention that she also had a reputation. Baynard was the one who had to go along with it. To keep her with him. Then the parties got a little out of hand. She found a man she liked much better than the rest. Some people say she left with him. Others say that Baynard killed her. But they never found the body."

"Oh, that's swell. So now you've got us searching through some kind of haunted house. Just keep your mind on what you're doing. Gordon, you stay here with Accum. We'll check this end. Then we'll move down toward the other. Shout if anything slips past us. Everybody ready?"

They were nodding, and they slowly worked across to search the corner to their right, moving around the triangle. They knocked the wood in case they might yet find a secret door. They crossed to search the other corner. Then they moved along the big wall, going around the triangle on that side.

"Nothing so far. But we've still got two partitions and the balcony. We've almost got him. Just be careful."

There was nothing in the far left corner, nothing in the right.

"Okay, he's up there in the balcony. He's got to be."

They started up the narrow stairs. But there was no room for four of them.

"This isn't working," Slaughter told them.

They were grateful for the chance to wait.

"Rettig, you stay back. You other three can go up. Rettig will be just behind you."

Rettig breathed out with relief. The other three were tense, their flashlights glaring up the narrow stairway.

"What about on top of those partitions?" one man said.

"No. How could he climb up?"

And in that brief distraction, faces turned out toward

146

the ballroom, everything began to happen. First, the snarling, then the hurtling body. It came off the balcony, a half-seen diving figure that swooped past them, slamming hard on Rettig, men now scrambling, shouting, bodies rolling on the floor. Slaughter heard the snarling, Rettig's screaming, as he tried to get in past the scrambling bodies. He saw Rettig struggling upward, something hanging on him. He saw Rettig falling backward then, the extra weight upon him as they crashed against the near partition, old board cracking, and the men were rushing forward with the net.

"Where is he?"

"Here, I've got him!"

Rettig kept on screaming. Then the net swung through the flashlight beams toward where he struggled with the figure on the padded bench beside the triangle.

"My Jesus, get him off me!" Rettig shouted, and he kicked, the figure thumping, snarling on the floor.

The net fell down. They had him. Arms and legs were lashing out, entangled worse with every effort. Slaughter pushed between his men and saw them roll the boy to get the net around his back and chest, and there was no way that the boy could get out. He was powerless, except for where he slashed his teeth against the net and snarled at them.

When Slaughter turned, he saw that Accum was beside him, setting down his bag and reaching in to grab a hypodermic.

"Keep him steady."

"You don't think we'll let him go."

Then Accum had a bottle, slipping in the needle, easing out the plunger to get liquid in the chamber. Standing by a flashlight, he pushed slightly on the plunger until liquid spurted from the needle, and he looked at Slaughter. "Pull his shirt sleeve up."

"You're kidding. In that net. I couldn't move it."

"Rip a patch out then. I need to see some skin."

And through the webbing, Slaughter tugged and

147

ripped the shirt sleeve. He was quick, afraid the boy might get at him.

Accum now was swabbing alcohol across the skin and leaning close to press the needle.

One loud yelp as Accum pushed the plunger. Then he straightened. "In a minute."

"What's these bricks here?" someone said, and Slaughter turned. Too much was going on.

"I don't—"

He saw where Rettig's fall had broken the partition. In there, as he shone his flashlight, he could see the wall of bricks. He glanced at Rettig who was slumped across the padded bench, his hands up to his throat.

"Are you all right? He didn't bite you?"

Rettig felt all over. He breathed, gasped, and swallowed, breathing once again. He nodded, wiping at his mouth. "I think I only lost my wind." He tried to stand but gave out, slumping once more on the bench. "I'll be okay in just a second. What bricks?"

"There behind you."

Rettig turned, still trying hard to breathe. "I don't know anything about them." He was swallowing again. "I don't think they should be here."

Slaughter didn't even need to ask him. Rettig was already going on. "I guessed that this one sounded different from the others. Much more solid, heavier."

"What's that supposed to mean?" a man was saying.

"Baynard's wife. I think we know what happened to her."

And the group was silent.

Slaughter felt where Dunlap had come beside him. They were peering at the small boy who was tangled, now unconscious, in the net.

"A little kid and all this trouble. Hell, I didn't really understand how little he would be."

They stood around the boy and stared at him.

"We'd better get him to the hospital," Accum told them. "You too, Slaughter. Rettig, you as well. I want to check the both of you."

148

"He never touched me," Slaughter said.

"The cat did. If this virus is like rabies, you're long due to start your shots. Rettig, I don't know. If you don't have a bite, there won't be any problem."

"But I wasn't bitten," Slaughter told him. "Only scratched."

"You want to take the chance?"

And Slaughter shook his head to tell him no.

"That's what I thought. Don't worry. You've got company. I need the shots as well."

"But you weren't bitten either."

"No. But with this bloody lip, I can't take any chances. Here, the boy is harmless now. You men can lift him. Stay clear of his head."

They looked at Slaughter, who was nodding. One man at the boy's legs while another gripped his shoulders, they were lifting.

"Christ, he doesn't weigh a thing."

"That's what I said. A little kid and all this trouble. It's enough to—"

Hollow and disgusted, he was watching as the men worked with the boy to reach the stairs. "Here, someone grab that corner of the net before we have an accident," he told the new recruit, and they were moving off their balance down the stairs.

Slaughter kept his flashlight aimed before him. On the second landing, they turned, headed toward the bottom, and he heard the idling cruisers now. He saw the headlights glaring through the open door, the mother and the father out there, and the woman from the group that ran this place, an officer beside them.

"Take it careful," one man said and paused to get a better grip around the shoulders. "Okay. Now I've got him." And they reached the bottom, moving through the hall to face the entrance.

"Rettig, you can tell that woman what we found up there. Those bricks could mean a dozen things, and none of them important."

"You don't think so."

"I have no opinion. But that damage she should know about."

They went out on the porch. The mother and the father now were running.

"Is he—?"

"Just sedated," Accum told them. "Everything considered, he's been lucky. Stay away from him. I don't want you contaminated. You can see him at the hospital."

They weren't convinced.

"It's simply a precaution," Slaughter said. "We don't know what we're dealing with. Let's put him in the back seat of my car," he told his men.

"You'd better set him on a blanket," Accum said. "We'll burn it at the hospital."

"We have to be that careful?"

Accum only stared at him.

"I'll get a blanket from my car," the father said and hurried.

"Good. That's very good. We need your help."

They moved now toward the cruiser. Slaughter pulled out on the back door, and the father spread the blanket.

"Thank you," Slaughter told him. "I know how hard . . ." He looked at where the mother stood beside the cruiser, crying. "This is hard for all of us."

They set the small boy in there. Accum leaned in, checking. He stayed, leaning in there quite a while. When he came out, even in the darkness out here, Slaughter saw how pale his face had suddenly become.

"I have to talk."

"What is it?"

"Over there."

And Slaughter watched him walking toward the forest. Slaughter waited, thinking, and then followed.

"What's the matter?"

". . . I just killed him."

"What?"

"I should have thought." He wiped his face.

150

"For Christ sake, make some sense."

"The sedative. I should have thought. The dog I found. I called a vet who came and took one look and gave the dog a sedative."

"But what's—?"

"The dog was in paralysis by then. The sedative was just enough to kill it. That boy in your back seat isn't breathing."

"Oh, my God."

"You understand now. I'm not sure exactly how this virus works, but it's damn fast, I know that much at least. He was maybe ready for paralysis. The sedative precipitated everything. It slowed his body down until it killed him."

"You can't—"

"You're damn right I can. I should have paid attention. *I just killed him.*" He was hoarse now, eyes closed, shaking.

Slaughter turned to see the father leaning toward the back seat.

"I don't—Something's wrong," the father told them.

Slaughter watched the mother crying as the father scrambled in. He saw his men, the cruisers, headlights on the mansion, saw the woman Rettig talked to start to run up toward the mansion. He could sense the moon above him, Accum near him shaking, as he felt his world begin to tumble all around him and a creature down there in the park below him started howling at the moon. Dunlap stood to one side taking pictures. Slaughter didn't even have the strength for anger anymore. He let the man continue taking pictures, flasher blinking.

PART TWO

57

He was drunk. He hadn't come back home till nearly one o'clock, and he had stayed outside just long enough to check his horses. Then he'd walked back to his house and with the porch light on had stared down at the cooler filled with tepid water and the beer cans from this morning. There were empties on the porch. There hadn't been a chance to clean up. Too much had begun to happen. But he didn't clean up this time either, simply glanced out at the darkness and then turned to go inside where first he flicked the lights to study one more cooler in the kitchen before heading toward the cupboard where he kept the bourbon. That was something which he almost never drank, but this night had been special, oh, my God, yes, and he almost didn't bother with a glass. He knew that would be too much weakness, though, and since he was determined to be weak to start with, he at least would set some limits. Reaching for the bottle and a glass, he fumbled in the freezer for some ice and poured the glass up to the top and in three swallows drank a third of it.

The shock was almost paralyzing. He put both his hands on the sink and leaned across it, choking, waiting for the scalding flood to settle in his stomach. Now he felt his stomach tensing, and he knew that he had eaten nothing since this morning, that he easily could throw the bourbon up. But then the spasms ebbed and he was breathing, trembling once as if his body had shrugged off the sudden punishment.

He leaned across the sink a moment longer. Then he poured some water with the bourbon, and he started toward the shadowed living room. He earlier had tried to get in touch with Marge, but she was neither at the station nor at home. He almost phoned her once again, but it was too late, and he didn't want to wake her. All the same, he needed someone he could talk to. He recalled as if he yet were there the father crying with the mother, cursing, saying that he'd warned them about so much force to catch a little boy. The hardest part had been the struggle with the father.

"No, you can't go in to touch him."

"He's my son."

"I don't care. He still might contaminate you. As it is, your wife might be infected from that bite."

It took two men at last to keep the father from the back seat of the cruiser. Dunlap had continued taking pictures. Oh, my Jesus, what a mess. And when he'd mustered energy to talk to Dunlap, there had been no sign of him. The man, his former friend, had sense enough to get away while he was able, likely fearing that his pictures would be confiscated. Slaughter didn't know if he would actually have grabbed the camera, but by then he had been scared enough to grab at something. It was just as well that Dunlap had not been around to serve that function. There was little doing by the time he looked for Dunlap anyhow. The mother and the father had been driven home. Accum had gone with the body to the morgue. The officers were shutting up the mansion till they'd come back in the morning to investigate. He himself had stood there in the darkness by his cruiser, staring at the mansion, and he'd heard that howling from below him in the park again, but he had been too weary and disgusted, not to mention frightened, to go down there. He had seen enough for one night, and he had the sense that he would see a lot more very soon. All he wanted was to sit here and anesthetize himself.

But not too much. He'd have to do a lot of talking in the morning. Dunlap, Parsons, Accum, the town council. Lord knows who else. There'd be many, and he wondered how he'd do it. He was certain that the council would request his resignation. Accum very well

155

might lose his job. Hell, never mind his job—his license. They had both been negligent. The father would press charges, sue them.

Accum had gone with the body. Slaughter wished he hadn't let him. "Don't you see I have to know?" his friend had begged. What difference did it make? The boy was dead. There wasn't time to bring in someone else to do the job. They had to know right now how this thing worked.

He sipped his drink and hoped that Accum would discover that the boy had died from other causes than the sedative.

But would the council trust his judgment?

Or yourself, he thought. Would *you* believe him? Do you trust him that much?

Yes, he thought, and when the phone rang and he reached for it, he guessed this might be Marge. It wasn't, just a dead sound on the telephone.

"Who is it?" he repeated, but there wasn't any answer. Slaughter wondered if this could be Accum or the father. "Is there anybody—?"

But the dial tone was buzzing, and he stared down at the phone and set it in its holder. Which he would have done regardless because from the field down by the barn he heard the horses. They were whinnying and snorting. Through the open window and the screen, he heard their hoofbeats skitter one way, then another. He was setting down his glass and rising from the chair. The bourbon made him dizzy, and he waited till his brain was steady before walking toward the door. He'd switched the porch light off when he came in, but now he switched it on again and stepped out, pausing as he glanced around, then turned left off the porch to face the barn. There was something different, and he had to think before he noticed that he didn't hear the insects. They were always rasping in the bushes and the grass. They had been when he drove in, parking, going down to check the horses at the start.

But now the night was silent, heavy, just the skittish

whinny of the horses, and he wished that he had thought to bring a rifle from the house. He had his handgun, though, and in the dark its range was good enough for any target he might see. This likely would be nothing anyhow. The horses sometimes acted like this if they sensed a snake or something like a coyote skulking down that dry wash on the rear side of the barn. Often all he had to do was calm them or else shine a light out in the bushes, and the thing would go away. But with the bourbon working on him, he had left his flashlight in the house, and he was wondering if he was in control enough for this. Considering the trouble that was going on, this might be something, after all.

Despite the moon that shone upon him, he came to the open barn door, reaching quickly in to switch on all the floodlights. There were two sets, one in front and back, which blazed out toward the dry wash and the field beside the barn and toward the house. His eyes hurt briefly as he stared at where the horses galloped toward the right and whinnied and then swung fast toward the left. Their pattern was a kind of circle as if both felt threatened on each side, and though they were a distance from the fence before him, he could see their wild eyes and their twitching nostrils.

"What the hell?"

The words were out before he knew he'd said them, and their sound, mixed with the horses' panic, startled him. He'd never seen them act like this. When there was something here that bothered them, they always made some slight disturbance and then shifted toward a better section of the field. But both were in a frenzy, snorting, twitching, galloping, and he was just about to climb the fence and go out there to calm them when he realized that they might be infected. Sure, a sudden change in manner. That would be a symptom. He could not afford to go to them.

But what else could he do? Assume that something in the darkness bothered them. He hoped that was the

157

case. He loved these horses, and he'd hate to have to shoot them. Well, get moving then. He realized that his reluctance was an indication of how much he had been frightened, and he took a breath, pulled out his gun, then forced himself to walk along the fence to reach the dry wash.

Floodlights brightened everything for fifty yards behind the barn. He saw the red clay, saw the bushes on the slope across there and the trees along the far rim. He glanced once behind him, fearful that there might be something crouched behind the barn, and then, his back protected, he walked slowly toward the near rim of the gully.

There was nothing at the bottom, just the red clay and the boulders and the branches he had thrown in there to stop erosion. All the same, he *felt* that there was something. In the field, the horses yet were skittering and snorting, and he didn't know exactly how to do this. In an average normal summer, he would have no second thoughts before he went down in the gully and then up the other side to check the bushes. After all, what normally could harm him? But this trouble made him reconsider everything. From certain points of view, he had to distrust every living thing. He couldn't bear the horses' panic, couldn't tolerate their agony, however; had to stop what they were doing, so he started down the gully when he heard the branches snapping. Over to his left, across the gully in the bushes, where the floodlights blended with the darkness. Stepping back now toward the rim, he walked along it, squinting toward the darkness. Handgun cocked and ready, he could not be certain if the branches snapped from something that came close or backed off. Then he heard another group of branches snapping, farther to the left, and he relaxed a little as he judged that it was something moving off. The branches snapped close to the first place he had heard them now, however—farther to the left again as well—and there was more than one thing out there, that was
158

certain. He was rigid, fighting with the urge to flee in panic like the horses. Keep control. That's just the coyotes. Sure, then why the hell have you quit breathing? When he heard the snapping once again and couldn't anymore pretend it wasn't coming closer, he reacted without thinking. With his instinct now in charge, he fired up in the air and saw the lean four-footed creature, furry, scrambling backward through the bushes. Then he saw the other, and another, and he might have shouted as he saw one coming nearer. He would never know for sure. He heard a noise down in the gully to his right, another on the far side of the barn, and he was running up along the fence beside the barn to reach the house. The horses galloped in a line with him, and then they bolted toward the middle of the field. He kept on running, hearing noises there behind him, not once looking, only gasping, racing, and he reached the house and burst inside, the door slammed shut and locked behind him. He dodged through the living room to reach the kitchen and the back door, which he locked as well. He closed the windows everywhere. He locked them, pulling down the shades, and he was reaching, gasping, for the phone.

"Hello? Uh—"

"Rettig, this is Slaughter. Pick up Hammel, and get out here."

"Chief? Is that you? I uh—"

"Rettig, don't ask questions. Just get out here."

"To the station? What time is it?"

"My place. Hurry up. I need you."

Slaughter told him once again and set the phone down, hearing how the horses whinnied beyond tolerance. He started toward the windows on that side, reaching for a blind to pull it up and see why they were sounding like that. But the phone rang, and he stood immobile, one hand on the blind while he was starting toward the phone. That god damn Rettig. What's the matter with him? When he crossed the room and grabbed the phone, there wasn't any voice, however, just the same dead silence. "Tell me what you want!" he shouted to the mouthpiece, but the silence just continued. Then he heard the dial tone again and scratching on the porch, and only one horse out there now was whinnying. He faced the front door, handgun ready, glancing at the window on the side close to the horses. But he couldn't even hear the one horse now, and he was scrambling toward the front blind, but the scratching stopped, and there was nothing.

58

Dunlap set the phone down. He was in his room, the camera and the tape recorder on the desk where he was sitting, notes spread out before him. He was almost out of cigarettes. He stared down at the pint of whiskey which he'd left here in the morning. Even though his body was in agony, he held firm to his promise not to take a drink. That promise was a recent one, though there'd been others like it many times before, but this time he was absolute in his determination not to break it. He had walked back to his hotel from the park. He'd seen the mother and the father leave, had seen the coroner go with the body, and he'd known that Slaughter shortly would be turning on him. After all, he knew too much. He'd even taken pictures—of the grieving parents, of the body, of the coroner who looked so guilty that an image of him would be damning. Dunlap understood that he had violated friendship. Slaughter would feel threatened and betrayed, and Dunlap couldn't take a chance on him. He hadn't come across a story this strong in too many years, since he had first been here in Potter's Field. Indeed, if this thing got much worse, and he was positive it would, it might turn out to be among the ten best stories of the year, and he was not about to jeopardize his comeback. Actually he'd run back to his room. He'd fumbled to unload his camera, looking for a place to hide the film. The room would be too obvious. He'd gone out in the corridor and braced the cartridge in behind a picture on the wall. He hid the tape from his recorder in behind another picture. He had all their voices from the moment they had reached the ballroom to the instant that the grieving parents had accused the coroner of negligence. Oh, it was all there, every blessed detail, and he meant to keep possession of it. Slaughter might come after it, but Slaughter wasn't going to get it.

Back inside his room, he'd locked the door, and that was when his glance had settled on the pint of bourbon. He was moving toward it, even twisting at the cap, before he stopped himself. No, that was how he'd ended in this dump. He'd ruined every piece of luck he'd ever had by drinking. But not this time. This time he was going to be a winner. He had lasted since the morning without booze, the first day he had managed that in years, and if he'd suffered this long, he could suffer just a little longer. Make it through the night. The melody to those words unaccountably occurred to him, and he was laughing. Face this one hour, then the next. That was how the A.A. people were successful, wasn't it? Sure, take this one hour at a time.

But though he'd laughed, his hands were shaking, and he set the bottle by the television. He went down the hall to drink some water, stripped and showered, and that helped, the hot sting of the water flooding all the tension from him, but he nonetheless was sick and wishing for a drink. The drink might even make him sicker, but he wanted it. Attraction and repulsion. So he put on fresh clothes. Why, he didn't know. He ought to go to bed, but he was thinking maybe he would take a walk. Instead, he sat down at the desk and tried a first draft of some notes, just to flesh out what was on the film and tape. He smoked and scribbled his impressions, in no special order, just to get the words down,

161

staring at the way his hand was shaking, and the sentences were scrawled so poorly that he almost couldn't read them. Why not just one drink? To brace you, get you through this. No, and glancing from the pint of bourbon, he kept smoking, writing.

Then he knew he had to have some sleep. He flicked the lights off, stretched out on the bed, and concentrated to relax his body. Hard, it trembled, and he eased the muscles in his feet, his legs, his torso, slowly moving toward his head. It might have been that he was even more fatigued than he suspected, or that slowly moving up his body was like counting numbers backward or repeating nonsense phrases, but his consciousness gave in before he ever reached his head. He woke in what he later learned was half an hour, almost screamed out in the darkness, but he stopped himself. He found that he was sitting on the bed, that he was sweating, and he stood up, switching on the light. He saw the insects that were flying through the open window, and he leaned against the wall and rubbed his forehead. He had seen that image once again, that strange, half-human, antlered figure, part man, part deer, part cat, God knows what all. And that grotesque beard, that body turning sideways, paws up, round eyes staring at him. It was horrifying. More than that, hypnotic, powerful, like magic, as if somehow it were waiting for him, drawing him, and one day he would see it. He was frightened by it, by the riddle that it represented. What was happening to him? If he kept seeing this thing, he would end up in an institution. Never mind an institution. He'd be in the crazy house. He couldn't stand this anymore.

He had to talk to someone, but he didn't know whom he could call. He crossed the room and grabbed the phone, surprised to find he told the desk clerk Slaughter's number. He was fearful what the man would say to him. He didn't know how he should do this, how he'd cancel the ill-will he had created. As the phone rang, he was tempted to hang up, but Slaughter answered,

162

and he found that he was speechless. "Yes, who is it?" Slaughter said and then repeated. Dunlap waited, paralyzed and muted. "Is there anybody—?" Slaughter said, and Dunlap set the phone back on its cradle.

That was stupid. What's the matter with you? Dunlap thought. But he knew what the matter was, all right, although he had some trouble to admit it. He was shamed by what he'd done tonight, regretful and embarrassed. What do you intend to do? he thought. You plan to give up those good pictures and that tape? You want to back off from the story? No, of course not. You're damn right you don't. Because that shame you're feeling is just one more way to be a loser. It's not your fault that the boy died. You're just here to write about that. You can go on feeling all the shame you want, but just make sure you get that story, just make sure your emotions don't intrude on how you make your living. They're a luxury.

He knew that he was right, but all the same, he kept on staring at the phone. Regardless of their broken friendship, he still had to talk to Slaughter, smooth things, fix them so he wasn't cut off from the story. Even so, he thought about it for ten minutes before picking up the phone again. He told the number to the desk clerk, and he waited while the phone was ringing. This time Slaughter's voice was angry. "Yes, God dammit, Rettig, what's the matter? Get on out here." Dunlap didn't answer. "Tell me what you want," the angry voice was saying. Dunlap set the phone back on its cradle. There was no way he could make a man who sounded like that sympathetic. He would wait until the morning. So he smoked his final cigarette and looked down at his notes, and then he did a thing which he had never done before, had never even dared because he was so bothered by it. Yet unsettled by his dream, the image fixed there in the background of his mind, ever turning, staring at him, he was forced, he didn't will it, but was passive, worked on, forced to sketch it.

He was staring at it, swallowed by its eyes. He kept

163

on staring, couldn't shift his head away. He felt a darkness in his mind begin to open, and he didn't weaken all at once. It took him several minutes, and he fought it, he would later give himself that credit, fought as hard as he could manage, but resolve diminished into pointlessness. He'd gone this long, he'd proved that he could last a day, and he was reaching for the bourbon.

59

Accum spread the injured portion of his lip and shoved the needle in. It stung, and he was too quick on the plunger so he felt the liquid spurting through the tissue. All he could be grateful for was that he held his breath and didn't squirt the liquid up across his lip, hence couldn't taste it. Human antirabies serum manufactured from the blood of persons who'd been vaccinated against rabies virus. That would help his system to produce the necessary antibodies and in tandem with a second kind of treatment was his best chance to survive contagion, if this serum even worked against this virus. He was wincing as he drew the needle out. He set it down, undid his pants and dropped them, pulling down his underwear and reaching for a second needle, which he pressed into one buttock. This injection too was antirabies serum, and he wouldn't need another needle until just about this time tomorrow. Even so, that didn't give him comfort because, if he winced to draw this needle out, tomorrow's shot would be the start of worse things. It would not be antirabies serum; it would be the second kind of treatment: rabies vaccine. Anyone who ever was injected with it didn't like to talk about it. First developed by an Englishman named Semple, it was rabies virus from the brains of rabbits, mice, or rats, which virus then was killed by incubation in carbolic acid. In effect, the dead cells helped the body's immunizing process. Although harmless in themselves, they caused increased rejection of the not yet rampant live cells that were like them. But the trouble was that not just one injection of the vaccine was sufficient. Fourteen were the minumum, and twenty-one were better. Each was given daily to the muscles of the abdomen. A clockwise pattern was required since the shots were so excruciating that the muscles became sensitive. And maybe you could bear the first five or the second, but the last few were an agony, and this was not a thing that he was looking forward to.

He didn't have a choice, though. He had indirectly been exposed, and if indeed he had it, this disease would surely kill him without treatment. There were only two examples in which persons had lived through the rabies virus, and there yet was doubt that they had really had it since their symptoms had been like encephalitis. With the treatment, he yet took the chance that he would die from this disease, that it would be too strong for his precautions, but the likelihood was small, and anyway, as he kept thinking, he just didn't have a choice. Even rare reactions to the vaccine, like a fever or paralysis, were nothing when compared with certain death. But all the same, the start of treatment didn't calm his fears. The dog had gone through preexposure vaccination. It had died regardless.

And the start of treatment didn't calm his sorrow either. He was thinking of the boy spread on the table in the morgue, of how he should have had the foresight not to give him the sedation. Both those parents. How could he absolve himself? He still could hear the mother shrieking. Well, he meant to find out everything he could about this thing. When he was finished, he would know this virus more than any other he had ever worked on. He had once been famous as an expert in pathology. That was in the East before his breakdown. Now he'd prove how much an expert he could be. That's

165

right. You think you know so much. Get moving. Now's the time to prove it.

So he tugged his pants up, buckled them, and thinking of the tests he would perform, he turned and started from his office. Owens would be here soon with the dog's brain to compare with what the autopsy would show them. In the meantime, he himself would use the simple test for Negri bodies. He would use as well a more specific test in which a thin brain smear was treated with fluorescent antirabies serum and examined underneath an ultraviolet microscope. To watch the symptoms of the virus, he'd inoculate a half a dozen newborn mice with portions of the boy's brain. He would even want a picture of the virus, using the electron microscope. Whatever this thing was, he meant to have a look at it, and when he opened up that body he would understand why the paralysis came on so quickly, why it worsened with sedation.

At he walked along the corridor, he saw the nurses staring at him. Word had got around all right, and fast as only people in this business knew to spread it. They were looking at a man whose error had been fatal to a patient. Then he told himself to get control. They maybe just were frightened by a thing they didn't understand. Or maybe they were startled by the grim way he was looking. Well, he didn't plan to ask them, and if they knew what was good for them, they'd stay clear of his way.

He reached the door down to the basement, and he thought of Slaughter, who would need injections, and the mother, and the man who had been bitten, and the man who owned the dog. There were too many details he had not attended to. And what was more, he needed sleep. And food, he hadn't eaten since this morning. Well, he'd do this and take care of everything. With Owens here to help him, he would find the time to call these people, get them down here for their shots. But he knew what he really wanted—just to find out what had killed this boy.

He reached the bottom of the steps and went through the anteroom. He washed his hands and put on mask and gloves and lab coat. Just to be exact, he even stepped inside protective coverings across his shoes, and then with nothing further to detain him, he was going in there.

Green tile on the walls, fluorescent lights up in the ceiling, bouncing off the green and twisted by it, steel sinks and the instruments, and then the guttered tables. Three of them, set sideways as he faced them, one behind the other, and the third was where his eyes were centered, on that tiny lump beneath the sheet. He walked both slowly and determined toward it, breathing through the clinging vapor that collected on the inside of his face mask. Then he paused and gently pulled the sheet back, staring at the naked body on the table. So small and so battered, all those bruises from the fury it had been through. There was caked blood on the lips which swollen, slightly parted, showed some damage to the front teeth. But those details weren't important. Even with them, he was striking. Blond and pale, angelic, even innocent. This was the first time he had ever worked on someone whom he'd treated as a patient. But then that was just the point. He *never* had a patient. That was why he had become a coroner—to free himself from obligations to the living, to avoid responsibility. Well, he had brought this on himself. He *had* become responsible, and he was pausing to eliminate emotion before reaching for the scalpel which he'd use to peel the hair away. He took a break and leaned close to select his point of contact as the eyes flicked once below him and then stared at him. But they were purged of any innocence, as old and stark as any eyes he'd seen, and they kept staring. While the hand came up, the room appeared to swivel, and his own hand to his mouth beneath his face mask, he was nearly screaming. He was stumbling from the hand. The boy sat up and leered at him, then crouched upon the table. Accum thought of old Doc Markle. As the

167

boy leaped toward him, Accum's instinct was to push the boy away, but with the scalpel in his hand, he struck the naked stomach. Blood was flying.

60

Marge had stayed on duty at the station until everything was finished at the mansion. There was nothing she could do up there to help, but she could free a man from night shift on the radio while he went up to lend a hand, and Nathan needed every officer in town. So she had got the news in bits and pieces from the radio, and when she'd found what at last had happened, she had done her best to keep from crying. Nathan didn't need the people he depended on to break down when he most required them. She couldn't help it, though, and she sat there, wiping tears, relaying messages. She knew the mother and the father. She had gone to school with them. They lived just two blocks down from her house, and she'd often gone to visit, see their son and bring him presents. Now the boy was dead, and she was crying. When the man she had relieved came back to go on with his shift, she yet was crying, and he sat with her until she felt okay to drive. "You need a little sleep," he told her, but they both knew that it wouldn't be so easy; there were many people now who wouldn't get much sleep tonight. And she had thanked him, starting from the building. He had asked her if he ought to go outside with her, but she had thought about the radio, with no one to attend to it, and she told him that he didn't have to. After five years now with Nathan, she had learned the value of control, and she was certain she'd be fine.

She reached the parking lot behind the station,

checked the back seat of her car, then got in, driving. Almost midnight on a Saturday, she normally would have expected lots of movement on the streets, especially outside the downtown bars, young trail hands come in for a weekend's fun, but she was not surprised when she saw little action. Just a few old cars, some pickup trucks, a couple men who stood outside a bar and sipped from beer cans. But in contrast with a normal weekend, this was more like quiet Tuesday, and she wondered if the word had got around already. Even so, the trouble wasn't only in the town but in the valley. All day she'd been hearing about mangled cattle on the range, and she suspected that ranchers, losing stock, had stayed home watching for some predators. As she drove through the outskirts, she saw many houselights on, and this late, that was hardly normal either. She was wishing that she'd had the chance to talk to Nathan, but he'd been so busy, and she didn't want to stay at home alone. She thought about the mother and the father, and when she came to her house, she didn't stop. She drove for two more blocks, and if the lights were on, she meant to go in and console them.

There were lights for sure, the whole house both in front and back. She saw the plumber's truck, the car before it. Both the mother and the father must be home then, and she parked her car, debating if she maybe was intruding. Well, she'd come this far, and after all it was her duty, so she got out, locked her car, and started up the sidewalk. She heard crickets squeaking as she peered now toward the lights in all the windows, wondering if someone else had come to visit, when she heard the voices. Loud: two men it seemed, and they were shouting. Then she heard the screaming, and the cool night air was still, the crickets silent now, as someone ran out on the porch in desperation. She had met this man, a neighbor. He was staring at her.

"Jesus, she's gone crazy!"

"What?"

But Marge now heard the snarling, and she almost

169

turned to run, but she was concentrating to move slowly forward as the window in the living room came bursting toward the porch, two people struggling through the jagged edges, falling, writhing on the porch. The mother and the father, mother snarling, father screaming, and the mother was on top where she was scratching, biting. Marge was yet a moment understanding. She was running up the steps.

"You've got to help me! Get her off him!"

"But she's crazy!"

Marge would later recollect how she had thought of Nathan at that moment, how she wanted him to say that she had done the right thing when an instant could make all the difference. She was pushing at the man behind her, shouting "Go get help!" as she was looking all around for something to subdue the mother. She was not about to grab the mother and get bitten like the father screaming there, but when she saw the thing she needed in one corner of the porch, she couldn't bring herself to use it. Warren evidently had been playing with it on the day before he died. She didn't want to touch it, but the father's screaming was too much, and she was reaching for it. Slipping on the broken glass, she moved in on the mother, raised the baseball bat up high above her head, and thinking about Nathan, started swinging.

61

Slaughter waited while they flashed their searchlights. Then he stepped out on the porch.

"What is it?"

"Don't you think I wish I knew?"

And they were looking at him. They were dressed in jeans and sports shirts, gun belt strapped around each waist. They saw that Slaughter had his own gun out, and they were drawing theirs as they walked toward the fence where he was pointing.

"Shine your flashlights."

Now the beams arced out across the field.

"But I don't understand this," Rettig said.

"Just keep your back protected. There was something out here. Hell, it came up on my porch."

Slaughter climbed the fence and flashed his light while they stepped down beside him. Then he started with them through the field.

"Your porch?"

"That's right." And Slaughter was embarrassed to admit that he had run in panic, that except for one shot in the air he hadn't tried to use his gun, that he had simply lost his nerve and locked his doors against what might be out here. He was feeling safer now with these two men to help him, but he couldn't shake his worry, and he wished they wouldn't ask too many questions.

"But what is it?" Rettig said again.

"I told you I don't know. I never got a look."

"Your porch, though."

"I was talking to you when I heard it. When I looked, it wasn't there."

And Slaughter saw what he was searching for and wished that he'd been wrong. He would have gladly confessed panic to these men if he'd been wrong. But with his flashlight aimed, he saw the fallen bodies in the field, and he was brushing through the sparse brown grass to reach them.

He was stopping, staring. They were mutilated so much that he—

"Some damn thing was out here, all right. God, I'm sorry, Chief."

"These horses. They were all I—"

He was stalking toward the gully. "I heard three of them up in the bushes, two more by the barn."

"Hey, wait a second, Chief."

And Rettig's hand was on his shoulder. Slaughter pulled it off. "Those goddamn—"

"*Wait a second.* We don't even know what we'll be up against. You say that there were five of them?"

171

And Slaughter had the image of that shadow. "Like a bobcat."

They were staring at him.

"You saw *five* of them?"

"I know it doesn't make much sense, but—"

"I don't care about that. Sure, a bobcat doesn't hunt in packs, but anything can happen. What I mean is, we need help to do this. We need better light."

"You want the sun to come up? What's the matter? They'll be long gone when that happens."

"You can find a tracker."

"Who, for Christ sake? There's no time."

"I'm sorry, Chief, but I'm not going."

Slaughter stared at Rettig. Then he turned to look at Hammel. "What about yourself?"

And Hammel shrugged then.

"You don't have a lot to say."

"I figure I'll just watch and learn."

"I'll bet you will."

He stared at Rettig. Then he faced the shadowed gully. Even with his flashlight and the moon, he didn't see much in the bushes, and his anger became fear again.

"Okay. You're right. It's stupid to go in there. Looking at these horses, I just—"

"We'll be sure to get whatever did this. Don't you worry. But not now."

He had to get away from here.

"Hey, what about the horses?"

"Leave them. Hell, what difference does it make?"

He heard them walking close behind him as he climbed the fence, and when he stepped down, from the house he heard the phone again. Whoever kept on calling, he was thinking, livid, he would make sure that they stopped it. He was running, cursing toward the house, but when he burst in, grabbing the phone, he heard a voice this time, and as he listened, in his mind he started running yet again. It seemed as if the last few days he'd never stopped.

172

62

He ran along the corridor, the nurses staring at him. He was pushing at the first door, running through the anteroom to push the second door. The morgue was like a shambles. There was blood and broken glass and scattered instruments. Accum leaned against a table. He had blood across his gown, his face mask hanging limp around his neck. His face itself was white in contrast with the blood. He looked as if he had been sick. His hands were shaking, and the man beside him, wearing street clothes, didn't look much better.

Owens. Slaughter recognized him as a vet whom he had seen from time to time, who, very good at what he did, was always frowning.

They were turning to him, and he glanced around. He smelled the chemicals, the sick-sweet cloying blood. He didn't understand this, drawing breath to speak, but Accum interrupted. "I just killed him."

Slaughter stared at him and then at Owens. He was puzzled, walking toward them. "Look, you'd better take it easy. When you called, you sounded like you'd had a breakdown."

"But I killed him."

"Yes, I know. You told me on the phone. You said that at the mansion. But you had no way of knowing that the sedative would kill him. What's this blood here? I don't understand what's happened."

"Christ Almighty, listen while I tell you. I just killed him."

Slaughter turned to Owens. "What's the matter with him?"

"Over there. You'd better take a look."

Owens had some trouble speaking. He was pointing toward the far end of the room, beyond the final table

173

where a smear of blood was dripping from the wall, and Slaughter felt his apprehension once again. He started forward, though a part of him was holding back. He saw a pool of blood beside the table, and he didn't want to, but he peered down past the corner of the table, and he saw the small feet on the floor now. Then he leaned a little closer, and he saw the boy, his belly sliced wide open, as the part of Slaughter's mind which had been holding back snapped forward, and he saw the face, in death so ugly, twisted and distorted. "Christ, you mutilated him!"

"No! I told you that I killed him!"

Slaughter swung around and glared. "You said that he was dead back at the mansion!"

"I was certain that he was. I would have bet my reputation."

"Bet your reputation!"

"Never mind that. I did every normal test, and he was dead."

"Well, then he—"

"Seemed to come back from the dead and tried to grab me."

Slaughter didn't understand the words. They made no sense. They had no meaning. He was staring. Then he understood what he'd been told, and he was stepping back. "My God, you've really had a breakdown. You've gone crazy."

"No, just listen. I don't mean that quite the way it sounds."

"I hope to God you don't."

"I mean the paralytic stage of this disease must have been aggravated by the sedative."

Slaughter kept on staring.

"He was so unconscious that his life signs couldn't be detected."

"What the hell is this now? Edgar Allen Poe?"

"No, please. I listened for his heartbeat, checked his breathing, even took his temperature when I got back here. Everything was negative."

174

"You did a brain scan?"

"I did *everything,* I told you. He was dead as far as I could tell. I started working with him on the table, and he looked up, and he grabbed me. I—"

"Just take this slowly. One thing at a time. You're saying he was catatonic. That's it? That's your story?"

"On occasion it can happen. Rarely. There are cases where a patient has been certified as dead, and he recovers on a morgue slab."

"Jesus, brain scans."

"Look, for years we thought a lack of heartbeat was a sign that someone died. Then we found out that a person's heart could beat so weakly that we couldn't even measure it. So we made up other tests. For body heat. For rhythms of the brain. The fact is, we don't know exactly *when* a person dies. A man goes into surgery. He's doing fine when suddenly his heart and brain fail. So he's dead. Five minutes later, though, he has his functions back. So tell me how that happened. You explain it. I can't."

Slaughter looked at him. He couldn't take the words in. "All right, let's assume your argument's correct. The sedative wore off along with the paralysis."

"He grabbed for me. We fought. I knew I couldn't let him bite me. Never mind how small he was. I couldn't let him reach me. He was leaping, and I had the scalpel."

They were silent, staring at each other.

"Oh, my God." And Accum pounded with his fist across the table.

Slaughter walked across to him. He put his hand up on his shoulder. "Take it easy."

"But I—"

"Take it easy. Everything is going to be all right. We know what happened to that hit and run we're missing. He was bitten before he came down here."

"And Doc Markle. He was scared to death."

They stared at one another.

"Something else. The mice died," Owens told him.

175

Slaughter looked at him. He didn't even need to ask. Owens was explaining. Accum stared down at the table.

"We have mice down at the lab for doing tests on viruses. Born and raised in sterilized conditions, as the parents were, and those before them, so we know they're not contaminated. We can study any symptoms they develop from injections we might give them and be certain the injections caused the symptoms. They're a way of isolating what we're dealing with and finding what will cure it. Anyhow, a standard test for rabies is injection of infected tissue into mice. If they live, then we're not dealing with the virus we suspected. If they died, then we have perfect samples of the virus from them to examine. Well, our first tests on this virus weren't conclusive. Oh, we knew that it was deadly, but the slides we studied looked a little different than they should have, so when he went up to join you at the mansion, I continued the tests. Instead of looking at the dog's brain, I injected several mice."

"And now they're dead?"

And Owens nodded.

"Well, that isn't new. You said that it was deadly."

"But the mice don't normally develop symptoms for at least a week. *These* mice died in just about four hours. It was like a sped-up version of the rabies symptoms. First, a subtle difference in behavior, then hostility, impairment, finally paralysis and death. The hostility was quite pronounced, although they didn't snap at one another, only at the glass enclosures. But the point is that instead of several days, this only took a couple hours."

Slaughter's mind at last adjusted. It was racing, making jumps in logic. "Show me."

Owens frowned at him.

"I want to see them. Show me where they are."

"I didn't have the instruments I needed. An electron microscope for one thing, so I came up here to—"

176

"Never mind. Just show me."

"Over there. I brought them with me."

Slaughter started toward the leather case beside the door. He stooped to press the catch. "It's all right if I open this?"

"The mice are in containers."

Slaughter pulled the lid up, staring at the glass containers, saw the white fur of the mice, and something else which he had dreaded but expected, lifting one container, showing it. Accum now had turned, he and Owens staring, and the mouse in there was snarling at them. Slaughter felt its scratching through the glass.

"But they were dead, I tell you," Owens said. He crossed to Slaughter, pulling out the other glass containers. In them, every mouse was frantic.

"You're quite certain?" Slaughter asked him.

"Don't you think I know when something's dead? As certain as *he* was when he examined that small boy."

The mice were frantic.

"I don't know what's going on here," Slaughter said, "although I do know that it's happening." He frowned then at the farthest table. "What about the boy? The mother and the father won't believe us when we tell them that he woke up and you had to kill him. I can't think of any way to tell them."

"Then we won't." And Accum finally was moving, coming toward them, color in his face now. "I'll continue with the autopsy. I'd have to do it anyway, to find how this virus works. I'll fix that slash across his stomach so it looks like it was necessary, and the three of us will be the only ones who know."

And suddenly they looked at one another, understanding the significance of their conspiracy, ever after their dependence on each other.

They were silent. Slaughter nodded, Owens with him.

"Owens, did you bring the samples for the microscope?"

"I've got them with the mice."

"Okay then, let's get started. Slaughter, if you go up to my office, you'll find all those books beside my desk. You'd better search the master index and read everything that you can find on rabies. That's not what we're dealing with. It's close enough, though, and we can't waste time from now on, telling you what we'll be doing."

Slaughter studied him, then looked at Owens. He was standing from where he'd been crouched beside the samples. "How long till you know?"

"At least a couple hours."

Slaughter glanced down at his watch and saw that it was three o'clock. "I don't look forward to today."

"For lots of reasons."

"They'll be coming to me with their questions."

"Well, let's see if we can find some answers."

Slaughter nodded, trying hard to smile but failing, starting toward the doorway.

63

It was growling underneath the porch as two men aimed their flashlights at it.

"Christ Almighty, did you see that blind man's body when it finished with him?"

"I don't want to talk about it. Shoot the damn thing."

"Here in town?"

"You want to crawl in there and catch it?"

"I don't want to even *be* here."

They were pulling out their guns.

The lights. It couldn't bear this. As it heard hammers click back, it was leaping.

"Jesus!"

64

It was stumbling up the stairs now. It had eaten from the bodies in the basement and had slept a little, but it wakened, and it couldn't stop this strange compulsion. It was moaning as it reached the kitchen, couldn't keep from going out to face the night, as it gripped the back door, stepping out, it heard the gunshots. It was snarling.

65

"This is what a rabies virus looks like."

Slaughter nodded toward where Accum pointed.

"Fine. Now here's a micrograph from the electron microscope. The virus from the dead dog."

Slaughter watched as Accum put the micrograph beside the book which they'd been looking at. He studied it.

He thought about it quite a while. "Well, this one's thinner than the rabies virus."

"Yes, that's one of several contrasts. Normally we say a rabies virus has a bullet shape, but this one looks like, I don't know—"

"A missile," Owens said, and they were glancing at him.

"Why not? All right then, a missile." Accum pointed toward the micrograph again. "A missile is in keeping with the speed of this thing anyhow. The point is that a lot of viruses are shaped in general like this, but none exactly like it. It's much sleeker, and while there's an indentation at the bottom, there's no sign of an appendage there. What's more, the nervous system of the boy was not infected."

Slaughter looked at him. He knew enough from what he'd read that rabies moved along the nervous system, fed off it, and finally destroyed it. He was frowning. "But I thought that—"

"Yes, I know. That shouldn't be. This thing is unlike any virus that I've ever seen. It did infect his limbic brain, however."

Slaughter didn't understand.

"The limbic brain. The part around which all other sections of our brain develop. Sometimes called reptilian, it's really more like animal. It causes our survival instincts, our emotions and aggressions. That explains why this boy acted as he did. Put simply, he became an animal."

"But what about the coma he went into?"

"Just don't rush me. Wait until I get to that. You ought to know that, when I looked at where the boy said he was cut by glass, I found some evidence that he'd been bitten. Not more than a day ago. To work that fast, it has to be transmitted through the bloodstream. It's selective. Only certain cells appeal to it."

"The limbic brain?"

And Accum nodded. "It produces rabid symptoms very quickly; passes through, let's say, a twelve-hour phase in humans, paralyzes and produces coma. Evidently when the brain shuts down, the virus becomes dormant. When the victim regains consciousness, the virus starts to work again. It's really quite efficient, feeding until it produces near-death, and then holding off until the victim can sustain it once again. But since it passes through the bloodstream, it would show up in the salivary glands, infect the spittle, and pass to another victim in a bite. If you were cut already, though, and came in contact with infected blood, you'd get it just the same."

And Slaughter reached up to the scab across his face. He started frowning.

"It's too late to worry, Slaughter. If you'd been infected, we'd have known about it yesterday."

"If what you say is true, there isn't anything that you could do about it anyway."

"That's right. Our vaccine would be useless. I got lucky too. I would have had it by now if this lip had been infected. As it is I gave myself two antirabies shots."

"I'll bet that was a lot of fun."

"Oh yeah, I liked it so much that I think I'll make a habit of it. Shit, I don't know what we're going to do."

"You say you never saw a thing like this? You never even *heard* about it?"

Accum shook his head.

"Well, I did," Owens told them, and they looked.

"I read about it. Nineteen sixty-nine in Ethiopia. A herd of cattle came down with a special form of rabies, little frenzy, just paralysis. They all collapsed. The owner didn't know exactly what they had. He gave them up for dead, and then they all recovered."

"That's impossible as far as I know," Accum told him. "Nothing can survive it."

"This herd did. The problem is they still retained the virus, and in several days they manifested symptoms once again. They had to be destroyed."

"You're certain it was rabies?"

"Oh yes, all the later tests confirmed it. And I read about another case in India two years ago, but this time it was water buffalo."

"But this thing isn't rabies. Any vaccine they developed wouldn't be of use here. Even if it would, there isn't any time to get it."

Owens looked down at the table, shrugging.

"Anybody want more coffee?" Slaughter asked them, but they only looked at him. "Well, I don't understand it. I mean, what would cause a brand-new kind of virus?"

181

"You tell me," Accum answered. "Hell, you want to know the truth? I wonder why it doesn't happen all the time. Never mind a thing like legionnaires' disease which evidently was around for quite a while, but no one diagnosed it. Never mind a thing like staph or gonorrhea which mutated into forms resistant to a drug like penicillin. Let's just go along with my contention that this virus is a new one. Asking what would cause it is like asking why our ancestors developed big brains from their limbic system and turned into humans. There's no ready answer. Evolution is an accident. A cell develops wrongly. Something happens to the DNA. We like to think that everything is fixed and ordered. But it isn't. Things are changing all around us, not so quickly that we recognize the change, but it's occurring, people growing taller, dogs whose breeds are now defective, dying out. We recognize extremes, of course. We call them monsters. But the really startling changes are occurring in those simple life forms which we hardly ever notice, those so small, so reproductive that they go through several generations in a day. Their time scale is much different from our own, much faster. Evolution has sped up for them, the chance for random variants. But evolution doesn't even have to be in stages. Quantum leaps can happen in an instant. Every time a person gets an X ray, tiny bullets zinging past those chromosomes. You want a model? Let's try this one. Let's assume we've got a dog. The dog has rabies, but the symptoms haven't shown up yet. The dog is hurt, though. Let's say that it's got a broken leg or some internal swelling, so the owner takes it in for X rays, and the dog is treated and gets better. But the damage has been done. The rabies virus has by chance been struck by just one X ray. Hell, it only takes one mutant cell which lodges in the limbic brain and starts its reproduction. Now the owner goes on holiday. He takes the dog up here. The dog goes crazy, and it runs away. Contagion now gets started."

182

"What you said about those dogs up in the hills. Psychotic animal behavior," Slaughter told him.

They were silent for a moment.

"Sure. Just two roads from the valley," Owens said. "The mountains are around us, so the virus has been localized. But why did no one ever recognize it until now?"

"Because, so far as I remember, no one ever tested for it. Ranchers maybe shot a few dogs and then buried them, but did you ever have a look at one?"

And Owens shook his head.

"Well, there you have it."

"But you told me Friday night that people have been bitten by them," Slaughter said. "They would have come in for the rabies treatment but, regardless, have developed symptoms."

"And they *did* come in for treatment, and there wasn't any problem. So the dog that bit them didn't have the virus, or the virus didn't mutate until later. That's no argument against the model."

"But the virus is so virulent that everything would have it by now."

"I don't think so. The attacks we've seen are plainly murderous. I doubt too many animals or people would survive them. Plus, the victims must be weakened by the virus. When the winter comes, it likely kills them. That's a natural control. We haven't studied any long-term consequences of the virus. Maybe there's a calming process. I don't know at this point."

"Why would it be showing up in town now?"

"You know why as well as I do. All it takes is just one dog to wander in. But I think there's another reason. Don't forget the winter was a hard one. It drives victims down from where their normal hunting routes are in the mountains. That's one version of a model anyhow. I might be wrong. At least it's something. What we do know, in addition to our tests, is that the victims are nocturnal. That was why the dead boy snarled the way he did. The moon was shining through

183

the upper windows. And that helps explain why so much trouble has occurred at night. The victims hide and sleep in daylight. Then they come out after dark, but now the moon is almost full, and they're reacting to it."

"One thing more. We know that they're not dangerous to one another," Owens said. "When I put several mice together, they ignored each other, staring fiercely at the light and lunging at the glass around them."

Slaughter thought about the shadows he had seen up in the bushes by his barn tonight. "You mean they hunt in packs?"

"Not necessarily, although it's possible."

"But what would make them do that?"

"Look, this virus gives control back to the limbic brain and makes it act the way it once did several hundred thousand years ago. To hunt in packs is natural. It's even a survival trait. An individual, at least in humans, is by contrast very recent."

66

It was higher in the mountains, staring toward the snow line. Then the sky began to lighten, and it raised its hand to shield its eyes as in the forest it saw antlers coming toward it, and it knew that it was home now.

67

Slaughter stood before the glass partition, numbed by what he saw. Cody, who had found the boy inside the mansion last night and been bitten, was now snarling, writhing to escape the straps that bound him to the bed. His throat was bandaged thickly, and the damage there might help explain the hoarse inhuman sounds he made, but Slaughter didn't think so. No, the virus was at work, and though the bed was padded so that Cody couldn't hurt himself, the violence with which he thrashed must surely have effects. The man was like a lunatic, and Slaughter thought again about what Accum said, about the madness from the moon. "It's just a guess," he told the orderly beside him. "Flick his room lights off, and maybe that will calm him. God, I wish that he'd pass out."

Even with the window as a buffer, Slaughter felt the snarling touch him. He was nauseated by the foam that drooled down on the bandage. Now the snarling, writhing, became more extreme. Cody tried to twist his head to bite the nearest strap around him.

"I can't watch this."

Swallowing, he glanced at where Marge waited at the far end of the hallway. She was peering through another window. Slaughter knew the mother of the dead boy was inside there, and he took one final look at Cody before walking slowly toward her.

"Hi, Marge," he was saying, understanding what she felt, and then he kissed her.

But she just kept staring toward the window. Slaughter watched her.

"I tried phoning, but I guess you weren't at home."

She didn't answer.

"Marge, I—"

"Nathan, I just hit her. There was nothing else that I could do. I didn't mean to hit her so hard. She was—"

"Take it easy."

"But she's got a fractured skull."

"I know that. Take it easy. You did what you had to. As it is, she's going to live. That's all that really counts, although they don't know any way to cure her." He reached out and held her.

He was looking through the window at the mother who was strapped unconscious to her bed, a skullcap

185

white around her head, an intravenous bottle draining toward the needle in her arm.

Marge was crying, and he held her closer.

"Take it easy. Why not go on home, Marge? Please. There isn't anything that you can do here. You'll be told whatever happens."

"Will you come with me?"

"You know I'd like to."

"But you can't?"

"You know that, too. The one thing in this world I'd like to do right now is stay with you, but I'm afraid of what's about to happen."

"Just an hour? You need rest as much as I do."

"Don't you know? I'm trying for a record. How long I can go without some sleep."

She didn't laugh, though.

"Marge, I wish that I could make you understand. I know that what you did was hard."

She studied him.

"I know that, if there'd been another way, you would have chosen it. She would have killed her husband. You did fine. I wish you wouldn't feel so badly."

"You would feel the same."

"Of course I would. But then I'd need a friend like you to say to me what I just said to you. I mean it. You did fine. I hate for you to worry. You're too special."

"Thanks. . . . It doesn't help, though." She was turning toward the window.

"All the same. Here, go on home, Marge. Please. You know that I'll get word to you."

"I'm frightened, Nathan."

"Come on. Let me walk you down."

He kissed her. Then he touched her arm, and she responded, walking with him down the hallway. Neither looked at Cody. At the corner, she glanced back once at the windows in the wall down there, and then she went downstairs with him. He touched her hair and watched beside the back door as she walked across the parking lot.

186

That lovely, tortured woman, he was thinking. When she raised that ballbat, she must have been in agony. He waved as she drove out, but tired, sorrowed, she just nodded, and he thought a moment before heading toward the phone inside the nurses' station.

68

"Slaughter? Eight o'clock? Can't this wait until a decent hour?"

"No, we really have to talk."

"Well, Jesus, Slaughter—"

"This is serious. We don't have too much time."

The line was silent briefly. "All right then. I'll see you at the paper in an hour. But this better be important."

"Oh, don't worry," Slaughter told him. "You'll wish that you didn't know."

"I do already."

Slaughter frowned and hung up. He was thinking that in all the years he'd lived here he had never been to Parsons's house, and then he wondered why just now he'd thought of that, with everything he had to keep his mind on. Then he guessed it was because of all the power games that Parsons liked to play. The man kept his subordinates away from where he lived because he wanted to dissociate them, keep them from assuming friendship. That way he intimidated them. But Slaughter didn't care much. He had never been afraid of Parsons, though in truth he didn't want to go through this with him, and needing to keep occupied, he went out, driving to the station where already, even early in the morning like this, there were calls about more prowlers, about mangled cats and dogs and cattle, about several missing persons. Well, it's just beginning, he decided. Then he did his best to shut his mind off as he cleaned up, washing in the men's room, changing from his sweaty shirt to one he kept inside his office drawer. No, Parsons wasn't going to like this, and a half an hour later, as the two unshaven men sat facing one another, it was worse than Slaughter had expected. Parsons had been fifteen minutes late, and Slaughter had been forced to wait outside the locked doors of the Potter's Field *Gazette*. Then Parsons had shown up, a sport shirt and a pair of nylon slacks. "No, not yet. Wait until we get upstairs," the man had told him, and upstairs the man had listened, then quite calmly answered, "You expect me to believe this?"

Slaughter frowned then before saying, "I don't know. I wish I didn't."

"Really, Slaughter, think about it. All you know for sure is that a boy came down with some disease, or maybe he just had a breakdown. Then his mother got hysterical and fought her husband. Cody has a raving fever. And that guide dog just went vicious. There's your explanation."

"You've forgotten Clifford's body."

"No, I haven't. Clifford was attacked all right and likely by a wild dog as you say. But were there any tests performed?"

"Just to find out what attacked him. At that time, we had no reason to suspect a virus."

"So the only tests were on that sick dog, and the evidence was very close to rabies."

"Accum—"

"Slaughter, I don't want to disillusion you, but everybody knows that he came back here because no one else would have him. He broke down in Philadelphia, and it would not surprise me if he made a crisis of this just to give himself importance. As I interpret what you told me, there's been no time yet to test the dead boy for this so-called virus. Granted that his brain had been infected, if what Accum says is true. But that could be because of many things. To do a proper slide

188

for the electron microscope takes at least a couple days. I gather that some steps can be eliminated if a person's in a hurry, which explains how Owens had his samples ready, but I know this much—slides from that dog's brain were made so quickly that we shouldn't put much trust in them. I'll need a lot more to convince me. Think about it as I told you. Which makes more sense? Rabies or a brand-new virus?"

"You weren't there to see the boy."

"But I heard all about it."

Slaughter looked at him.

"Sure, what's the matter, Slaughter? Did you think I wouldn't know? I run the goddamn paper. I'm the mayor. I have all kinds of people watching for me. If those parents choose to prosecute, Accum is in trouble. He administered a sedative without the normal cautions. Now of course he's going to say a virus killed the boy. He surely won't incriminate himself. His word on this is hardly what you'd call objective. And that's something else I want to talk to you about. We'll leave aside for now the issue of this woman you employ who hit the mother with a baseball bat, although I wonder why you haven't charged her and I'm positive that there'll be lawsuits. Let's just concentrate on Accum. He's the last man I'd have chosen to do tests on that boy. He—"

"It's not important. If you'd seen the boy, you'd know he wasn't acting normally."

"But that's exactly what we pay you for. To deal with things like that. You've had it fairly easy, Slaughter. Not too much goes on here. Now the first time something different happens, you come waking me on Sunday morning with your crazy notions about sealing off the valley and exterminating all the livestock."

Slaughter stared at him. He kept his fists gripped tightly by his legs where he was sitting, and he felt his face go warm, and he was trying to control his breathing.

"I said if it came to that. I don't know if it's necessary. I'm just asking your opinion."

"Well, it *isn't* necessary. Let's relax a minute, Slaughter. Let me talk about my job a little. I was mayor for many years before you came here. Twenty of them, all told. I was mayor when all those hippies came to town, to name an instance, and I knew that there'd be trouble, plus I knew that all I had to do was flex my muscles and arrange to herd them out of town. I didn't, though, because there would have been complaints about that, people saying that, while no one likes hippies, still we should have let them have a chance. And so I waited for the opportunity. Their foul mouths and their dope and garbage got extreme, and still I waited because I knew people shortly would come begging me to move them, which precisely is what happened. Now I got what I intended, but I did it diplomatically. Does all that make some sense to you?"

Slaughter only shrugged at him.

"The truth is that the people always know what's best for them. A proper leader only goes along with what they tell him," Parsons said. "That's why they've kept me as their mayor all these years. Because I understand that. All I want is what they tell me. So you say there's going to be an epidemic. Well, that's fine. Let's wait and see. The evidence is inconclusive, but I'll keep an open mind about it. Even so, the steps which you suggest are inadvisable. Exterminate the livestock, all the animals around? Now really, Slaughter, what if there's no epidemic, what if this is just a case of poor tests and a biased coroner? The people would come for our heads. They'd want someone to pay for all the cattle that were killed, and I don't think you earn enough for that. Even sealing off the valley. Christ, this valley's livelihood is cattle. If a rumor starts that all our cattle are diseased, we might as well destroy them anyhow. There won't be any way to sell them. No, we'll wait and see. If there's indeed an epidemic, we'll hear from the people what to do. They'll

190

tell us, and their choice will be the right one, and we'll all survive this with a conscience, just the way we did with all those hippies."

"But the difference," Slaughter said, "is that nobody died because you waited. On my desk right now, the messages are piling up, and there'll be more until the valley's in a panic. Not just mangled cattle. Not just Clifford and that boy. We're going to wade through corpses before long, and nothing's going to help those people."

"But you haven't listened to me, Slaughter. There's no other choice. Okay, you want to argue. Here's the end of it. You'll go on as if everything is normal. You will quarantine whoever's been exposed, if indeed there is a virus, which I doubt. You'll pick up any dogs or cats or even chipmunks if they seem a little strange to you. But you'll stay calm and tell the people that the situation's in control. And listen to me, Slaughter. If you even hint about an epidemic, your ass won't be worth the nail that stakes it to the courthouse door. Is that clear enough? Is that an order you can understand?"

But Slaughter only stared at him.

"Can I at least get on the radio and tell the town we've found a case of rabies?"

Parsons thought about it.

"Yes, I see no problem. After all, we do have evidence of rabies, and the town should be informed for its protection. But don't dare to mention cattle. That's a different issue altogether. Now I have to get back home. I'm late for church, and I have people coming afterward for brunch."

He stood, and clearly Slaughter was expected to go with him. "Oh, yes, what about that magazine reporter from New York? That man named Dunlap?"

"He's still here."

"Well, get him out of here. That's all we need is for these rumors to get printed. Have him leave this afternoon."

"But what if he's not finished?"

"Oh, he's finished all right. He just doesn't know it. Get him on the train, and while you're at it, get yourself cleaned up before too many people see you. Really you don't look so good. The job is maybe too much for you."

Slaughter almost laughed. You bastard, he was thinking. You don't miss a chance to stay on top of people, do you? They were walking toward the door, and Slaughter had his fists clenched, felt the way his face was warm. He waited until Parsons went before him, thinking this would be the way to handle things: he'd better keep his back protected.

69

He was in the phone booth, but the line was fuzzy, and the noises from the other end distracted him. "Look, Altick, I can't tell you why I need them, but I—"

"Just hold on." To someone in the background: "Put them over there. I'm going with you. I don't want that chopper to take off without me. Good. I'm sorry, Slaughter. Everything is frantic here. I'm listening."

"I need some men," he told him louder. "I can't give you reasons, but I'll maybe have to borrow help."

"There isn't any way."

The voice was much too final.

"But—"

"No, listen to me. I need everybody I can muster. I sent five men with some dogs to find whatever's picking off these cattle. There are several ranchers missing. And my men—"

"But—"

"It's my men. I mean my *men* are missing. I don't like the way I'm feeling. If you'd called five minutes later, I'd have—" Noises in the background. "I said wait until I'm ready. Yeah, we'll need those things as well. Just take them to the chopper. Slaughter, there's no way for me to help you. I've got too much going on here."

"But—"

"I'm sorry, Slaughter."

There were other noises in the background, and the line was disconnected.

Slaughter put the phone down, staring at it. Sure, another escalation. By now, he had grown accustomed to the burning in his stomach, but he hadn't yet adjusted to the way his mind was nagging at him. Everything was moving too fast. There was hardly any time to think. His talk with Parsons. Now state troopers missing. Things weren't bad enough, he had to worry about Parsons.

He was stepping quickly from the phone booth, moving toward the hotel desk. He knew that he had planned this since he'd said good-bye to Parsons, though he wouldn't have admitted it. But why else come directly here? He could have used the phone back at the station.

"Gordon Dunlap," he said to the old clerk in the jeans and denim jacket.

"What about him?"

"Dammit, tell me where to find him."

And the clerk was staring as he fumbled through the cards to find the number.

Slaughter started up the stairs as he was told the number, shouting "Thank you" past his shoulder as he ran up to the balcony and scanned the arrows showing which rooms were on which side, darting to the left and down a hallway, staring at the arrows once again. The halls were twisting, turning. He came to a corner, and he saw the door along a dead-end corridor, and he was racing past the pictures on the wall. He knocked, but no one answered.

"Dunlap. Wake up. This is Slaughter."

No one answered.

"Dunlap." He was knocking. Then he tried the door-knob, and it wouldn't move. But as he leaned against the door, the catch gave way. The door was swinging open.

Dunlap hadn't even shut the door tight. He was sprawled across the bed, his clothes all wrinkled, soaked with something. On the floor, there was an empty whiskey bottle, papers, cigarette butts, broken ashtray, toppled chair.

What happened here? He smelled the sickness, stepping back, then going forward, staring at him. Dunlap didn't seam to breathe. He wasn't moving. Slaughter grabbed him. "Dunlap, wake up. It's important."

Dunlap didn't move, though. Slaughter shook him. "Come on, Dunlap. Wake up." Slaughter felt to find a heartbeat. Then he had it, and at least he didn't have to worry about that much. "Dammit, Dunlap." He was shoving at him. Dunlap groaned and tried to turn, but Slaughter wouldn't let him. "This is Slaughter, Dunlap. Wake up. We've got problems."

Dunlap groaned again. His breath was putrid, and too rushed to mind that, Slaughter hefted him across his shoulder, stumbling down the hallway toward the bathroom. When he set him on the toilet, he unbuttoned Dunlap's shirt, but that was taking too much time, and he just ripped the shirt off. Dunlap tilted so he almost fell, and Slaughter eased him to the floor and got his pants off, shoes and socks and underwear. The underwear was soiled, and Slaughter threw it in a corner. Dunlap groaning, Slaughter slid him in the bathtub, and he turned the shower to its coldest. Dunlap woke up screaming.

"Take it easy."

Dunlap kept on screaming.

Slaughter slapped him. "Hey, it's me. It's Slaughter."

Dunlap blinked at him. His eyes were red. The sickness that had caked around his lips and chin were rinsing off, and he was frowning, head to one side. He

194

looked as if he might begin to cry, and then his body heaved.

"It's all right. I'm here with you," Slaughter told him. "Get it up and out of you."

He studied Dunlap, water spraying on the both of them, as spasm followed spasm, and then Dunlap sighed and leaned back coughing in the bathtub. He was crying.

"What's the matter? Nightmares?"

Dunlap only shook his head.

"Well, I've got work for you. I need you sober."

Dunlap turned to him. The water kept on spraying.

"While you're stunned like this, I need some answers," Slaughter told him. "And I think right now that you won't lie to me. I need to know if I can trust you."

Dunlap closed his eyes and shivered, ice-cold water spraying on him.

"You tell me," he answered weakly.

"I don't understand."

"You know already what you want to hear. You don't need me to answer."

"Listen, buddy," Slaughter said and dug his fingers into Dunlap's shoulder. "You're not quite so drunk as you pretend. I want to hear the answer."

"Sure, all right, I'll say that you can trust me."

"If you screw up, you'll wish that you'd never met me."

"*You can trust me.* Hey. My shoulder."

Slaughter saw the way the skin was turning purple, and he eased his fingers off. He leaned back, sitting on the toilet seat. "I need a man to cover me," he said at last. "A man from outside who has no involvement in this. I want you to watch me every second, check out everything I do and keep a record. There'll soon be some trouble, and I want to know that I'm protected."

Dunlap had his eyes shut as he shivered in the ice-cold spray of water.

"Do you hear me?"

"Is it that bad?"

"It's that bad."

"Hell, I'd be crazy not to go along with you."

"You'll be crazy if you do. There's just one stipulation. All I ask is that you wait until I say that you can publish."

"Now I—"

"I don't want to have to worry about you. I have lots to watch for without that."

The water kept on spraying. Slaughter felt his wet shirt clinging coldly to his skin.

"All right, so long as no one else is in on this."

"It's you and me."

"A deal then."

Slaughter sat back on the toilet seat. He didn't know exactly where to start. "You said you wanted some good story. Here's the damnedest thing you ever heard."

And Dunlap now was looking at him.

70

Hammel didn't like this. He'd been told to do a follow-up on anybody who had been in contact with the virus. It was not enough that he'd been wakened in the middle of the night, that he had seen those mangled horses, that he'd almost had to hunt those bobcats. No, he'd been assigned to check the owner of the dog that Accum yesterday had found; and as the new man on the force, he always got the worst jobs. He was peering through the screen door, and the television was blaring, but the owner didn't answer. Hell, the television this loud, who could hear if someone knocked? He pounded now and shouted. But the television was the only answer. Oral Roberts. Hammel tried the door, and it came open.

"Anybody home?"

He stepped in, staring at the beer cans.

"Where the—?"

196

Try the bedroom or the bathroom. To the right, he saw the hallway, and he walked along it. "Anybody here?" He found the bathroom first and squinted in there, smelled a fetid odor. As he stepped in, he was almost sick. He saw the toilet bowl where no one flushed it.

"Jesus."

And he turned in reflex, but the hall out there was empty. Next, a kind of study, papers strewn, a lamp-shade broken. But the bedroom was immaculate, not one thing out of place, the bedspread smooth as in the Army.

"Fine. I'll try the basement."

But he thought that he would phone for help first. Clearly something wasn't right here.

As he turned, he heard the scratching in the closet, pulled the door, his gun drawn, and the owner was upon him. Hammel's only talent was his youth and inexperience. Another officer might have been tempted to dodge back, to point the gun and tell him not to do this, or reminded of the chance for lawsuit, to avoid the risk of hurting. If the officer had been an older man, his reflex might have failed him. But in Hammel's case, he didn't have the chance to dodge or think or balk. He was too frightened. He just shot the owner's face in.

70

They were staring at the packing crate.

"I normally don't come in on a Sunday, but we've had a lot to do," the foreman said. "I saw the broken window back there, and I should have called you right away, but I was thinking of our inventory, so I came in and I checked the place."

Get to it, Slaughter thought but didn't want to say it, didn't want to make this worse by showing his emotion. He was glancing fast at Dunlap, who was staring.

"So I looked around, and there was nothing missing, nothing I could tell at least. I even counted through the stock we just got in on Friday."

It was cold in here, the floor cement, the warehouse laced with shadows. They were stepping closer to the packing crate.

"And then I saw these empty crates here. We unloaded several freezers from them just before we quit on Friday, and I don't know if you understand this, but I like to keep things neat. It's like I spend more time here than I do at home, and anything that's out of place, I'm bothered by it."

"Sure, I understand." But Slaughter was impatient, frightened.

"Anyway, we left the lids off. We were running late already, and I figured I'd come in today and finish. Well, the lid was on this crate. It shouldn't be. It wasn't when we quit on Friday."

Now the foreman pulled the lid off. Slaughter looked in.

"Jesus."

What he saw had been a woman, still was in a sense, except her clothes were ripped and dirty, and her face and top were smeared with bloodstains, dry and crusty.

Slaughter sensed where Dunlap peered down past him.

"I don't know," the foreman said. "You tell me how she got here. I was scared enough to almost pee my pants. Who killed her? Why'd they put her in here?"

Slaughter had some trouble speaking. "Who else knows about this?"

"Just yourself. I wondered if I ought to call the morgue, but then I thought I'd better call you first."

"You did the right thing. Listen, you've had quite

198

a shock. I recommend you go home while we handle this. Pretend it's really Sunday. Come back in the morning. We'll be gone by then."

"I want to help, though."

"You've done what you should have. I'm impressed you kept control the way you did. Just go home. Let me handle it."

The foreman looked relieved as Slaughter reassured him. He stayed half a minute longer. At the back door, he glanced toward them once.

"I'll call if I have questions," Slaughter told him, and the foreman nodded, leaving.

Slaughter waited until he could hear the car out there, until its engine faded. He was looking now at Dunlap.

"You take notes on everything I do," he told him.

"But—"

"Just pay attention."

Slaughter leaned in, feeling for a pulse. There wasn't one. He pulled the eyelids, and there wasn't any cornea dilation. He had brought a pocket mirror. Now he held it underneath the nostrils, but there wasn't any vapor.

"Is she dead?"

"She looks that way to me."

"Except she isn't."

"No, if what you say is true, I guess she isn't."

"We could take her to the morgue, but she might wake up, even though it's daylight."

"And then come at us?"

"That's right."

And Dunlap shivered.

"Now you've seen me check for life signs, and you're satisfied from all appearance that she's dead. The most that they charge me with is desecration."

Dunlap stared at him as Slaughter drew his handgun, leaning in to cock it.

72

She had walked the twelve blocks from the depot. With her suitcase and her purse, she had been awkward, but she'd ridden in the bus until she'd reached Cheyenne, and there she'd realized that she had been in such a hurry that she hadn't taken several things she would be needing, plus the money in the bank account was half hers. She'd been stupid, not to mention hasty. Sure, all right, she'd gone to bed with Orval, but she'd done that mostly to get Willie angry. She had never planned to leave. She'd hoped that Willie might get jealous and appreciate her if his brother thought she was attractive. Orval, though, had managed to convince her that for safety she should run away, and now that she was back, she didn't know what she was doing. She saw Orval's car with Willie's in the driveway, and she braced herself for all the shouting that would happen, but when she stepped in the house, she only saw the mess, and she'd be shouting now herself as she called out for Willie. No one answered. But she knew they never walked, and with their cars here, they'd be close, so she now stepped inside the kitchen, and she saw the blood that led down toward the cellar. Oh, my Christ, they killed each other. She was rushing down there, staring at the blood upon the stairs, and then she saw the bodies stretched out in one corner. Orval, and a woman she had never seen before, and Willie with a knife stuck in his chest, and they were mangled. She was shrieking until someone came inside and found her.

73

Slaughter didn't know how this was going to end, or
even if. He stared down at the bodies in the corner.
They'd been slashed and beaten, and some portions had
been gnawed. He didn't know how much more he could
take. He'd passed beyond revulsion into shock.

He turned to Dunlap. Willie's wife was upstairs with
a doctor. Winston was the officer who first had reached
here, thin, asthmatic, but a good man. Though his face
was pale, he looked as if he still could do his job.

"I guess you heard what Hammel found."

"He shot the guy."

"He could have ended in the cellar like these other
people. God, I talked to Willie Thursday night. I saw
his brother."

"Chief, I don't mind telling you I'm frightened."

"Think about it. All through town. How many other
bodies in the cellars?"

They were silent, staring everywhere except at these
three bodies.

"Well, I don't have any choice. I phoned the state
police. They've got too much to deal with on their own.
I'm going to call the state militia in."

And then he realized he couldn't do that. Only Parsons could, and even then, the governor would have to
give permission. There was hardly any time. The night
would soon be on them.

"What about reserves in town, the Army?" Winston
said. "They're here already. You don't have to send for
them."

"I'll use them. Lord, the only logic I can see is to go
from house to house and check the cellars. Before sundown."

"What about these bodies here?"

"We'll leave them."

"What?"

"They're something's stock of food. Don't ask me how I know this, and don't ask me where it went. We searched the house. It isn't here. But I'm damned certain, once the night comes, if its hunting doesn't go well, it'll—"

"—come back here and eat some more?"

And they were almost sick to think about it.

"I have lots for you to do today," he said to Winston. "But by sundown you come back here and you wait. When it comes down here, don't ask questions. Make sure of your target, and then shoot it."

"But that's murder."

"And these bodies here are murder too, and what we're dealing with has changed the rules. What's normal doesn't matter now."

74

It struggled down the street.

It crawled on hands and knees and tried to shield its eyes from sunlight, but the pain was too intense, and all it did was crawl on blindly. It was snarling, foaming at the mouth, although it didn't do that willingly. The broken white line stretched before it, and it wavered to one side and then the other as in agony it tried to move directly down the center. Objects angled past it, beeping. It heard voices, sensed the people crowding near it, and it snarled at them and bared its foamy teeth and kept on crawling. How it got here, it could not remember. Trees and grassland it remembered. But this hot black surface and this white line, it could not recall or understand. It just kept struggling down the white line. Someone screamed nearby. More objects inched past, beeping. And the pain. The awful pain. It fell, face cracking on the hot black surface, squirming forward on its stomach, white line stretching forward from its nose. It pawed now at its skull. It jerked its head. The murmurs gathered closer. It was snarling to protect against them.

75

Rettig stopped the cruiser, puzzled by the crowd that filled the main street. He saw cars and trucks stopped, drivers getting out, people on the sidewalk pointing, others coming from the side streets, from the Sunday restaurants. He stepped out from the cruiser, putting on his hat, and handgun loose inside his holster, he was moving forward. What the hell was *this* about? He'd seen so many bad things in the last few days that he had no idea what more worse could happen. And this morning. Word had got around so fast that even for a small town it was startling. People in a panic, leaving town or gathered in small groups and talking wildly. He had seen three traffic jams this morning, had been forced to waste time clearing them. He'd shot a frenzied dog, had helped its bleeding owner to the doctor. He had found a mangled woman by a laundromat. But now a mob that filled the street. He didn't like where this was heading.

Weak from lack of sleep and scared because the town would shortly be in chaos, worried for his family, he had told them not to leave the house for anything. He'd called his sister down in Denver, made arrangements for his wife and kids to go there. They were packing right now, and he didn't know how many other people had found out what soon would happen, but he knew that many others had made plans to leave the town as well.

But all the same he thought he guessed what to

expect now—more of this but surely nothing worse. Yet even as he walked up to the crowd to part it, he was sensing something that was far beyond his knowledge, something that when he reached out to shift the crowd as if he pulled a screen away would show him some dark final truth which ever after would change everything.

He heard the words but didn't understand them, couldn't make them out, a snarled fog-throated muttering. He pushed more through the crowd and stopped and stared, and it must once have been a person, but its trunk was cloaked with rags which maybe once were furs. Its arms and legs were bloody. It was snarling, drooling, jerking, hair down to its waist and falling all around it, beard down to its navel, face dark from the dirt and scabs, and bugs were crawling on it as it leered up, blinking. "Own oom," it was choking. Rettig didn't understand the sounds. He stumbled back against the crowd, his heartbeat racing. Then he understood. The choking, rasping, barking.

"Throne room," it was saying.

"Throne room," it repeated.

"Throne room, throne room, throne room."

76

Nature had reclaimed the place. New trees had grown around the stumps from which the wood had come to build the mess halls and the sleeping quarters. Weeds and bushes choked the lanes and the parade ground. Walls had toppled, roofs had sagged, and doors were off their hinges. In the buildings, animals built nests among the spider webs and sawdust from the insects that had nibbled holes inside the logs. A bird sat in one broken window, scanning, blinking at the desolation.

Years of dust lay on the floors, and hornets buzzed around their hive up in one corner. Faded slogans, symbols, Day-Gloed red and green, were on the walls, a skull and crossbones, flags with rifles for the stripes and bullets for the stars, a skeleton across a pentagon. From down below, a wind was blowing.

77

They were standing near the figure in Emergency.

"Does anybody know him?" Accum said.

"...*It*, you mean."

And they all turned to Rettig.

"I don't know exactly *what* I mean."

The figure wore a gown now, top part showing just above the sheet that covered him. His beard was trimmed, his hair was cut, an intravenous bottle hung beside him, leading to the needle in his arm. Though he was motionless, unconscious, straps restrained him.

"I do," Dunlap said, and they were looking, and his face was strained. He didn't speak for several seconds. "Slaughter wouldn't know, of course. The rest of you, I don't see why you haven't understood by now. He's from the compound."

They were staring.

"What?"

"The tattooed number on his wrist there. Quiller had them all tattooed before he let them join the compound."

"Christ, he's right."

"But they're all gone now," Slaughter told him.

"Are they?"

"No, I go up hunting through there," Rettig told them. "It's deserted, has been for a lot of years."

"That doesn't mean they didn't move to some place

205

else. The winter plus the murder. They decided on a better place."

"But where?"

As if in answer, now the figure squirmed beneath the straps. He shook his head, unconscious, flared his nostrils, moaning, "Throne room."

"What?" And Accum frowned.

"He's saying 'throne room,'" Slaughter told him. "I don't understand it either. He was moaning that when Rettig found him." Slaughter didn't like the smell in here. Although the figure had been bathed while he was strapped down in the bed, the room yet stank from rancid meat and sweat and mildew, and the sharp sweet smell of medicine mixed in with these things nauseated him. "Where has he been living anyhow?"

"The throne room," Dunlap told him.

"Very funny."

"No, the place has clearly some importance to him. Maybe if we asked him."

"He's unconscious. You can see that."

"I don't care. Let's try it."

Slaughter looked at Accum.

"I don't know. He's very sick. All right, I don't think it could hurt him any more than what he is already."

"But it's pointless," Slaughter said.

"What difference does it make? Let's try it." Dunlap bent down by the figure. "Can you hear me?"

"Careful," Slaughter told him.

Dunlap nodded, moving back a little from the figure. "Can you hear me?"

There was no response. He waited. Then he said again but softer, "Can you hear me?"

Now the figure squirmed again. He hissed once. Then he settled.

"You're with friends now. Talk about the throne room."

"Throne room." That was croaked, but they could hear it.

206

Dunlap looked at them. He spoke more softly to the figure. "That's right. Talk about the throne room."

"Red room."

Dunlap frowned. He looked at them again.

"It could be blood." And Accum frowned at them for answer.

"Maybe," Slaughter told him. "Or it could be something he remembers from when he was just a kid. There isn't any way to know."

And suddenly the figure on the bed was screaming. They were staring at the figure as the scream swept louder all around them. It rose higher, strident, body twisted, agonized, and then as suddenly as it began, the scream diminished, and the figure settled, moaning, on the bed. They kept on staring. People gathered at the door.

"There's nothing you can give him?" Slaughter said to Accum.

"I won't risk a sedative. The only thing that we can do is watch to see what happens."

"What about these lights, though? Can't we dim them?"

"He's unconscious, so they shouldn't bother him. But why not? I don't see a need for them." He walked across to flick the lights. The room was shadowed now, lit only by the dim lights on the rack above the bed.

The figure didn't stop his moaning, though. He jerked his head from side to side. Then gradually he seemed a little calmer.

"What about the red room? Tell us all about it," Dunlap said.

There wasn't any answer.

"Red room," Dunlap said again.

And then in answer, "Red room, red room, antelope."

"I told you this is useless. He's just babbling," Slaughter said.

"Or else he's saying what's important to him," Dunlap answered.

"Then you tell me what it means."

207

"You know I can't."

"Of course you can't. We have to find out where they've gone. If there's some kind of red room, I sure want to know what's in it."

"Where, though?" Rettig said. "Those hills are used for camping, fishing, hunting. Someone would have found them."

"Could be someone did. You'd better check your missing persons file and any inquiries you might have had from other sections of the country," Dunlap said. "You never know how far back this might take you."

"Slaughter, would you mind explaining what this means?"

The new voice thundered through the room. They stiffened, turning toward the doorway, Parsons braced there, looming over them, and then they turned toward Slaughter.

"We don't know yet. We were—"

"In the hallway."

"What?"

"I'm waiting, Slaughter."

Parsons stepped back out and let the door swing shut. The room was silent as they looked at Slaughter.

"Well, I guess I knew that this would happen."

"What would happen?"

"Nothing. Guess I'd better get it settled." Slaughter faced the door and pulled on it. He saw where Parsons waited.

Parsons knew enough to let the door swing shut before he started, though. "I told you not to let that magazine reporter see this! You were told to get him on a train the hell from town!"

The nurses at the far end stared at them.

"I don't think I can do that."

"If you want to keep your job, you'll—"

"Parsons, look, we really should have got to know each other. It's too late now, but I'll try to make you understand. I've been through situations like this many times. Back in Detroit, we'd have some trouble,

208

and the pressure would be on our supervisors, so they'd look around for someone to put blame on. We learned early how to come out looking squeaky clean. Now this town's in a *lot* of trouble, and you're going to need a fall guy, but I'm damn sure that it won't be me. That man in there is closer to me right now than my jockey shorts. I don't go anywhere, not even to the men's room, without bringing him along. Because I want to guarantee that I'm protected, that he writes down every move I make, so that if you have any accusations, any tricks you want to pull to keep your lovely reputation, there'll be someone else's word beside your own."

"I'll have you—"

"Listen to me. I'm not finished. So you want to sit back, let things happen. Well, that's not the way I plan to do this. If I have to, I'll declare a state of martial law. I don't have the authority, but when I'm finished, there'll be lots of time for us to argue. In the meanwhile, I'll at least be doing something, which is more than I can say for you. It could be that I'll make mistakes. Okay then, I'll take blame for them. But there is no way in this life that I'll take blame for your inaction."

Parsons glared at him. "You'll wish you never came here."

"Maybe. But just think about your options. If I'm right, then you'll reach out and take the credit. If I'm wrong, then you know who to point at. But this man is my insurance. He's my witness to protect me. I'm in charge now. Don't forget it."

"Oh, I won't forget." And Parsons was so full of hate that he was trembling. "Years from now, I'll still remember you, but you won't be around to know it."

209

78

Owens didn't want to do this. He came into Slaughter's office, and he saw where Accum, Rettig, and another man whom he had never seen before, were turning to him.

"Good. I'm glad that you could make it," Slaughter said.

"But not for long." And Owens pointed out the window toward the line of traffic moving out of town. "Tonight there won't be anybody left here."

Slaughter looked at Owens, then at where he pointed. "So the word spread fast, and folks are leaving. That can help us."

"To do what? Protect a ghost town?"

"That's exactly what I didn't want to hear. You've worked a lot on this. I thought I could depend on you."

"But what's the use? You know that we can't beat this."

"We can try."

"Well, you don't have a family. My wife and kids are packing right now."

"So are mine. That doesn't mean I'm going with them," Rettig told him.

Owens looked at him and then at everyone. His gaze was disbelieving. "You guys still don't get it, do you? All that we've found out, the way they don't like light and how they come out in the darkness, how the moon affects them, how the incidents have been increasing."

Slaughter frowned and shook his head. "I still don't understand you."

"It's the moon. The moon's been getting fuller, and tonight it's at its fullest. This whole valley's going to be a madhouse."

They were staring at him.

"You're a cop. When you were in Detroit, you surely noticed how the crazies started acting up when it was full moon or when seasons started changing. You don't even need to be a cop to notice it. Just talk to doctors or to me about the way my animals begin behaving. Talk to people at complaint departments out at Sears or Ward's or anywhere. The moon does crazy things. And now tonight it's not just full moon. It's Midsummer's Eve. They didn't pick that night by accident. We've got a virus that affects our limbic brains and makes us act the way we did when we first started. You'll see hell tonight."

And everybody stared at him, their faces drained of color.

"Jesus."

"Yes, you've scared me," Slaughter said and looked down at his desk, then at the window, then at him. He took a breath. "Yes, I admit it, and I guess that, after what I've seen, you're likely right that anything can happen now. But I don't know what I can do about it."

"Leave before you don't have any choice."

"I can't allow that."

"Why?"

"Because I have a job."

"That's just as crazy as the things you've seen. You won't do any good, and even if you do, who's going to thank you? Parsons? He looks out for you know who. You think the people in this valley will be grateful if you die for them? Don't you believe it. They'll just say you didn't have control, that you were foolish. Take the chance and get out while you can."

"But it's not for the town I'm doing this. It's for myself. If I run now, I couldn't tolerate myself. And I don't think that you could run out either."

"No? Just watch me."

And they did. They waited, staring, and he looked at them, and for a moment, it seemed certain that he moved to walk away, but then he didn't.

"Something wrong? You're bothered?" Slaughter said.

Owens kept on looking at him.

"Maybe you had something more to say?"

But Owens only looked at him.

"I tell you what. It's daylight. Things won't get too bad until tonight. Just stick around a little. Tell your family to leave, that you'll catch up. And in the meanwhile, keep on helping us the way you did just now. You've given us more information that we had. I don't know how to use it, but you're really quite important."

Owens kept on looking. "Till tonight at sunset."

"That's no more than I could ask for."

And then Slaughter did a strange thing. He reached close to shake with him, and Owens seemed a little better, and the other men relaxed then.

"We're a team again. Let's do it."

79

Parsons pulled the roadblock toward the two-lane highway. It was like a sawhorse, only bigger, longer. He had found it by the roadside where a highway crew had been repairing asphalt, and he pulled the second one across so that the both lanes now were barricaded, and he faced the backed-up traffic. His intentions were uncommon to him. All his life he'd learned to occupy a still point, to let power channel through him rather than be active and pursue it. He had earned his station simply by agreeing to what everyone already was committed to. That government is best which governs least, he always said. A public servant's job is not to lead, instead to follow. And for twenty years of being mayor, he found that notion was successful. Now it failed him. From his house outside of town, he'd seen the people
212

leaving, had received the phone calls of complaint and of desertion. He had begged his friends to stay and trust him, but that moment when, if he had only acted, now was past him, and he saw the town dissolving, saw the power he had passively received dissolving with it. For the first time in his life, he was a failure. More important, he would never occupy his same position. If the town were ever saved, if people ever came back, they would surely not be loyal to him. They would change things, choose a new mayor, want to do things differently, and he would be like presidents who once were influential, leaders who were set aside and even an embarrassment. He knew that these analogies were grandiose, but this had been his country, this town in this valley. He had ruled it absolutely, and he couldn't bear a time when he would be deposed and useless.

Both his roadblocks set up and his shotgun in his hand, he stalked ahead toward where the first car waited. He was bulky, towering above the car. That was the first thing he had learned, to use his size, his presence. "Turn around. We have to work together on this."

"Get those roadblocks out of there before I ram right through them."

"And what then? If everybody leaves, there won't be anyone around to stop this."

"Look, the guy next door was mangled by his German shepherd. Two doors down, the husband went berserk. I know of twenty people who've been missing since last night. Something's going on, but it's been covered up, and I don't plan to wait around to find out what it is."

"I'll shoot your tires out."

"And what about the other cars behind me? You don't have the shells for that. Just clear those roadblocks. Let me on my way."

"I can't permit that. We don't know what this thing is, but if I let you from the valley, you'll be spreading it. This valley, starting now, is quarantined."

He knew that he was being contradictory, that what he'd said to Slaughter went against what he was doing now, but he was in a fight with Slaughter, and if using Slaughter's tactics meant success, then he would use them. What was more, the situation was so uncontrolled now that this tactic really was the best way, and besides, as he was saying to the driver, "If you leave now, if this valley goes to hell, you won't be coming back. There won't be anything you want here or can trust here. Take a stand, for God sake. Go back into town and fight this."

All the cars were lined up, honking, drivers getting out and massing toward him. He was ready with his shotgun. "If you'll trust me, I can show you how to beat this."

They were yanking at his roadblocks.

"It's the compound. Don't you see it?"

Yes, he knew about that too. He had informants everywhere, and he'd been talking to them since he'd been with Slaughter. There were yet a few things he didn't understand, but he knew just enough that he now had a scapegoat. Plus, they really were the enemy, and if he'd worked this angle seven years ago, he knew that he could work it once again. He stared at them.

"The compound?" They were pausing with the roadblocks in their hands. "But they're long gone."

"I'm telling you that they're still in the mountains. Oh, they moved to some place else, but they're still up there, and they're crazy. God knows what all they've been doing, but they've picked up some disease now, and they're coming to the valley. Oh sure, I know that cats and dogs have got it too, but we can handle them. The compound is the thing that I'm afraid of."

It was prehistoric argument that took advantage of their tribal instincts, conjuring the image of some foreign thing that no one understood and hence that everyone was fearful of. He almost was ashamed to use it, but he nonetheless believed it, all those hate-filled recollections of the sixties, latent, ready to be triggered,

214

and his anger was intense enough now that he wanted to get even. Damage Slaughter. Get this town back as it was for him. Oh yes, by God, the way that Slaughter spoke to him, he meant to see that someone paid.

He waited as they stared at him. "You don't remember how things were back then? They're going to come down here and kill us unless we make plans to stop them."

They were staring.

"I don't even need you. I'll go see the ranchers. *They* know what's important. *They* know how to keep what they've worked hard for. I'll go find some *men* who aren't afraid!"

And now he felt emotion stirring in them. In a moment, he would ask if anybody knew the people who'd been murdered. He would tell them about Slaughter, how their chief was so inept that he himself, their *mayor,* was forced to come down here and take charge of his people.

80

Slaughter stared down with the others at the map. They'd made arrangements for their message to be broadcast on the TV and the radio, for everyone to stay inside, to keep away from animals, from strangers, to report a bite or any odd behavior, then to call his office for assistance, and to watch for cruisers that were out in force along the streets. He himself had got in touch with the Reserves in town, and they were massing now to search the streets from house to house. He glanced down at his watch. "You know these mountains more than I do. Tell me where the compound is."

"It's too much area to figure," Rettig told him.

"Yes, but—" Slaughter paused and rubbed his forehead. He'd been having pains there for some time now, lack of food and sleep, the tension building in him, and his argument with Parsons. He was hoping he could handle this, but he was overwhelmed by what he faced, gradually more doubtful. "Yes, but there must be a couple places you can think of, caves or canyons where a group of people could live undetected."

"If you want to think about it that way, there are hundreds. I remember as a kid we didn't even have terrain maps for those mountains. Hunters, fishermen, oh yeah, they go all through there, but I used to know an Indian who lived there as a hermit for three years and never came across another person."

"What you're telling me is that we won't find any answer."

"What I'm saying is that we don't have the time for trial and error."

"Look, there has to be some logic to this," Dunlap said.

They turned to him, the city man who planned to tell them about mountains.

"Logic? Where the hell is logic?" Slaughter said.

"You're trying too hard. Think about it. Quiller kept two hundred people. Some of them died from the cold that winter. Others likely snuck away. But all of them? I don't believe that now. You're looking for a place that's big enough for, let's say, fifty people. And it's high, where people normally don't go. Away from all the public trails."

"Okay, I buy that," Rettig said.

"But," Slaughter told them, "that still doesn't get us anywhere."

"You'd know the way to do this if you still were in Detroit. Think of everything that's happened as a group of crimes you're plotting on a grid of city streets. Diagram it for the pattern."

"But there *isn't* any pattern."

"Sure there is. Which section of the valley has been losing cattle?"

216

"Over here. The west side."

"And the ranchers who are missing?"

"To the west."

"The field where you found Clifford?"

Slaughter started drawing X's on the map. "We'll need a list of everything that's happened." He was wishing Marge were here to help him. Then he realized his own place was in that direction, and he shivered as he understood that what he'd seen last night had not been bobcats.

"Draw some lines up. Intersect them."

They were grouped around the table.

"Well, it's high up. That's what you expected."

"High enough that people don't go up there much. You see there are no trails marked."

"What's this scattered line here?"

"That's the railroad that went up to where they used to mine the gold back in the old days. It's all broken down now."

"Mine the gold? Mine *what* gold?"

"This was once the richest section of the state. Back in 1895. There used to be a town up there."

And Slaughter felt the chill begin.

"Dear God, and we were just too dumb to see it," Owens said.

"The ghost town," Rettig said. "They called it Motherlode. It's hard as hell to get there now that we don't have the railroad up there. I mean, there's no wagon road, no trail. That's why they build the railroad in the first place."

"Motherlode, and there are shafts that cut in through the rock walls. If you knew what you were doing, you could live up there a long time. All those miners did."

"And now the compound," Slaughter said.

"And now the compound," Owens echoed. "There's no telling what we'll find up there."

"I'm sorry, Slaughter."

Parsons's voice came strong across the room. They turned and looked beyond the glass partition toward

217

the group of men with rifles who were coming through the main door, standing in the middle of the larger office. Parsons was ahead of them, looming huge and staring through the glass partition.

Slaughter frowned and told him, "You keep barging in."

"Well, this will be the last."

The room was silent now. The shuffling feet had stopped. The officer on duty at the radio was staring, and the three men who'd been answering the phones were halting in mid-sentence. They made brief remarks and set the phones down. Almost at that moment, all the phones were ringing once again.

"Pull the jacks on those things," Parsons said.

They looked at Slaughter, then at Parsons.

"Pull the jacks, I told you."

He was walking toward them as they leaned down quickly, pulling at the jacks.

"That's better. Now we won't be interrupted. Well, come on then, Slaughter. Let's get moving."

"Why?"

"I just declared emergency conditions."

"I don't—"

"This is what you'd call a citizen's arrest."

"You're joking."

"Am I smiling? Move before I make you."

"But you can't be serious."

"I'm not prepared to argue. It's a known fact that you wouldn't follow orders."

"That's because you didn't want to deal with this."

"Do I appear as if I'm not prepared to deal with this? You're not convincing, Slaughter. You've been acting on your own without authority. Your methods have been irresponsible. You've let this thing get out of hand while you and Accum here and Owens were conspiring to hide the evidence of murder."

"What?"

"The boy that Accum slashed down in the morgue. The boy was still alive. You think that I don't know
218

about that? Once I figured that the parents would be suing us, I had a second autopsy performed. That slash is hardly what you'd call professional. Oh, Accum did his best to make it seem a part of his procedure, but he didn't do it well enough. We're holding all of you until we learn the truth about this."

"Not including me. I don't know anything about this," Dunlap told him.

"But you've seen enough to be a circumstantial witness. Slaughter bragged about that."

"What about myself?" And that was Rettig, stepping forward.

"I have nothing I can claim against you. Actually I'm putting you in charge, although I'm still suspicious of your friendliness toward Slaughter. Make one move to help him, and you'll join him. This department's been in bad shape for too long. I mean to put some muscle in it. *I won't ask you anymore,*" he told them. "Rettig, take his gun."

"Do it," Slaughter told him. "There's no choice. Believe me, I'll make good on this."

And Parsons started laughing. "Sure you will. In your own jail. Let's get this finished."

Rettig looked at Slaughter, took the gun. The men with rifles stepped ahead to form a cordon, and the four men went out, guards around them.

81

Rettig stood there, silent. Glancing toward the window, he saw people in the front yard, mostly men, and they were angry, holding weapons. He was suddenly exhausted.

"Tell me what that bastard thinks he's going to do," the officer beside the radio was saying.

"He's afraid that Slaughter will outclass him."

"But that mob out there. He's instigating them."

"He's doing what they tell him. That's what he'll say later, and that's always been his pattern. Oh, he'll get away with this all right, and he'll come back with twice the power that he started with. I hate to say it, but no matter how you look at it, we've got some bad times coming, and there isn't any way to stop them."

He was looking out the window as the people shifted so that Parsons could go through, haranguing them.

82

He started feeling strange now. They had warned him this might happen, but the bite had not been deep across his finger. Lots of scratches on his face and neck, but just the one slight bite where he had reached up to defend himself against her. When she'd started last night, he'd assumed that she was crazy from her grief. Their only child and he was dead now. Then he'd vaguely understood that even grief could not account for how she acted, and he'd tried to get away from her. She wouldn't let him. If that woman hadn't clubbed his wife, he doubted that he would have had the strength to fight her off much longer. Now more grief. His wife unconscious. He was sorry that his wife had needed such strong force to be subdued. He wondered if their lives would ever regain normalcy. He worried that his wife might even not survive.

And now the knowledge of the virus she and Warren had contracted, of the virus he himself might harbor. They'd explained to him that, if he had the sickness, he would demonstrate the symptoms in the next full day, and they had put him in this chamber. *Locked* him in the chamber really. It was padded, floors and walls and ceiling, without windows. It was for hysterics, and the thought of what he might become was reinforced by these conditions.

He glanced at his watch. They'd let him keep it, which to some degree was comforting. He saw that it said three o'clock—fourteen hours since he had been bitten. Maybe he'd survive this, but he felt the strangeness in him. Only grief? Depression? Was it something else? Was this the way it started.

Angered, suddenly he punched against a padded wall. He kicked it, cursing. Yesterday his life had been perfection. Driving home with Warren from the doctor, he had felt relief and happiness, togetherness. Now all that was destroyed for him. His son was dead. He punched the padded wall again. He growled at it. So easy to imagine how this day could have been different. Then he understood that he had growled just now.

He stood immobile, startled. No, he'd just been angry. It was nothing. But the sharp salt smell of sweat in here was powerful. He sniffed. It was exuding from the walls. He stepped close, sniffing. This was how it started then, he guessed. There wasn't any question. Though he should have felt more fear, he knew, his grief and anger now subdued had wearied him. He didn't at last care. And maybe that passivity was part of this thing too. He didn't have a choice. It forced him to accept it.

And that sharp salt smell of sweat. He leaned close, sniffing. He was licking. And he realized that he was licking, but he couldn't stop himself. The urge was irresistible. His tongue lapped rough against the canvas. For an instant, he could recognize his double personality, but then analysis was past him. When they came ten minutes later, he was raving.

83

Parsons waited in the field beside the fairgrounds. There were many who were here already, but he knew that soon there would be more. He'd sent his messengers to all the ranchers in the valley. Men from town were driving in, and he saw ranchers coming now as well. He climbed up in the Jeep and raised his bullhorn.

"Listen to me." Amplified, his words burst strident toward them.

They were turning, faces tense from expectation. Motions rippled through them. Then the group was still, and they were waiting.

"You all know the trouble that we've got. I need some volunteers to bring your neighbors to the fairgrounds. We'll inspect them to make sure they're not infected, and we'll keep them here until the trouble's over. In the meantime, I need other volunteers to search the houses. If you see a cat or dog that looks suspicious, shoot it. We have sedatives for any person with the virus."

"What about the compound?"

"First we get the town in order. After that, we'll stop whatever's out there. Don't worry."

They were murmuring. He pointed to the captain of the Potter's Field Reserves. He had to get this moving.

84

They were sleeping in their hiding places through the town, the men and women, children, who were missing, who had felt the savageness come on them and had sought out shelter from the sunlight. There were dogs and cats and other animals as well. In closets, unused cisterns, attics, every place that was in darkness.

85

In the mountains, in their caves, their leaf nests, and their burrows underneath a maze of logs, they slept and murmured. Antlers scraped together. When the moon rose once again, they would come out to face the night, and in their haunted minds they dreamed about their sanctuary, moaning for the banquet of the town spread out below them.

86

Four men in the cells downstairs, two other men with rifles watching them. The guards were leaned back in their chairs against the wall. There was a desk, a door that led out to the stairs up to the main floor, and a second door that led through to the tunnel toward the courthouse. That way prisoners could be escorted to the judge without their ever going outside, and the tunnel was both dank and fetid, odors which came underneath the bottom of the second door and filled the cell room. Slaughter had been down here only when he was required. Certainly he'd never been a prisoner, and he was understanding the humiliation, vowing that he'd make things better if he ever got the chance, although that didn't seem too likely. He was finished in this town. He knew that Parsons had been much too clever for him. He was sickened, and the damp oppressiveness around him didn't help things.

He at least had got some sleep. At first he had been anxious, pacing back and forth across his cell. He'd tried to reason with the guards, but they had only looked at him and didn't answer. His three friends who were imprisoned with him, when his arguments had lagged, exchanged diminishing complaints, then gave up, sprawling in defeat across their bunks and finally were silent. Slaughter gave up with them. In his weariness, he slept.

The cells were in a row, four units with a prisoner per unit.

Accum, who was puzzled how he'd let himself become committed to this. He had been a star once, back in Philadelphia, but his preoccupation with the dead had led to disassociation from the living. Each night he'd stayed later, working longer on the bodies. They had been his final truth, and all it took was one slight, gentle touching of a young girl's lifeless shoulder to alarm him. He had glanced up, and his supervisor stood within a doorway, looking at him. Neither said a word. There wasn't any need. The next day he'd resigned and come back here to Potter's Field where he'd been born and raised and where his father, the physician, had been powerless to save his cancer-dying mother. Here he'd tried to get his mind in order, and now after all his distance, he was close to being prosecuted for his rare involvement. Yesterday when he had found the virus-ridden dog, he should have phoned the station and been done with it. Instead he had become committed, and now surely he'd be forced to . . .

Owens, who was worrying about his family waiting for him. He had been denied a chance to call them, and he wished that he had left the office upstairs when he'd said that he was going. But he'd stayed for stupid reasons, loyalty to people other than his family, to these men who'd said that they had need of him when his first duty was toward home. Now he would maybe face a jury because Slaughter and the coroner convinced him that they all would lie about the boy's death. What had he been thinking of? What power did these men have? Did he want that much for them to like him? He'd be punished for protecting people whom he had no obligation to, and he was wishing now that with his family he had fled to some new place beyond the . . .

Dunlap, who a while ago had dreamed about that antlered figure, turning, staring past its shoulder at him. He had never dreamed it with such vividness, as if each visitation were more real, more clear until he'd wake up one last time and see it crouching there before him. But it wasn't in his cell when he awakened. Just the memory of what had happened, and beyond the bars the two guards who leaned, chairs against the wall, and held their rifles. He was sweating from the dream and from the absence of the alcohol which gave him strength. His hands were shaking as they had all day and yesterday, and he was thinking that if he could only have a drink his troubles wouldn't be so fierce, he knew that he could handle this. But in a way he was delighted. In his agony he at last had got his story, and if Parsons thought that his imprisonment would keep him from the truth about this, Parsons didn't know how good this loser once had been, though he was not a loser any longer. He would find the truth and neutralize the dream and save himself. He clutched at every instant, wondering what . . .

Slaughter, who was thinking of five years ago and old Doc Markle and the secret they had shared. He had

225

never told the old man, and the old man never had alluded to it, but they understood their common knowledge. Slaughter was a coward. Seeing Clifford, walking through that moonlight field, trapping that dead boy, he'd felt the old fear rising in him. Hell, he'd *panicked* in the field and at his house. He'd lost complete control. He didn't understand now how he'd come this far. His bluff of manliness to all his friends, his arguments with Parsons. They were overcompensations, last attempts to keep his self-respect, because the one thing that he wanted was to get the hell away from here, to free himself from any need for strength and courage. Five years he had coasted. Parsons had been right. In fact the mayor had done him quite a favor. By imprisoning him, Parsons had relieved him of his burden. Slaughter silently was grateful. He had argued with the guards to let him free, but he had known there wasn't any chance, so arguing was easy, even pleasant. But the thought of old Doc Markle had enlivened ancient guilt, and he was caught between conflicting notions. Stay here. It's the safe place for you. Find a way to get out. Prove that you're still worth a shit. He told himself he didn't have a choice. Regardless of his shame, he was imprisoned. Sublimate the shame. Get rid of it.

The night was deep upon him. Through the tiny windows high along one wall out there, he heard the howling and the shooting and the screaming. Thank God that you're in here, that you're safe. But he was growing angry at himself, at Parsons, at this trouble. He was just about to argue with the guards again. Though useless, that would help suppress his tension. Then the door was opened at the far end, and he stared as Rettig stepped in.

Both guards stood now, careful.

"Take it easy," Rettig told them. "Watch out for those rifles, or you'll maybe shoot your mouths off."

They looked puzzled, shifting nervously. "You're not supposed to be here," one man said.

"Oh, really? Well, I'll tell this woman here to take the food back." He was turning.

"Wait a minute. What food?"

"For the prisoners. They haven't eaten."

"No one fed us either."

"Well, I'm sorry that I didn't think of that."

"Hey, you just bring the food in."

"I don't like this," his companion said.

"It's only food, for Christ sake. What the hell, I'm hungry."

"Yeah, but they might pull a trick."

"We've got the rifles. Bring the food in."

"If you're certain." Rettig shrugged.

"Just bring it in."

"Okay then." He went toward the door and gestured.

Marge came in. She had two baskets, looking at the four men in the cells and in particular at Slaughter. Slaughter tried to smile, but she seemed nervous, and the last few days had aged her. Slaughter couldn't stop his sorrow for her.

"Hi, Marge."

She just looked at him. "I thought you'd maybe like some food."

"Is something wrong?"

"The woman that I hit."

"Yes, what about her?"

"She died half an hour ago."

87

It struggled in its airless prison. It had crawled inside this storage chest to sleep, and now it felt the night beyond there, and it needed to get out. The latch had

227

snapped. It pounded on the lid which wasn't moving. It was sweating, gasping. Muffled screams went weaker.

88

He was stationed at this intersection, watching as the drunk came near him.

"Hey, you shouldn't be here. Everybody's at the fair-grounds."

But the drunk came lurching closer, stumbling in the moonlight. As the officer reached out to stop him, he discovered that this drunk was something more than that. The awful eyes were closer.

89

When he saw the dog lope down the street, he shot it.

Someone screamed then.

"That's my dog you shot!"

90

The things had found each other in the darkness. They had crawled out from their sheds and basements, from the trunks of old abandoned cars. They formed in packs and stumbled down the streets, and volunteers who had been searching houses fled in panic. Sometimes they found strength to form their own groups, and they stood beneath the lights of intersections, shooting at the antic horror they were facing. Dogs and cats had formed in packs as well, and now they merged together, one great swirling furor, snapping, hissing, pressing forward. All through town, the sound of gunfire crackled.

91

Winston wondered what the shooting was. He'd done his job all day and with reluctance had come back here to this basement as he had been ordered. He had flashed his light at these three bodies, and he'd huddled by the washer in one corner where, if something came back for its supper, he would have a chance to shoot it where it poised upon the stairs. He waited as the gunfire worsened. He heard screaming outside, but he concentrated on his duty, almost glad that he was in here. Then the gunfire lessened, and he thought he heard some movement. He was tensing. Over by the stairs. He had his flashlight ready. Wait until it's down here. Make sure that you hit it. He heard scraping, but the sound was not what he'd expected, or from where he thought it would be coming. Understanding, in a panic, he now flicked his light, and Orval had arisen, lurching toward him. Winston shot and kept shooting.

92

They were sorting through the baskets, looking in the thermoses. They shook them. Everything was fine.

"Okay, you stand back here while I distribute them."

The one guard walked past Rettig, left some sandwiches before each cell. He set down plastic cups and then the thermoses.

"You listen. Just as soon as I step back, you reach out for them. Since you've only got two thermoses, you'll have to pass them to each other, but as soon as you're done pouring, put the thermoses back out in front where I can see them. I don't want somebody throwing them."

Slaughter didn't care. He kept his gaze on Rettig. "What about outside?"

"Don't ask."

And Slaughter glanced down at the floor and then at Marge. He cleared his throat. "Well, listen, thank you, Marge."

She didn't answer.

"Hey, take care of her," he said to Rettig.

"That's a promise." Rettig looked at where the two guards stared at him. "Don't get excited. I'm already gone." Then Rettig scanned along the cells and paused, and he was leaving. "See you, Chief."

"Take care now."

And the door was closed behind where Rettig left with Marge.

The four were silent, studying the guards.

"Get started," one guard told them. "Let me see if it's been drugged. I'm hungry."

Slowly they were crouching, reaching. Slaughter was the last. He chewed, his mouth like dust, the meat-loaf sandwich tasteless.

"Here, I'll pour the coffee." Thinking of the shooting outside, he reached through, unscrewed the cap. He poured the coffee into several plastic cups and passed the cups along.

But one cup he was careful to keep only for himself. Because as he had poured, a slender pliant object had dropped with it, splashing almost imperceptibly, so soft and narrow that it didn't rattle when the guard had shaken both the thermoses. He didn't dare to see if anyone had noticed. He just went on as if everything were normal. Then he stood and leaned against his bunk and chewed his sandwich, stirring with his finger at the coffee. This he knew. He wasn't going to drink the damn stuff, though he did pretend, and then his finger touched the object. It was like a worm. He felt it, long and slender, pliant. But what was it? For a moment, he suspected that it maybe was explosive, but that wouldn't do much good because there wasn't any way to set it off. Besides, the noise would draw attention. Rettig wouldn't give him something that he couldn't use. This wasn't plastique then, so what else could it be? He leaned to one side so that no one saw him as he picked the object from the coffee, glancing, dropping it back in the coffee. It was red, just like the worm he had imagined. But he couldn't figure what it was or how to use it.

"Christ, this coffee's awful," Dunlap answered.

"Just shut up and drink," the first guard told him. "I was right," he told the second. "There's some kind of drug in it. They'll shortly be asleep."

"Or worse."

"That's all we need. Well, they can throw up all they want to. I'm not going to help them. You remember that," he told the prisoners. "If anybody's sick, he's on his own."

And they were setting down their plastic cups. "It's true. This coffee's rotten," Owens said.

"Don't drink it," Accum told them.

Now the first guard started laughing.

Slaughter stood and walked close to the bars. "Well, I don't know what's wrong with you guys, but this coffee tastes just fine to me. If you don't want it, pass the other thermos down."

"Be careful, Slaughter," Accum told him.

"I know what I'm doing. Hell, I'm thirsty."

"Suit yourself." And from the far end, Owens passed the thermos down. They moved it, hand to hand, along the cells, and Slaughter set it by the thermos he had poured from.

"I'll save this for later."

"If you're not too sick," the second guard now told him, grinning.

"You guys don't know what you're missing."

"I think that you'll show us soon enough," the other guard was saying.

Slaughter shrugged and went back to his bunk, pretending that he sipped and liked the coffee. "All the more for me." And he was yawning. As he lay back in his bunk, he wondered if another worm were in the second thermos and if he would figure what it was and how to use it. On the wall, the clock showed half past twelve now.

93

At the fairgrounds, people huddled in the stands and peered off furtively toward all the chaos sounding in the town. They heard the shooting, screaming, closer. Children whimpered. The arena and the field beyond it were deserted, and the shadowed mountains loomed beyond, the moonlight glinting off the snowcaps. Parsons for the first time now was worried. He had been so confident that he would be successful. But he understood now that he'd brought these people to a central place, that as a group they were a target, and that all the fury out there was converging on them.

"Form a line with rifles!" he was shouting.

94

They were watching from this ridge above the fairgrounds, staring at those once familiar objects down there. Nervous, glancing toward the moon and trembling, they were howling, but the people down there were distracted, didn't bother looking toward the mountains. Then this ridge here was deserted. They were backing from it, moving lower through the forest. They were eager for the taste which, though it sickened, yet they craved, and as they shuffled through the underbrush, they heard the rumbles from the town spread out below them.

95

Slaughter waited in the darkness. He was lying on his bunk, pretending sleep as through his half-closed eyes he glanced out through the bars toward where the two guards, having dimmed the lights, were tilted in their chairs, their heads against the wall. He knew he had to act soon, but if *too* soon, he would rouse them, and they would discover.

He was cursing to himself. He had been safe. A cell to keep him occupied while everything went on without him. Now the force of choice was on him once again, and if he didn't act, he knew that Rettig then would understand him. Did it matter? Yes, he finally decided. He would not relive his past humiliation. He had come here for a fresh start, and if he ignored this opportunity, he never would feel whole again; he would have chosen a progressive pattern of defeat; he'd just keep moving pointlessly. Of course, he could pretend to Rettig that he hadn't understood the objects in the coffee, but he didn't know if he would be convincing. Even so, he wouldn't be convincing to himself. He had to do this.

Cursing to himself, he studied both the guards. Then he sat up slowly in his bunk. Because he finally had understood these objects in the coffee. They were obvious, so much so that he wondered why he took so long to realize their purpose, that he wondered how much smarter Rettig was than he had ever guessed. The plan was simple to the point of genius. Perhaps that was the reason Slaughter took so long to figure it. The objects in the coffee were pure phosphorus. The liquid kept them from igniting. That had been the word that solved the puzzle for him. Thinking yet that these things were explosive, he had wondered how to detonate them. Detonation made him think of fuses, bright light burning. But the blast would warn the guards. These things must have a silent function then, but if they were indeed explosive, how the hell could he ignite them? Since he seldom smoked, he didn't carry matches. Bright light, matches and their phosphorus, ignition, and he had it, suddenly in high school, watching as his teacher drew the worms of phosphorus from jars of water, waiting as the worms, exposed to air, abruptly were on fire. Later he would think how close he'd come to missing the significance, but now he understood and didn't have a choice.

He got up slowly from his bunk and walked with caution toward the bars. He saw that all his friends were sleeping. He stood motionless and waited for some action from the guards. There wasn't any, and he knelt to reach through toward the second thermos. Then he slowly opened it and poured the coffee into plastic cups.

234

Another red worm slid out, dropping. So there *was* another one, and he was reaching in the cup to grab the worm and drop it quickly in the cup that held the other, coffee safely over them. There was one thing yet that bothered him. He knew that phosphorus was poison. If some portions had dissolved, the coffee might yet make them sick. But then he thought that its foul taste might not be from the phosphorus but from the way the coffee was prepared to make it taste bad. Rettig hadn't wanted anyone to drink it. So they all had tried a sip and spit it out. They maybe would be fine.

He watched the guards and guessed there wasn't any point in waiting further. He dipped in the coffee, grabbed the worms, and as they dripped, he pressed them to the bolt that locked his cell. He wouldn't have attempted this if he'd been in a new and well-made jail. But this place had been built in 1923. When he had first come down here, he had been appalled. Oh sure, the locks would hold if someone lunged at them or tried to break them, but the metal wasn't pure enough or thick enough for him, and he had asked permission to revitalize the jail, which the council had denied him. What did he expect? they asked him. Hacksaws or a bomb? There had never been that kind of trouble here, and if he did his job right, none of that stuff would get in here. Well, he had a trick to show them now, and he was grateful that they hadn't acted. Phosphorus burned at high temperatures. Though not sufficient to melt steel, the heat would weaken this poor metal, and the lock seams weren't that good to start with. Hell, he didn't have a thing to lose. He had to try.

He stepped back, but the phosphorus remained inert. Or maybe he was wrong, and these things weren't what he had figured. No, the coffee still was dripping from them. They weren't yet exposed to air. The coffee had to dry, as suddenly he saw what seemed to be a spark, and in a flash the phosphorus was burning. White hot, sparks, a thick cloud rising. He was staring toward the guards. The hiss was louder than he had expected, like

235

a thousand sparklers blazing on July Fourth, and the one guard moved a little in his chair as Slaughter lunged against the cell door.

But it held. The phosphorus kept blazing on the bolt and lock seams, and he lunged again, and this time he could see the seams begin to part. The guard was shifting in his chair and in a moment would be fully wakened. Slaughter lunged against the door again, the metal clanging, and abruptly he was weightless, stumbling forward, almost falling as he realized that he was out, the cell door swinging free, the phosophorus yet hissing, blazing. He kept stumbling, arms out for his balance, as the guard was sitting upright in his chair, and Slaughter lunged against him. While the guard fell, chair upsetting, Slaughter grabbed the rifle, and he swung to grab the rifle from the second guard who now was sitting up as well, his face grotesquely startled, wincing from the rifle blow against his forehead, falling. Slaughter dropped one rifle, aiming with the other, and the two guards paused where they were halfway to their feet now, and the worst part had been managed.

"Stay exactly where you are. Don't move or even fidget," Slaughter told them.

"How the hell—?" They stared from Slaughter toward the dimming remnants of the phosphorus.

"What is it?" Accum said.

The men were moving in the cells.

"It's nothing. We're just getting out is all. Remember," Slaughter told the guards. "Don't even scratch your noses."

He was shifting toward the table, pulling out the drawer and grabbing for the keys. He watched the two guards all the time he edged back toward the first cell, Owens waiting.

"Here. The big key," Slaughter told him, and he moved again to watch the guards while close behind he heard the scrape of metal as the key was turned. The cell came open. Slaughter glanced at Owens coming out. He concentrated solely on the guards then as the cells were in their sequence unlocked and the men came out.

"But how did—?" Dunlap said.

"I'll tell you later. You two, get on in there." Slaughter pointed toward the guards.

They hesitated.

"Dammit, move, I told you." Slaughter started toward them, and they raised their hands.

"Okay. We're moving."

"You get in the first one. You get in the fourth."

"But why—?"

"No reason. Just do what I tell you. I just want you separated. Move, for Christ sake."

And they did, and Slaughter watched as Accum bound and gagged them, using belts and strips of cloth torn from the bunk sheets. Accum stepped out. Owens shut the doors and locked them.

"Bring the keys. The other rifle."

Dunlap was already half across to reach the one door.

"No, we're going this way," Slaughter told him. "That way leads upstairs. This other one is where we're going."

Dunlap's face was puzzled.

"You'll see."

Slaughter went across and took the keys from Owens. He unlocked the second door and swung it open. Then he flicked the light switch in there, and they saw the damp, slick, brick-lined tunnel.

"It leads toward the courthouse. There's no time."

They moved through. Slaughter stared once at the two guards in their cells. He waved and stepped inside the tunnel where he shut the door and locked it. Then he turned, and they were running.

It was slippery in here. Some condensation on the ceiling dripped down on them, and the tunnel echoed from the clatter of their footsteps. Slaughter saw the vapor from his breath and felt the damp brick chill and kept on running. He was forced to stoop his head as he ran underneath the lights that hung down from the ceiling. Then the tunnel curved, and they were at a second door.

"It's locked. I have to use the key."

But when he fumbled with the key, it didn't work. The door stayed locked.

"What's going on here?"

Then he realized the door had not been locked at all. What he had done just now was actually to lock it.

"Who the hell—? I'm going to fix them."

But in his position he could not fix anyone. He worked the key and turned the handle. Slowly, wincing as the door creaked, he was pushing, and they faced the darkness.

"There's a hall. Just follow it. You'll reach some stairs."

Now Slaughter flicked the lights off.

"But we—"

"I don't want to be a target. Feel along the hall."

They inched on through the darkness. Here the floor was tiled. It echoed smoothly from their halting footsteps. Owens struck an object, groaning.

"Quiet."

"There's a table."

"Quiet. People might be up there."

So they kept on inching forward. Slaughter felt ahead. We should have made the end by now, he told himself, and then his boot struck wood, and he was gripping the banister.

"We made it," Owens said, but Slaughter didn't take the time to caution him. He just continued up the stairs, and everything was dark up there as well, except that with some windows moonlight spilled in, showing first the front door, then the big main hallway. Out there, he heard shooting.

"Quiet," he was saying, and they stopped while, breath held, he was listening. "We'll use the back. For all we know, there could be guards out in the front. I didn't come this far to let them catch me."

238

He was moving down the murky hallway, and the layout in here was the same as at the station. He passed silent offices and reached the back door, staring out, then looking at the others, pulling at the door, and stepping toward the moonlight.

Screaming, shooting.

"Over there. My car is in the lot behind the station. If we're careful, we can take it."

He was shifting from the sidewalk toward the grass, his concentration on the shooting and the parking lot across there as a man stepped from the bushes by the courthouse, then another person. Slaughter, thinking of the two kids in the grocery store who shot him, almost raised his rifle, firing. But he didn't see a reason finally to kill these two. All right, so he'd been caught. Well, he had done his best, and he was waiting, rifle resting in his arms, as Rettig came up close to him.

The men behind were sighing.

"Christ Almighty," Owens said.

"It took you long enough. I almost gave up waiting. So you figured what that stuff was."

"How come you're so smart to think of that?"

"I didn't. Marge did." Rettig turned to Marge, who stepped now close beside him. "She remembered what you said about the cells downstairs, how you complained that they were weak."

"I'm glad it wasn't you. I was afraid that I'd misjudged you."

"Thanks a lot."

"So tell the rest of us."

But Slaughter only stared at Marge and then reached out to touch her. "Thank you."

He could see where she had recently been crying.

"Look, that woman, I—"

"It's all right," Marge was saying. "Maybe dying was the best thing for her." She was blinking.

Now the gunfire and the screaming out there worsened.

Slaughter stared a moment. "What the hell is going on?"

"It's Parsons. He had everybody taken to the fairgrounds."

"Jesus."

"That's right. Now they're all together in the open."

Slaughter turned to them. "I don't know what we're going to do, but we're all useless standing here. The fairgrounds."

"Count me out." And that was Owens.

Slaughter looked at him.

"My wife and kids."

"There's no need to explain yourself. Go on. We'll talk about it sometime."

"Sure."

Except they both knew that they wouldn't.

Owens lingered.

"Hey, you waited until sunset. You made good on what you promised."

"Sure."

And Owens looked at him, then shrugged and moved as if to speak but then thought better, slowly backing off, then turning, walking down along the courthouse, disappearing in the shadows.

Slaughter watched him.

"Here, Chief," Rettig said. "I'll get another gun belt." He was pulling, handing it across.

The weight was satisfying. Slaughter strapped it on. "Your family?"

"My brother's with them. They packed out this afternoon."

"That's all that Owens wanted too, I guess."

And Slaughter stared off toward the gunshots. "Let's get to it."

"Watch out when you reach the parking lot. Parsons has some men inside the station."

"I don't plan to advertise. You coming?" Slaughter said to Accum.

"I have work to do."

And Slaughter nodded. "What about yourself?" he said to Dunlap.

"I intend to see the end of this."

And Marge was standing there before him. "If you think you're going anywhere without me, you're plain crazy."

"We might all be."

They were starting toward the parking lot.

96

The group that Hammel was in charge of had established their position by two cars which they had used to block a side street. They were staring at the mob which stumbled toward them, and perhaps because he'd shot a man already, Hammel hesitated. But the others, squinting in the glare from corner streetlights, gave in to revulsion. They were shooting, but as Hammel looked around him, he saw other figures coming down the street beside him, and he pointed with his handgun. He was shouting, "Fall back! They've outflanked us!" Now his men stared to their right, then straight ahead. They swallowed, and abruptly they were running down the street and toward the fairgrounds.

97

Slaughter got there too late, or in other senses, just in time. The people now were panicked. They were huddled in the bleachers as the shooting thundered closer. Many had abandoned their slight cover, grouping in the field, and Parsons had arranged a line of men with rifles, staring toward the outskirts as the first band, these policemen, burst out backward from between two houses, shooting at some targets out of sight. They broke then, and they ran to reach the fairgrounds. Parsons told his men to hold their fire until the officers were safe behind them. Next another group came running from a side street, these civilians, and another group, civilians yet again, appeared. "Just hold your fire," he was saying. But a dog loped into view, and someone shot it. Other people now were shooting. "Dammit, hold your fire." But then another group came rushing toward them. These had once been neighbors. Now they were no longer human, snarling, drooling, jerking in a rage. The shots were deafening.

98

The house was dark when Owens reached there. He heard shooting two blocks over, saw his car parked in the driveway. He was running toward the house. Then something moved among the shadows. He was turning, and he saw the dog. He reached the steps. He tried the door, but it was locked. The dog was coming. Shouting for his wife, he smashed the window, reaching in to turn the lock, then scrambled in here, shut the door, and heard the clawing. From the back door. *Oh, my God, they're all around me.*

They were shuffling through the forest. Now the trees were thinning, and the slope was merging with the flatland. They heard thunder from the fairgrounds, and they rushed ahead; their appetites were gnawing.

Slaughter swung the cruiser, siren fierce, around a corner. He saw men lined up and shooting all along the street. He saw the things come lurching from the side streets toward him, and he swerved the cruiser up across a yard where he kept going, smashing through a hedge and then a fence as, in behind the men, he saw them shooting. Then the cruiser reached the big fence of the fairgrounds, and he jumped out, Marge and Dunlap with him.

Parsons ran across. "You've got to help me."

"Christ, you should have thought of that before. The floodlights in the front there. Get them on." And Slaughter drew his handgun.

"I don't—"

"Get those floodlights on. Their eyes can't stand the light."

Then someone near them said, "I'll do it. I know where the switches are."

The man was running.

Slaughter squinted toward the bodies out there dropping from the gunfire, and he thought that, after all, this might be handled as some people screamed from in the fairgrounds. They were pointing toward the field behind them. Slaughter stared, and even with the gunfire, he could hear it. Howling in the forest. As a cloud obscured the moon, he just had time to see the forest moving, and then Dunlap screamed to see the antlers.

101

Rettig had been bothered. He had watched as Slaughter drove with Marge and Dunlap toward the fairgrounds. Then he'd gone inside the station, where he'd found another gun belt. He was thinking about Owens, why they'd ever let him walk back into town alone. The wife and children wouldn't be there. They would either have left town, or else they would be waiting at the fairgrounds. Rettig pulled up at the house and saw the dogs around it, howling, snarling, saw the windows broken and the door where it was clawed down to thin wood, and from the cruiser, he was shooting.

102

First the antlers, then the deer appeared, and after them the smaller creatures, driven by the horror that pursued them. They came bursting from the forest, one great panic, eyes afright, stampeding.

Slaughter stared, heard Dunlap moan behind him, heard the screaming from the people in the fairgrounds, and he knew that every moment up to now had only been a preparation. He imagined he saw hockey sticks, a countless number, clicking in the for-
244

est, showing there above the bushes. He was paralyzed with fright. He knew that nothing worse could ever happen, and then sanity was gone from him. He saw the bushes parting in a turmoil, and the figures snarled out, charging toward the fairgrounds, each a hideous concoction, part man, part deer, part wolf, cat, and bear, a dozen other things, a monstrous bestiary from the forest. Those parts which were human were abnormal. Noses missing. Ears and fingers gone, and stumps were limping.

Slaughter blinked. Then he was moving.

"Marge, I need your help."

He didn't look to see if she was coming after. He was certain that she would.

It was just coincidence that, when the fairgrounds weren't in use, the city parked its trucks here. Why else had this happened? To permit him his salvation. Even as he thought that, he was certain he was crazy, but he saw the truck before him as he knew it would be waiting, liquid inside that the workmen used to kill the insects in the trees, the word INFLAMMABLE across the side. He even knew that when he climbed inside he'd find the keys, and in a vision knew that he would find the several flares beneath the seat.

He gave them to her. "Pull that hose down from the back."

"But Nathan—"

"Do it. Flick the lever. When this truck gets moving, spark the flares and throw them in the liquid."

Two things happened then which made him know that he was doing right. The cloud moved on. The moon appeared. The monsters out there cowered, shrieking. Then the floodlights arced across the fairgrounds, and the wails of agony were mounting.

Slaughter turned the key. The engine roaring, he was flicking at the pressure switches. He heard liquid back there spraying as, the truck in gear, he rammed it forward. He was aiming at them, rushing.

And they saw him, and they started toward him, one close object for revenge.

He almost let death have him, so excited was he, but he weakened, and he yanked the gearshift into neutral, steering as he stepped out on the running board. He saw them closer, aimed and jumped and rolled. Then, shoulder awkward, he was racing. As the flares blazed suddenly before him, he heard something close behind him, heard a shot. Then he was diving, and the scorching flame swept past him, feeding toward the truck.

The blast was like a mushroom cloud exploding. Flames went up and up and spread. His clothes were smoking, and he flailed to stop their burning. Metal fell around him, and the crying of the damned was everywhere. Then nothing.

103

Marge had taken off her jacket, hitting at him to put out the fire across his shirt. She smelled the charnel flesh but knew that it was not from Nathan, it was from the things out there. And people were around her, helping.

Slaughter moaned and stumbled, reaching out to hold her. He was blinking at the thing which almost had run fast enough to get him. It was dead now from the gunshot in its forehead.

"Who—?"

"I'm good for something, Slaughter."

That was Parsons, and they looked at one another.

"Even so, you won."

And Slaughter faced him. "No. The hockey sticks. My nightmare?"

"What?"

"The others in the front."

246

"They're dead."

And Slaughter turned to view the mass of burning bodies.

"But what *are* they?"

104

Rettig heard the blast from over near the fairgrounds, but he didn't have the time to wonder. He had shot the dogs around the house. Now he was going in and shot another dog upon the stairs. He shouted, heard no answer, searched the house, and shot another dog up on the second floor. He tried the bathroom door, but it was locked, and when he crashed in, found where Owens huddled in the bathtub.

"Goddamn dogs. I'll never touch another one."

105

They stared down at the bodies, antlers bound by rawhide to the heads. The monsters wore the skins of bear and bobcat—Slaughter thought about what he had seen behind his barn—the tails of wolves, and they were bearded, hairy. Fingers, ears, and noses missing.

"From the frostbite," someone said then. "It's the hippies from the compound."

Dunlap even now was moaning.

"But what happened to them?" Slaughter said. "These antlers. I don't—"

"No one will until we find where they've been living."

106

Accum watched the bodies coming in. The job would take him days, and nights, my Jesus, yes the awful nights. He knew that once this burden had been finished he would never want to look at death again. The beauty was destroyed for him, the truth which he had lived for. He would leave here. He would work to heal the living.

107

Parsons stood before his office window.

"We're both at a standoff," Slaughter said. "The way I see it, we can either fight each other or else work together on this."

Parsons didn't look at him. His back turned, he kept staring out his office window.

"By tomorrow morning, there'll be strangers here, the newsmen and the government, the lawyers," Slaughter went on. "There's a lot of loose ends, and I think we'd better settle what's between us. I don't blame you. I'm prepared to guess you did this for what you considered proper motives. I behaved the same."

And Parsons kept on staring toward the night out there.

"This trouble isn't over," Slaughter added. "When I think about the details. We both need each other's help."

And Parsons turned now. Then he swallowed. "I don't have a choice."

248

"And I don't either."

"What do you suggest?"

"The fairgrounds were a good idea. Oh, the timing was all wrong. The place was good, though. In the morning, we'll keep everybody out there while we finish searching through the houses. Now that people understand, we'll have cooperation. Every animal in town will need a quarantine, but we'll have men from outside to arrange that."

"And the cattle?"

"I don't know. We'll have to watch and see."

And Parsons looked as if his twenty years of power weighed too heavily. "I don't see how this thing can end. The animals up in the mountains."

"Just the western slopes. We'll have to kill them."

"That's impossible."

"I know it."

"Just one animal that has the virus. If we miss it, then the cycle starts again. And we're assuming that the virus has been localized, but what if something took it past the mountains?"

Slaughter nodded.

108

Accum stared in through the window at the figure in restraints upon the bed. It periodically would snarl in its delirium, and although Accum was exhausted, he was fascinated. All night as the bodies had come in, as he had worked with them, he had been bothered by a thought he couldn't formulate. From the condition of this figure from the compound, he assumed that its infection had been rampant for some time. He didn't understand how anyone from up there had survived the virus this long. Now as he kept staring toward the figure, he began to feel his thought grow stronger. There must be a form of adaptation. He had been assuming that the virus became dormant once the coma set in and then reasserted as the victim regained consciousness. But what if he was wrong? What if resurrection meant the virus had been killed, that only its effects remained? Contagion would be limited to just the first few hours. What was more, this figure then would have some dead cells from the virus which in tandem with the figure's antibodies were the start of a vaccine. And Accum started smiling. He would work to conquer death. He filled with pity for this figure in there, thinking of the hell that it had been through.

109

Dunlap dreamed about the antlers.

110

Two days later it was all revealed to them, the final sanctum. They went up in trucks and vans until the trails stopped. Then they moved on foot through crevices and canyons. Next, the railway trestle. It was angled toward a ridge up there. The central part had years ago collapsed, but near the cliff, the beams had yet retained their strength, and Slaughter climbed up, Marge and Dunlap, Rettig, Hammel, Accum, Parsons, all of them and many more. They climbed up on the windy top and saw the draw which angled higher. At the farthest end, they found the secret.

"Christ, it's like a thousand years ago."

"Much longer. Try *ten* thousand. Thirty, forty."

They were staring at the ice age. Snow on peaks above them, they had come to Motherlode, but she was different. Shacks and corrugated metal structures long ago had fallen. In their place were crudely molded wooden hovels, stones for tools, and rotting carcasses. The streets were like a midden heap, and everywhere the people turned, they saw the totems, antlers perched on boulders, bears' heads on thick stakes, the piles of bones, the skeletons arranged in crazy patterns.

All around them, wind was howling.

"They regressed."

And people turned to Accum.

"In their minds. They went back to the threshold, to the start of things. They really were like animals."

"They worshipped them."

And now they turned to Owens.

"It's a death cult."

"Over here!"

And someone now was shouting from a tunnel.

Slaughter started toward it, others close behind.

They saw the paintings, dye and crushed rock blended, ocher, black, and green, the animals, the bear and deer, the antelope which leaped in rampant silent beauty, clubs and rocks as if in flight to strike them.

"God, it's wonderful."

They scanned their flashlights at the bear who came back in the spring, the antelope and deer which, when the cunning of the hunt was ended, willingly gave up their lives for others.

People moved now farther down the tunnel. Slaughter lingered.

"What's the matter?" Marge was saying.

"It's just, since it ended, I've felt different."

"Better?"

"Yes, I think so. But I never told you. When I started toward the truck, I had the sense that something forced me, that I wasn't in control, that I was moved."

"I'm sorry, but I—"

"I don't understand it either, but I had the sense that I had done this long ago before."

And Marge was staring at him.

"Parsons."

"He did what he thought he had to. I don't blame him. Nothing matters."

"Accum."

"He'll be leaving."

"Owens."

"He won't ever touch an animal again."

"And Dunlap?"

"No," they heard from somewhere down the tunnel. "No."

They moved along it, and they found the crypt, the chamber for their burials, the bodies which, laid out with beads and weapons, bits of food, had no doubt been expected to return as many others had from their deep virus coma.

"Sure, a death cult," Slaughter echoed. "There was no way they could die, they felt. They kept on coming back."

"But others didn't."

In here, skeletons were present, maggots on the recent dead, and some who very well could be alive.

The stench was awful, sinking deep inside their lungs and nauseating.

Men were gagging.

"Dunlap?"

He was nowhere.

Slaughter saw the farther entrance, and he walked through and saw Dunlap.

And three other things.

His flashlight swept across the red Corvette. The incongruity was chilling, how they'd ever got it up here and what madness at the last had prompted Quiller to harangue his people to transport it.

He had found the red room, yes the throne room, for the second thing was Quiller, rotting in the driver's seat, his hands upon the wheel to drive for all eternity, his antlered head turned upward.

Toward the third thing.

Dunlap stared unblinking toward it.

Slaughter aimed his flashlight. Up there near the ceiling, turning, round eyes leering, was the blackened outline of a nightmare, antlers, wolf's tail. . . .

Slaughter had to glance away. He turned to Dunlap. "Hey, what—?"

But he knew that Dunlap never now would answer. He was somewhere else, in other time.

As Slaughter reached to touch him, Dunlap moved, his hands upon the Corvette, kneeling.

Slaughter looked behind him. He saw Marge and Accum and the others.

"Oh, my God."

But that was not from them or Slaughter. It was Dunlap.

"Oh, my God." The echo reverent. At peace at last, he'd found his story.

111

Slaughter sat upon his porch. Inside he heard where Marge was cooking, and beside him, in the rocking chair, he saw where Dunlap stared off toward the mountains.

"Oh, my God," the man was saying, though he didn't say that often now, and Slaughter, sipping from his beer can, walked across to him. He straightened Dunlap's blanket.

"Hey there, pal, you'd better not catch cold. You want some beer?"

And Dunlap kept on rocking.

"I don't mind. Here, sip from mine."

And Slaughter raised the can, but Dunlap drooled the liquid which had once been his main motive.

"Now he's got religion," Slaughter told himself. "Well, maybe that's not bad."

For in his own way Slaughter had it too. At peace at last, he thought about the vaccine Accum had developed. And the two kids from the grocery store were gone. The valley had returned to normal. Maybe better things were coming.

Marge was standing in the doorway.

"How's the chili?" he asked, smiling.

"Well, I don't know why we gave you phosphorus that night. Your recipe would melt those bars for sure."

He started laughing.

"How long before Rettig and the others get here?" she was saying.

"Half an hour."

"Then we've got some time."

"I still don't know a way to make it last that long."

He kept on smiling.

"Well, I guess I'll have to teach you, but that's not exactly what I meant."

He waited.

"There's a thing I never understood: why, when you started toward that truck, you chose me as your backup."

He was thinking. "I suppose you were the only person I was ready to entrust my life to."

They were silent.

"Guess that says it, huh?" he asked her.

"I'm not certain."

"Would you trust your life with *me*?"

"That's *very* certain."

"Next month?"

"Next week would be better."

She was smiling. Slaughter started toward her. From the field beside the house, he heard his newly purchased horses gambol in the sunlight. But the sun
254

dipped toward the mountains as a coyote howled up in the foothills.

Dunlap raised his hands in blessing.

"Oh, my God," they heard him murmur.